Greig Beck grew up across the road from Bondi Beach in Sydney, Australia. His early days were spent surfing, sunbaking and reading science fiction on the sand. He then went on to study computer science, immerse himself in the financial software industry and later received an MBA. Greig is the director of a software company but still finds time to write and surf. He lives in Vaucluse, Sydney with his wife, son and an enormous black German shepherd.

Also by Greig Beck

Alex Hunter series

Beneath the Dark Ice
Dark Rising
This Green Hell

Return of the Ancients

The Valkeryn Chronicles Book 1

Greig Beck

Momentum

First published 2012 by Momentum

Pan Macmillan Australia Pty Ltd

1 Market Street, Sydney 2000

A CIP record for this book is available at the National Library of Australia

Return of the Ancients: The Valkeryn Chronicles Book 1

EPUB format: 9781743340127

Kindle format: 9781743340264

Print format: 9781743340271

Cover design by XOU Creative

Copyedited by Gareth Beal

Proofread by Laura Davies

Macmillan Digital Australia: www.macmillandigital.com.au

To report a typographical error, please email errors@momentumbooks.com.au

Visit www.momentumbooks.com.au to read more about all our books and to buy books online. You will also find features, author interviews and news of any author events.

About this Book

Arnold Singer is just like any other fifteen-year-old boy growing up in the suburbs – average height, average looks. The love of his life thinks he's a geek ... that is if she notices him at all. Pretty normal, and pretty boring, really.

But this normal life is about to change forever. On a school science trip to watch the test firing of a new particle accelerator, Arn is caught up in an accident that propels him into an extraordinary new world.

In this new land, Arn is the last human alive. It is populated with mysterious and bloodthirsty creatures, some of whom want him dead, while others see him as their only hope for survival.

Can Arn survive in a hostile world and save his new friends? Or has he arrived in time to witness the fall of a mighty empire?

An epic tale of love, betrayal and war in a world both familiar and terrifying.

Acknowledgements

To the team at Momentum – Joel for making the future live and breath, Marketing Mark, Gareth Beal in editorial, and all the rest. Every one of them creative, patient and good humoured, and I thank you all.

For my father, still watching over my son from above. We all miss you big fella.

Great is the sorrow in the land of the gods when Odin, the father of time, is swallowed by the great wolf, Fenrir.

Ragnarok – The final battle at the World's End
Ancient Norse mythology

Prologue

And So, The Prophecy Begins

The king sat astride his armoured horse, drew in a deep breath and exhaled slowly as he looked out across the bloody plain below him. Broken bodies and armour were strewn over the entire field, and the smell caused him to bare his teeth and growl deep in his broad chest. He turned to an approaching warrior, and nodded for him to speak.

'No survivors, sire.'

The king turned back to the field with sad eyes. 'I know; I could already sense it.'

He snorted as if to expel the sickening odour of death, and shook his head in disbelief. 'But how? Two hundred of our mightiest warriors cut down. How does that happen? They wouldn't dare to attack us in broad daylight – they're nothing but assassins, cutters of throats in the dark.' He turned to the warrior once again. 'But if not them, then who – who would dare it . . . who *could* dare it?'

'Sire!'

The king spurred the horse to where another figure crouched down looking intently at something in the mud. He pointed and moved his gauntleted hand over the shape, and then looked up to the king.

'A print – a Slinker, I think . . . but the size. Impossible.'

The king stared at the shape in huge print with its knife-like claws, then looked away towards the horizon. 'I have heard legends of the giants from the dark lands.' He looked around at the carnage. 'Whoever did this did not just want to win the day, but wanted to grind us to dust. This was nothing but bloody savagery.'

He looked up at the sky, noting the position of the sun – mid morning

1

and the heat was rising. They needed to get their fallen below ground before the scavengers came. He felt exhaustion weighing heavily on his shoulders. It was not his age or his armour, but the feeling of impending danger that seemed to drag the strength from his frame. He had fought many wars, but none had caused the sense of disquiet that he now felt deep inside his chest.

Another warrior plodded through the mud and stopped to look up at the king, his mouth working, but no words came.

'What is it?'

'Sire, some . . .'

The king waited for a few more seconds. 'Speak, Karnak. Fear nothing.'

The warrior drew in a breath. 'Some of the bodies . . . have been . . . partially eaten.'

The king lowered his head and shut his eyes. He nodded slowly. 'May Odin give us strength and wisdom, for I fear a war like no other comes to Valkeryn.' He turned to the warrior. 'See that the princess is brought in from the forest.'

Karnak tilted his head. 'And if she won't come? Last time she put an arrow into a warrior's leg.'

The king spun around on him. 'Tell her it's the king's order. That girl needs to start behaving more like a royal charge, and spend less time daydreaming or testing her arm in the forests.'

He dropped the horse's reins and reached up to lift the silver helmet from his head. He ran one hand up through his hair, and looked around, scanning the ridge.

The breath caught in his throat – a silhouette on the rise. *It could not be* . . . He blinked and tried to speak, but no words came. All he could do was lift his arm to point. At last he found his voice. 'Have I gone mad? Karnak, do you see?'

The tall warrior followed his gaze and then frowned in bewilderment. 'Then I am also mad, sire. I see, but it is impossible – they are a myth.'

The sun dropped a little lower and the silhouette disappeared. The king dropped his hand, and nodded. 'All things are possible in these darkening days.'

'Shall we go after it, sire?'

'No. Events will unfold as they are meant to.' He turned to the warrior. 'And so, the prophecy begins.'

Chapter 1

Becky And The Boob Monsters

Arn ran out to the waiting bus. His large dog bounded beside him, trying to leap up and catch the loose cords of his backpack that flapped as he ran. He turned to the dog. 'No Jess, stay here – sit.'

The big black shepherd sat down hard, struggling to obey the command. 'Go home, girl. See you soon.'

He leapt up onto the bus – hopefully for one of the last times, considering his dad had agreed to match him dollar for dollar when he went new car shopping this weekend. Visions of girls fighting to be the one to sit next to him in his new SUV were quickly replaced by the smiling face of just one. Who was he kidding? There'd only ever be one girl for him.

The doors groaned shut behind him, and the bus lumbered away from the kerb. He flopped into a seat and turned to the boy next to him. 'Wazzup?'

Arnold Singer, Arn to his friends, and the only Native American at Naperville High, had dropped down next to his best friend, Edward Lin, who had his head buried in a comic book. Arn looked over Edward's shoulder at the coloured panels, catching sight of a superhero lifting a car in one square and then bringing it down on his foe's head in another.

'At your age, don't you ever get bored with that stuff? I mean, how smart is that guy anyway? Every single time, he solves his problems by braining someone – why can't he outsmart them for once? I mean, how intelligent is he?'

Edward spoke without taking his eyes off the comic. 'HunterMan outsmart them? Sure, maybe he should give them a good talking to . . . or maybe he could hand out pamphlets about anger management or how we should eat more fibre – that'd be pretty cool, wouldn't it?'

3

He turned to peer at Arn over the top of his glasses. 'You know, Arn, I'm the smartest kid in our class – straight A's all the way, and you know what I get for that? Every week, I get smashed by the meatheads, and laughed at by your make-believe girlfriend and her gang of mutant boob monsters. Oh yeah, did I tell you that I suck at gym and track? So comics like this are for people like me, who would just once like to be able to solve their own problems like this dude does.'

'Sure, violence is always the answer . . . *dude.*' Arn laughed, but understood his friend's feelings of alienation. Arn was the only Shawnee to have ever won a scholarship to the school – and some acted like they resented him for it. For a start, he looked different – with his straight, sharp nose, shoulder-length black hair and eyes so dark, his mother sometimes called him *Shadow* for their being so deep and mysterious. Average height, smart, okay at gym and track, and sort of good looking – different, but unremarkable.

He looked at his friend and smiled sympathetically. He could get straight A's if he wished, simply because he was a Native American; there were plenty of teachers and administrators at the school determined to try and give him a leg-up – he'd refused every one of them. If he couldn't make it simply by being himself, then he didn't want to make it at all.

He nudged Edward, who was trying to go back to his reading. 'And hey, who doesn't like boob monsters?' Arn chuckled and stole a quick glance over his shoulder to the rear of the bus. Rebecca Matthews was in her usual seat, chatting animatedly with two of her friends. *Make-believe girlfriend Becky and the Boob Monsters* – Arn smiled at Edward's insightful name for the group.

While Arn sat smiling, Becky caught him looking, and for the split second their eyes locked, Arn felt the usual electric tingle travel from his toes to his scalp. He knew he blushed as his face suddenly felt hot and tight. For her part, Becky's mouth turned down in one corner, and she looked away.

So beautiful, he thought . . . *and so unattainable.*

*****

The bus slowed to pick up more students. Arn sighed and tried to make himself more comfortable for the long trip ahead. Today was science excursion day – an entire day devoted to visiting the Fermilab particle collider at Batavia. Apparently there was to be a test firing of the new acceleration technology the company had developed – *atom smashing day*, Edward had called it. Their class was chosen to attend because of its grade point average prominence in the state.

He loved science, but had an idea what to expect from the lab visit – a robotic voice would count down to some sort of initiation event, lights flashed on monitor boards and screens, ignition would be called, everyone's breath would be held . . . and then a technician would say, *test run complete*, and that'd be it. Everyone would be invited to look at rows of numbers scrolling down a computer screen. *Riveting!*

It was going to be a far cry from what science fiction writers had described in countless novels he had read in the past. The reality was always uneventful – and mind-numbingly boring.

More students filed past seeking seats, and as Edward flipped another page in his comic, as if by magic, it disappeared from his hands. He and Arn stared up into the comically brutish face of Steve Barkin.

Naperville High was ranked in the top five per cent of colleges nationally, but looking up into the face of Barkin made Arn wonder whether every now and then someone bubbled up through the academic cracks – just to ensure that life didn't become too comfortable for the normal people.

'Whatta you, six years old?' Barkin sneered, baring his teeth.

Arn looked at Edward, who sat staring up, not saying a word. Barkin leafed quickly through the comic.

'Are there pages stuck together in here? You know, from where you been drooling over the muscle man in his tight superhomo clothes?' He brayed at his joke, and then started to read some of the comic's panels. His lips moved and his eyes narrowed in concentration.

Arn shifted and tried to look out the window, but he felt the hot waves of humiliation coming off his friend. In his mind he could hear a little voice repeating over and over: *Stay out of it, he hates you even more, just stay out of it* . . . As usual he ignored it.

'Take it slowly, Steve – a few big words in there.'

Two piggishly small eyes lifted from the page. They blinked as if their owner was taking a few seconds to register, in some deeply buried memory centre of his brain, that they were meant to be insulting.

'You got somethin' you want to say, Singer?'

'Just that you should try 'em, before you rag 'em, Barkin.' Arn kept his face serious.

'Kiddie comics? They're for nerds and dweebs – like you two *min-or-ity* creeps.'

Arn ignored the jibe, but pressed his attack anyway. 'Not comics, Einstein; I meant reading in general.'

'What did you say, Chief?' Barkin's eyes narrowed to two angry slits.

C'mon Arn, pull back before you cop it. As usual, Arn's mouth and brain never agreed on a strategy.

'I think you heard, redneck.'

The slits widened and Barkin's mouth opened a little, as if about to deliver another insult or a stream of unintelligible cursing, just as the deep voice of Mr. Beescomb, their physics teacher, rolled down the aisle of the bus.

'Seats . . . now.'

Barkin's mouth snapped shut and instead returned to its familiar sneer. He ripped the comic in two and threw the halves back at Arn and Edward, hitting neither.

'You pair of jerk-offs.' He leaned over Arn and whispered, 'Beats me why they ever let you in here – quotas, I reckon.' He straightened. 'I'll see *you* later, Singer.' He lumbered away, first towards the front of the bus, and then changed his mind and bullocked his way down the back, where he stopped in front of Becky and her friends.

Arn watched for a second, and then sighed, turning back to the front of the bus, where he noticed the eyes of Mr. Jefferson the driver momentarily fixed on him in the small overhead mirror.

Edward held up the two halves of his comic. 'Thank you Arn; that went well.'

Arn shook his head slowly with his mouth turned down in distaste. 'He doesn't scare me.'

'Does me.' Edward stuffed the comic fragments into his bag.

Chapter 2

Fire In The Hole!

Arn was jolted from his dozing by the bus driving over speed humps. They were passing a roadblock on a side road outside of North Aurora. He yawned and craned his neck to get a better look at a group of squat, grey, fortified buildings in the distance.

Men in green fatigues stood out front in pairs – military for sure. He could just make out one of the buildings, built like a concrete-and-steel blister with a flat iron door – not a roller door, but more like a solid heavy plate and marked with a lightning bolt held in a gauntleted fist.

He nudged Edward. 'Fire in the hole!'

Edward looked up and blinked several times like a mole coming to the surface of its burrow, and then focused on what Arn was nodding his head at. He snorted. 'It's an armoury. Rumour even has it they have experimental mini-nukes down there – shoulder mounted – like an RPG, but could flatten a mountain range. That structure is just a cap; it's supposed to drop down twenty storeys below the ground to a command centre. If the big one drops, the brass can keep belting out the orders from down there.' He sat back again.

Arn scoffed. 'You're making that up.'

Edward shook his head without looking up from his comic, and did his best Yoda voice: 'Internet a wonderful place is. Try you must, travelling there some day, young Master Singer.'

Arn laughed, looked back one last time, then relaxed back into his seat. *Mini-nukes*, he thought. *Cool.*

*****

About an hour later, and now late morning, the school bus turned into Pine Road and motored towards an enormous three-legged iron sculpture that reminded Arn of one of the Martian ships from *War of the Worlds.*

'Quick, look up.' Edward pushed Arn's head closer to the window so he could watch as they passed below the weird sculpture. He then said, 'It's called Broken Symmetry; it's sort of an illusion. From below, all three legs look exactly the same, but . . .' He held up his finger as they continued under, and then past the sculpture. They looked back at it. '. . . But when you see it from the side, you can see that all three legs are different sizes.'

'Hey yeah, you're right – spooky.' Arn watched the sculpture recede for a moment and then sat back.

Edward also sat back and reopened his comic book. 'It's actually made of the deck plates from the USS Princeton.'

'Well, you're a mine of information, aren't you?' Arn didn't doubt for a minute that it was true.

'I don't *always* read comic books, you know.' Edward raised his middle finger.

Arn laughed and looked forward through the window towards their destination. Mr. Beescomb had told them in their briefing that it was Fermilab's main auditorium, and Arn could see a tall building looming up in front of them that looked a little like two bits of sagging white bread stacked together. He grunted and nudged Edward. 'And what's the story with the weird building?'

Edward looked up at the structure for a second or two, then shrugged. 'Dunno – wino architect maybe.'

They passed various personnel on the ground, walking large dogs. Some looked to be security personnel, but others wore white smock laboratory uniforms, and carried electronic notepads as though they were testing the animals. Arn counted at least two dozen huge beasts before the bus pulled away from them. One of the wolf-like creatures paused to stare, its eyes creepily intelligent as it watched the vehicle pass by.

*****

The old wheezing bus squealed to a halt, and no sooner had it stopped than the entire group of students erupted from their seats.

'Okay everyone, we have landed. Thank you for flying with us today.' It was Jefferson the driver. His eyes in the rear view mirror stared back at them.

Edward went to stand up, but Arn stopped him. 'Let's give it a minute, okay?'

His friend looked at him for another second, and then over his shoulder, his eyes going from Steve Barkin to Becky and her friends. He shook his head. 'Please don't try and say anything to her – at least not while Barkin is with her.'

Arn shrugged. 'Don't worry.'

Arn had turned in his seat to watch her begin to come down the centre aisle, while Steve Barkin, still seated, kept up a constant stream of bad jokes and Neanderthal babble from behind. He saw Arn looking towards her, and he leaned forward in his chair to stage whisper something to her, causing her eyes to flick towards Arn for a moment.

Arn fumbled in his bag as she drew near. She slowed and smiled, raising her eyebrows. Arn gave her some folded pages, and she quickly looked at them, smiled again and winked, before turning away to the front of the bus.

Arn quickly added, 'I'll see you on the field trip. I can do up the other notes as we go.' She might have sort of half nodded – at least his ego hoped she did.

Beside him, Edward groaned. 'Please tell me you're not still doing her assignments for her.'

'No way . . . just a few tips and things, that's all.' Arn got to his feet, not wanting to look his friend in the eye.

Edward dragged his pack over one of his shoulders. 'I don't know why you chase her. She obviously only knows you exist cause you're her personal homework slave. Besides, I don't think she'd ever date a . . .'

Arn spun at him. 'A what?'

Edward shook his head furiously. 'No, no, I meant that she used to date Barkin – doesn't that tell you something? Even if it's only about her taste in cavemen.'

'*Used to date,* buddy . . . *used to date.*'

Edward surveyed the damage to his comic. 'Anyway, thanks for going in to bat for me.'

Arn shrugged. 'You'd do the same for me.'

Edward looked at him for a moment, and then looked away. 'Sure.'

As they neared the doorway, Mr. Jefferson cleared his throat. 'Putting yourself in harm's way for a friend is a noble thing. Some might say courageous.'

Arn turned and shook his head, feeling his face redden once again. '*Ahh*, it was nothing. Not really courage . . . more stupidity, I think. I'm sure I'll get some payback later.'

Jefferson cocked one eyebrow. 'You know, courage is about being scared, but acting anyway.' He chuckled. 'Or you can think of courage as fear that never stopped to think.' He laughed and reached out to slap Arn on the shoulder.

Arn chuckled. 'Okay, thanks.'

Jefferson winked and turned back to his steering wheel, glancing in the rear side mirror in preparation for pulling away from the kerb.

*****

He stepped down and walked a few paces from the doorway. Edward was immediately at his side and was looking over his shoulder as Barkin and Otis jumped from the last step onto the grass. 'That guy sure knows how to hold a grudge, doesn't he?'

Arn grunted, but didn't look back. 'Maybe if we just let him give us one each in the breadbasket, he'll get it out of his system.'

Edward snorted. 'We? Hey, you first, and we'll see how it works out.'

Arn laughed and then spoke out of the corner of his mouth while looking up over the heads of the other students. 'Gimme a minute.' He threaded his way through the milling students as Beescomb leafed through some paperwork.

Arn walked towards Becky and her friends, racking his brain for something cool or funny to say to her. He gulped. By herself, she intimidated him, but her friends . . . now *they* had cutting sarcasm down to an art form.

He stopped behind her, his lips moving in rehearsal. Monica Struan, standing at Becky's shoulder, saw him first. 'Oh God, no.' She smirked and nudged Becky, who turned, smiling. Her face dropped slightly when she saw who it was.

Seconds passed as his mind refused to give up any pearls of wisdom, or even humour. His face grew hot. Becky's friends started to snigger. At last he managed to stammer something.

'That metal sculpture was an optical illusion.'

She frowned. 'What?'

'I mean, if you look at it from one angle it looks symmetrical, and from another angle it . . . doesn't.'

The frown stayed in place, and she quickly looked over her shoulder at her friends, perhaps to see if they were still watching – they were, intently, as though something amusing, embarrassing, or hopefully both, was about to take place.

Becky turned back to him, her expression morphing from a frown to a look of haughtiness. She took a half step back as though his mere presence was dragging down her street cred, and allowing him to be in her space would mean his nerdiness would somehow rub off on her. She folded her arms and raised her eyebrows questioningly.

He nodded quickly. 'It was made from the deck plates of . . .' Arn shut his mouth and just grinned, or tried to. He guessed it looked more like one of those faces that chimpanzees pulled when they were scared.

Then she sort of came to his rescue.

'So, the notes?' she asked, with a small shrug.

'Yeah, *ahh* yeah, that's what I was trying to tell you. I was going to include the sculpture in my notes for you. Make a good starting point.'

She tilted her head, and her expression softened. 'Thank you for doing the notes for me, Arnold.' She smiled as she looked over her shoulder, perhaps this time feeling her cred was moving back up the cool scale by having someone do her work for her.

Now, ask her, he thought. 'Any time. Hey, I was wondering if afterwards, we . . .'

Beescomb began calling them to order. Becky mouthed, *gotta go,* and turned her back on him to move into a huddle with her friends.

'Okay, well maybe later,' Arn said to her departing back, and then shrugged, knowing she probably either didn't hear him, or had already blanked him from her consciousness.

'Ahh, unrequited love – the toughest love of all – especially when you're the *unrequitee*.' Edward watched as Becky and her friends giggled and pranced away like a small herd of colourful, long-legged deer.

Arn sucked in one cheek and then exhaled.

'Be even better if she liked *you*, and not just your note-taking skills.' Obviously, Edward wasn't ready to give up salting the wound.

'Sooner or later she'll see me – see the real me – and see how I feel about her.' Arn kept watching her as she flicked hair that shone in the sunlight.

Edward slapped his friend on the shoulder. '*Ha*, you're dreaming. Maybe *someone* will, one day, but I'm not so sure it'll be Becky Matthews. I think you're just too . . . *different* for her.'

'*Hmm*, different? Real feelings are blind to differences.' Arn shrugged. 'Besides, got to start somewhere.'

*****

Steve Barkin was one of the last on the bus. He sat next to Otis Renshaw and watched tight-lipped as Arn laughed and joked with Becky as they stood among the other milling students.

Otis followed his friend's gaze outside the bus, and spoke out of the side of his mouth. 'You used to date her, didn't you?'

'Ages ago.' Barkin kept watching.

Otis nudged him. 'Well, better watch out; Sitting Bull's going for it.'

'Never happen. She'd never go out with an Injun charity case. Anyway, so what? I dumped her. She was high maintenance, kept hassling me.'

Otis nodded. 'Well, she's certainly over you now.' He laughed and sat back.

Barkin shrugged and blew air from his lips in an *I don't give a crap* type of way. Then when he noticed his friend had turned to stare out of the opposite window, his eyes narrowed and drifted back to where Arn and Becky stood.

You just wait, he mouthed, and sprung up, heading for the door.

*****

Arn and Edward turned away from Becky and looked straight into the dead-eyed faces of Steve Barkin and Otis.

Barkin put his hand on Arn's chest and pushed him. 'You should leave her alone.'

Arn pulled an incredulous face. 'Leave her alone? Why? Your property is she, Barkin, huh?'

Barkin shrugged. 'Listen *Pawnee*: stay away for your own good. Besides, she thinks you're weird. We *all* think you're weird . . . and don't belong here. Just piss off back to the reservation . . .' He looked at Edward. '. . . And take your boyfriend with you.'

Edward seemed to shrink at being included in Barkin's spray. Arn felt his face get hot again. 'Really?' Arn turned to Becky and her friends. 'Becky!'

She turned. He made writing motions in the air and yelled, 'Catch up later!'

She nodded and turned back to her friends, and they started to head to where Beescomb was gathering all the students.

Arn turned back to Barkin. 'We write to each other all the time . . . and you?' Barkin opened his mouth, but Arn cut in. 'And it's *Shawnee,* not *Pawnee.* We've been here nearly four hundred years – I think it's you who doesn't belong.' He pushed past him, and he and Edward walked towards the class group.

Edward waved his arms in front of them to clear a path. 'Comin' through, dead men walkin'.' Edward looked up at his taller friend. 'He is so gonna kick your ass.'

Arn shrugged. 'Probably, but it was worth it to see that look on his face.'

'The *I'm gonna kill you* one?' Edward laughed. 'You know, it'd be worth it if she liked you as much as you liked her.'

Arn just sighed.

Chapter 3

The Speed Of Light

The group moved like some many-legged organism towards the main entrance of the giant, sagging sandwich building. Arn was amazed by how modern the interior was, how clean, how . . . sterile. But something else struck him as strange – it was almost empty.

'Where is everyone?'

A balding, smallish man was making his way towards them, and Arn's voice must have carried in the library-like hush of the high-ceilinged building.

'Mostly under your feet. Like just about everything else in the Fermilab community.'

Beescomb cleared his throat and walked forward to introduce himself. The small man nodded, shook his outstretched hand, and held out his other hand for the paperwork. He quickly scanned it, and then stepped back from the shadow of the larger teacher so the students could see him.

As he did, a number of large dogs raced up, pushing in between the crowd and quickly sniffing pockets, bags and fingers. Some of the girls squealed, and Arn reached down to pat one of the largest dogs, who gave his fingers a quick sniff before racing off after a discreet signal from its keeper.

'Don't mind them,' said the small man. 'Just working members of the security detail. In those few seconds they were among us, they searched for everything from explosives to drugs, and even for excessive nervousness – they miss a lot less than the most sophisticated electronics. In fact, you might be interested to know that Fermilab is breeding some of the best and smartest guard dogs in the entire world: increased intelligence, size, and a higher tolerance to ionising radiation – our new guardians if you like.' He gave a small nod, like a bow. 'My name is Dr. Albert Harper, and I'm the chief physicist working on the Tevatron project. I'd like you all to follow me to the theatre for a short background briefing before we descend for the test-firing.'

A couple of hands shot up, but Harper held up his own like a traffic cop. '*Whoa*, not yet. I'll take questions following the presentation – we simply cannot be late; the project has cost about a billion dollars, and is being monitored and managed by a very large, very expensive, and very impatient team.'

He laughed as though he was joking, but Arn knew the head scientist had got his message across: you're on my turf and my time – jump to it.

The group filed into the amphitheatre, and Arn let his long hair fall forward over his face to try to avoid seeing a glaring Steve Barkin skulking at the rear.

Before the last student had sat down, the theatre darkened and Harper's voice droned from speakers around the room.

'Welcome to Fermilab . . . funny name right? He peered around the room, his eyebrows raised and an ironic smile indicating no answer was really expected.

'Well, the science community you've come to today was originally home to the village of Weston, and was once little more than farmland. In fact, you might see some of the first barns still around the place. There's even a small burial ground with tombstones dating all the way back to 1839. We still maintain it out of respect for the original inhabitants.'

Arn kept his mouth shut, even though his, and Dr. Harper's, concept of *original inhabitants* differed by about 250 years.

Harper continued. 'We weren't always called Fermilab though. We actually started out as the National Accelerator Laboratory when President Lyndon B. Johnson himself commissioned it in 1967. But, in 1974 the laboratory was renamed in honour of Nobel Prize winner, Enrico Fermi, one of the most famous physicists of the atomic age and . . .'

Edward's hand shot up, and at the same time his voice sprang from the dark next to Arn. 'The father of the atomic bomb.'

Harper pointed to where Edward's voice had risen, and nodded. 'Yes, yes he worked on the Manhattan Project, but did you know he also developed the world's first nuclear reactor, and contributed to the development of quantum theory, nuclear and particle physics, and statistical mechanics?' Again the eyebrows went up.

Harper's voice had become momentarily rushed as though responding to a challenge. He paused, staring in Edward's direction for a few seconds before he smiled, and smoothly changed back to talking about the facility, his voice once again relaxed. 'Since those early days we have grown, adding extra circumference, accelerators, and too many upgrades to mention.'

Harper waggled a finger in the air. 'Although there is one worth mentioning.' A giant image appeared behind him of a ruby red cylinder – glass-like, perfect – a magnificent stone. 'Diamonds used to only be a girl's best friend, well, now they're the nuclear physicist's greatest gift. They are unparalleled in their transmission of heat and light, and are virtually indestructible. Our friends down under at Australia's Macquarie University found that their optical properties far surpassed anything else at the unique wavelengths required for high-powered laser technology. And red was best, because it allowed a pure beam without all of white light's additional, fractious particles.'

Hands went up around the room – *where was it found? Is it expensive? Is it here? Can we see it?*

Harper waved the hands down. 'For a start, we didn't find it, we grew it. Took over a year to create this single, three-inch structure via chemical vapour deposition – the result, after cutting and polishing – a lens of perfect, consistent clarity. And, at US ten million dollars, it was a fraction of the cost of using a natural diamond. Not that you'd be lucky enough to ever find one like it.'

Harper looked at the image of the red diamond for a few seconds, the red glow reflecting on his shiny face as well as an expression that was a mix of pride and adoration. 'Yes, we've come a long way.'

He lifted one arm theatrically to motion towards the screen. 'To where we are today.' Pictures of rolling green fields and forested countryside were displayed against a backing soundtrack of birdsong and soft music. It faded out, dream-like, to be replaced by images of the massive Tevatron collider.

The view shot into the sky, and panoramic pictures from miles overhead showed the size and scale of the gigantic Fermilab project. The physicist recited his lines with great enthusiasm – the world's second most powerful proton-antiproton collider – four miles in diameter, but able to send particles around its gigantic ring at 99.999 per cent of the speed of light, completing the four-mile trip nearly 50,000 times per second. The objective was to smash those particles together at a rate of almost two million collisions each second.

Arn nodded in the dark, scribbling notes without looking down at the page. *Cool*, he thought. He turned his head to the left and saw the presentation screen reflected in Edward's glasses – tiny copies of the Tevatron in each of the lenses. He smiled – his friend's face was rapt with awe. Turning slowly to his right, he saw that the light made Becky look even prettier. Again, he wished he could think of something cool or funny to say, but gave up in case he sounded like a jerk . . . again.

He slowly eased back in his seat, and snuck a look over his shoulder to where Barkin and his friends were seated. Huddled together, their faces were also lit up, but by something Barkin was holding on his lap – a portable PC game, probably. *Grades are gonna be looking good again this year, Stevo*, Arn thought and chuckled softly.

Arn turned in his seat, happy that he wasn't the focus of the dimwit's attention for at least a few moments, just as a new image appeared up on the large screen, and Dr. Harper was moving into presentation wrap-up mode.

The new pictures were of the void of space and distant galaxies, and Harper was talking about the connection between physics and astrophysics, and how their project would assist in solving the mysteries of dark matter throughout the universe.

A crude drawing was attached to the lower corner of the image – a rough cartoon, but its point was clear. Darth Vader was holding up a lightsaber next to some crudely scrawled words: 'The dark side controls the universe – dark matter holds it together – and dark energy determines your destiny.'

'Dark energy determines your destiny' – *good quote*, Arn thought, as the lights came up.

*****

The student group was herded from the amphitheatre and down a long corridor, before being shown to a set of large steel doors. Behind them, heavy

17

clanking and whirring could be heard until the giant doors slid back to reveal a grey service elevator large enough to fit ten elephants – or twenty boisterous teenage students – with ease.

Arn and Edward stayed near the front, and Becky stood to the side, chatting animatedly with her friends. As the doors slid shut, from the rear came the familiar voice of Steve Barkin: 'Smells like a thousand butt cracks in here' – followed by the nasal sniggering of his close friend, Otis Renshaw.

Arn tried to stop himself, but couldn't resist. 'Only you would know what that smelled like, Barkin.'

The lift erupted in laughter. Even Becky covered her mouth to hide a laugh and Beescomb scowled from under his brows, but didn't say a word. Beside him, Edward rolled his eyes, before shooting Arn a clear *you are really asking for it* kind of expression.

The lift continued down for another few seconds, and Arn noticed that Becky had moved a little closer to him in the crowd. *Hmm,* he pondered – *insults, the way to a girl's heart.*

*****

Steve Barkin felt his face burn. He watched Becky smile and mouth something to Arn, which he bet was about him. The guy was making him look like an ass in front of his friends, his former girlfriend, and the entire freakin' class.

He couldn't believe it. If she ever dated Singer, Barkin would be a laughing stock. Becky Matthews and the redskin? *That . . . was . . . not . . . going . . . to . . . happen.*

Before this trip was over, he'd have to think of a way to take him down a peg or two.

*****

Like the Pied Piper, Dr. Harper led them to the Tevatron control room. Beescomb was content to bring up the rear to ensure no solo explorations took place. After being ushered through another door, Arn's expectations soared. He was amazed by the sheer number of screens and monitors that completely covered three of the four walls in the near freezing, barn-sized room.

The core of the Tevatron, the entire ring, the collision points, the magnetic resonance fields – everything was being scrutinised by both human and electronic eyes that missed nothing. Several technicians continued to tap away at recessed keyboards, or stared intently at graphs, calibrations and rows of numbers scrolling down their screens – but none turned, or even acknowledged the college party in any way. Just as Arn was thinking they were probably bored by the continual parade of tour groups, Harper spoke up softly from the back of the room.

'Excuse the technicians. The new laser acceleration will be test-firing this morning, and as you would expect, it has created a lot of excitement and anticipation. Also, each firing has a considerable dollar cost associated with it, not to mention months of planning and preparation. So the teams are all pretty focused. Perhaps we can chat to them after the firing, and they can tell us about their results. Okay?'

A few shrugs and bored looks didn't daunt the bookish scientist, and he continued to point out different areas of the room and their team members, and talk a little more about the role of each section.

Arn and Edward were at the front, and craned their necks when Harper described to the group where each of the collisions would take place. He finished by telling them that, though they would be observing the test-firing from here, he was also going to take them down to the lowest level where the collider ring was housed – to the actual *collision ground zero*. Arn heard his friend breathe the word *awesommme* as they were escorted from the control room.

They went down in the enormous lift once again. This time when the giant elevator doors slid back they revealed a cavernous room the size of an aircraft hangar, complete with high roof, fortified concrete walls, and little else except for a set of steel doors at the end. They reminded Arn of the type you see on a submarine.

Harper looked briefly at his watch and then called everyone together. He leaned towards Beescomb and said something softly that caused the teacher to nod and fall in behind the group, perhaps to ensure that no stragglers wandered off. For his part, Beescomb was beaming. *The most enthusiastic kid in the group,* thought Arn.

While he talked, Harper led everyone towards one of the submarine doors at the far end of the cavernous chamber. Once Beescomb had corralled everyone in a huddle behind Harper, the Fermilab physicist entered some codes into a small silver keypad, waited until a row of red lights turned green, spun the wheel on the door, and then pushed it inwards.

The strange smell was the first impression Arn had of the shaft – metallic, sharp . . . reminding him of a short circuit or a smell he encountered once during a plasma discharge display at a science fair. *Ozone*, sprang to his mind.

Arn looked one way, then the other – the tunnel stretched away in both directions. Lit to a surgical brightness, it only disappeared as it bent into the start of its four-mile loop, hundreds of feet further away.

Harper stood like a showman, with his hands on his hips and a proud smile on his face. 'The Tevatron's particle collision track . . .' He opened his arms wide, flat hands pointed in each direction of the tunnel. '. . . Runs like this, nearly uninterrupted for miles. I say *nearly* because the only stop is the collision point where we monitor what happens when we smash the particles together.'

'Where?' The question had come from behind Arn, but he had the same query. *Where was the collision point? For that matter, where was the Tevatron track?* The tunnel seemed to be bare, except for some grey pipes on one side of the wall that looked more like normal basement plumbing. At a minimum, he was expecting some sort of gigantic, reinforced pathway that housed the power of subatomic particles, moving at the speed of light.

Harper nodded and pointed to the thickest of the grey pipes. Arn nearly groaned; it was no more than waist thickness – there were no flashing lights, no shiny steel casing, no coiled wires . . . just a damned ordinary-looking pipe. *Where's the magic?* he wondered, sighing and jotting a few more notes.

Harper turned to his left, and waved them all to follow as he set off, passing small doors built into the side of the tunnel's walls, talking as he went.

'Beams of particles travel through a vacuum, surrounded by super powerful magnets. These magnets bend the beam in a large circle, and by using a series of accelerators we eventually get the little critters gaining speeds close to that of light.' He stopped and looked around at the small group, smiling as though he had just imparted a valuable secret. He waited for a second or two, perhaps to see if there were any questions; when there weren't, he turned back and waved over his shoulder for his charges to follow.

After another five minutes of walking in silence, broken only by the hint of a background hum of electronics, Harper stopped the group at a section of the tunnel where there was an enormous bulge in the pipe – like those tabloid pictures of an anaconda that has just swallowed someone's cat. Circling the bulge was a metallic ring that had spikes, knobs and strange devices covering its entire surface. *At last*, Arn thought. *This is more like it.*

Dozens of cameras and monitoring equipment studded the walls and the ring itself. Harper looked at the bulge of sophisticated electronics lovingly, and rested his hand lightly on it. He turned, his face bright with pride.

'Speeds close to light . . .' He paused, his gaze taking in their faces. '. . . That was – until today. *Today*, we use the photonic laser accelerator.' Like a game show host, he briefly indicated a broomstick-wide pipe that entered the bulge. At its centre was a dazzling red stone – the diamond. It glowed softly and looked . . . warm.

Harper continued. 'Normally, once the particles are travelling at 99.999 per cent the speed of light, we collide them . . . but not today. Instead we are going to fire the laser at the particles and accelerate them even further. Will we actually attain the speed of light? Our computer modelling says we might. Our modelling also says we might even . . . *exceed* it!'

He took his hand off the ring, but looked back at it lovingly. Arn wondered if he was going to pat it like a favourite pet.

'What if you create a black hole? Could it destroy the planet – eat the mass of the Earth down to nothing?' Becky had her chin out and was on her toes, asking the question over the top of taller kids' heads.

Good on her, thought Arn.

Even cynical Edward, who had sidled up next to him, whispered, 'Someone's been paying attention to your notes after all.'

Harper chuckled softly. 'Good question, miss. Could we create a black hole – a dark matter anomaly? It's certainly possible. There are many strange and exotic particles we're hoping to create. Some we probably don't even have names for yet.' He looked around for a few seconds to build up some suspense, obviously enjoying the theatre of it all, before his eyes found Becky again. 'But do I think it will absorb the Earth? No. Even if we create a heavy-gravity particle, it will be so miniscule that it won't exist long enough to absorb matter, or give off any dangerous X-ray or gamma radiation. It will exist in our reality for perhaps a millionth of a second, and will be seen and experienced only by the computers . . . from in there.' He pointed to the bulge.

'But it's possible?' It was Edward's turn. 'And what about wormholes?' Edward's voice rose and echoed in the tunnel, but his small stature made it hard for Harper to find him among the group.

Arn nudged him. 'Way to go, Skywalker.' He laughed at his friend's determination to inject some science fiction into Harper's science fact.

Dr. Harper gave up trying to find the new voice and looked as if he was going to ignore Edward, when the young comic book buff spoke again.

'Even a dark matter anomaly the size of a pinhead could theoretically create a distortion in space and time. That's true, isn't it?'

'Well, I . . .'

Edward jumped in again. 'Theoretically, it could actually unpick a thread . . . open a doorway – a one- or two-way entrance to somewhere else . . . to some-*when* else.'

Harper held up his hands and raised both eyebrows. 'Wormholes, time-travel, strange particles . . . exciting, isn't it? The possibilities are endless. You're a good group.' He was silent for a moment, once again drawing up the suspense. 'Every experiment in particle physics is a leap into the unknown. You could well be witnessing history today. Each of you may go home on the bus, and be able to say, *today, I saw the future.*'

'Oh, brother,' whispered someone from the back of the room. Arn turned to see Steve Barkin sneering.

Mr. Beescomb clapped, and tried unsuccessfully to get the class to join in with him for a few seconds – before giving up and settling for just clearing his throat and offering some words of praise on behalf of the college.

*****

Steve Barkin gradually managed to drop a little behind. *Bumbling* Beescomb was clearly preoccupied with the ongoing discussion he was having with the dump's chief dweeb, and not watching each of his charges.

Barkin was sulking, bored, and ambled along, placing his hand on the levers for each of the small doors. None of the levers budged an inch, until . . .

One of the doors opened smoothly and silently. Barkin looked down to see the lock panel was registering green, not red indicating a sealed door. He quickly looked inside – a smallish room with maintenance equipment, some suits with glass face-panels, and rows of thick boots and gloves.

He snorted. It reminded him of one of his online games about mutants in the future, where everyone wears biohazard suits and spends all their time either shooting at, or being shot at by zombies. How the zoms managed to shoot guns, when they couldn't even speak, was beyond him.

He went to pull the door shut, then he paused. A smile drew one side of his mouth up, and he closed the door quietly. *It'll be perfect*, he thought.

He quickly caught up to his friend Otis and grabbed him by the arm, pulling him back to the rear of the group. In a few seconds he had explained his plan, and Otis grinned and nodded enthusiastically.

Barkin sniggered as he imagined how his plan would work. He just needed a little diversion, and then Singer would look stupid and be in trouble all at the same time. *Perfect*, he thought again.

*****

Arn was fascinated by technology. Any sort of groundbreaking wild science attracted him like a moth to the front porch in summer. Ever since his father had brought home a book on the ancient Greeks, he had been filled with an insatiable hunger to learn more – not about their politics, culture, or even their art – but about their machines.

He dropped back, telling Edward he'd catch up later. He sketched the particle collision track in his notepad, wrote a few sentences he'd expand on later, and then spent a little time looking at the back of Becky's head. Her long dark hair shone in the artificial light of the ring chamber. He wondered what it felt like – silk, he bet . . . and probably smelled like apples – wild apples, whatever they smelled like. But it just sounded right. He sighed.

Overhead, red domed bulbs started to flash and turn – like upside down ambulance lights, but without the accompanying scream of sirens. Harper looked from the lights to his watch, clapped his hands once, said a few words to the group to round things off, and then started herding them back the way they had come. Arn stepped back as they pushed past, quickly finishing his notes.

He hurried to catch up, and as he was about to pass one of the submarine doors, he noticed that Barkin's friend Otis was talking animatedly to Beescomb up ahead. He couldn't imagine what it was about, as he doubted this field trip would have been high on Otis's *interest-Richter Scale*, or whether he even understood what it was about. Arn shook his head. *Strange*, he thought – the way Otis hung onto Beescomb's arm, like he was guiding him.

Just as Arn was wondering where Otis's partner in crime might be, from behind him he felt his T-shirt being pulled out of his jeans, and then up and over his head. He was spun around, and a fist to the stomach up under his diaphragm knocked the air from his lungs, and any words from his mouth. The blow made his legs go weak, and he doubled over. Just as he felt himself falling, he was wrenched up and dragged to one side.

The flashing red lights, which made the inside of his T-shirt pulse red every second, suddenly went dark, and he was pushed to the floor. A familiar voice sneered, 'So long, Singer – I hear radiation shrinks your balls. But that shouldn't worry someone who didn't have any to start with.' There was a soft, cruel laugh, the sound of a door closing, and then . . . complete darkness.

Arn rolled over and sat up, pulling the shirt down from his head. He blinked. Everything was so dark, it was as if his eyes had been painted black. He managed to gulp air into lungs that still didn't want to fully inflate, and he got to his feet holding his arms out in front of him.

He was like a blind man who had lost his cane. He couldn't tell if he was in a room as big as an aircraft hangar, or as small as a broom closet. He certainly couldn't hear the sound of his college group anymore.

*****

The class was herded back into the lift. Edward tried to ask some questions, but Harper, distracted, kept checking the time and apologising for keeping them so long. The laser test-firing must have been nearing its countdown.

The lift took them back up towards the monitoring room. Harper turned to the chattering class and put his finger to his lips before he opened the door. He spoke softly to Beescomb and pointed to the rear of the room, and then went to join the technicians.

The room, which was so quiet before, was now a hive of frantic activity. Edward wondered why they had needed to be silent, as instructions, countdowns, and equipment checks were shouted from one scientific team member to the next.

Edward narrowed his eyes to concentrate on the multiple screens and display panels within the room, his gaze at last resting on a digital clock counting down in hundredths of a second – there was little more than four minutes remaining.

He stood on his toes and looked for his friend.

*****

Arn slowly felt his way around the room. His outstretched hand and fingers drifted over locker doors, then some empty space, and then . . . He jerked back his hand, his heart pounding hard in his chest for an instant when he thought he felt a person there, standing quietly in the impenetrable dark.

He swore softly as he gripped the sleeve, and began to laugh in relief – it was just some sort of suit. Feeling around some more, his hand brushed across the top of a bench, knocking a plastic cup to the floor and sending a ballpoint pen rolling across its surface. Finally his fingers closed on a small plastic cigarette lighter.

He flicked the wheel, but other than a spark from the flint, there was nothing. He tried again and again – but obviously there was no gas. Still he held it out and flicked the wheel a few times more, spying the outline of a door in the split-second illumination. He stuck the lighter in his pocket and felt about the door until he came to the locking mechanism. He found, as he had hoped, that the door locked from the outside, but not from the inside. There was a button. He pressed it and pushed – the door swung open easily.

'That's one I owe you, Barkin.'

He stepped from the chamber and looked left and right. He was close to the laser acceleration track, and not far from where the ring bulged around the pipe. With all the cameras positioned there, he expected he'd get someone's attention pretty quickly.

Barkin is going to pay for this, he thought, and jogged towards the bulge, leaning in close to the mechanism and waving his arms.

25

*****

'Moving into ignition lockdown.' The room fell into silence. Even the chattering students were silenced by the suspense as they watched the screens.

A computer-generated voice counted down from thirty seconds: *Twenty-nine–twenty-eight–twenty-seven–twenty-six* . . .

One of the technicians was on his feet pointing. 'Wha . . . what the . . . there's a kid in there!'

The room descended into shouting, panic and confusion. Beescomb went as white as a sheet as he recognised the figure on the screen. His mouth opened and closed, but no words came.

Twenty–nineteen–eighteen–seventeen . . .

'Shut it down, shut it down!'

Barkin smirked at the rear of the observation room and nudged Otis. Harper grabbed and lifted one of the technicians from his seat, taking control of his command board. The scientist's voice had gone up several octaves as he screamed over his shoulder, 'Abort, abort! For God's sake, abort!'

Five–four–three–two . . .

The synthetically calm computer voice intoned, 'Laser firing commencing.'

The room froze as if time had stopped. There was no sound or movement as everyone watched the screens. Edward held his breath.

The photonic diamond glowed, turning the chamber, and their screens an infernal red as the particles, which were travelling at a fraction under the speed of light, were given an extra kick by the laser.

On the screen, they could see Arn stop waving and turn to look at the bulge. The screen blurred slightly, like it was recording something behind a gauze veil. Then Arn blurred as the veil thickened and became more like a waterfall of oil.

Edward sucked in a breath in horror. Arn seemed to bend unnaturally for a moment, his body distorting, his mouth opening in a silent scream of pain and confusion. The Hadean red glow of the diamond, coupled with Arn's horrific contortions, made it a scene straight from the pit of Hell.

The display went black.

The only sound Edward heard was Becky screaming Arn's name. *She actually cares after all*, he thought with surprise.

The screen came back on.

Arn was gone.

Chapter 4

Weird Things For Company

Excruciating pain, dizziness and nausea. Light, then swirling colours, then darkness. Arn fell with a thump into mud and shards of something hard.

He blinked. There was nothing in front of his eyes. He sat up and pushed the heels of his hands into them and rubbed hard. He opened them again – there wasn't the faintest ray or particle of light. His head hurt, reminding him of the time he had spent too long at the beach and got too much sun on the back of his neck.

It was like he was still locked back in the storeroom. *Or have I gone blind?* he thought dismally. He held out a hand, and waved it around – nothing.

He sniffed. There was a rank dampness, and something else unpleasant. He held his breath and strained to hear – there was faint dripping coming from somewhere far away. Arn stood and reached out again. He took a few steps, groping in the darkness like a blind man, and then his hand touched a wall. It was slick with slime.

He flicked his fingers. 'Yecch.'

Arn stepped sideways and his head banged into something metallic, showering him with flakes of what he assumed was rust. He swore loudly, and after the echo died away, he heard something in the distance – a movement, like a shuffling or dragging.

'Hello?' No response. The noise stopped. 'Hello, anybody there?'

It started again; this time it was closer. There came a soft murmur.

Arn remembered the cigarette lighter in his pocket, and pulled it free, frantically spinning the strike wheel. A split second of spark showed he was in a long tunnel. Plenty of debris, but he could navigate it.

The soft murmur came again, followed by a sound like a child giggling. 'Who . . .?'

He was breathing hard through his mouth, and felt his heart thumping in his chest. The shuffling was closer, and he spun the lighter's wheel again.

He shrieked, and fell back. There had been a ghastly face, all milky eyes and chisel-shaped teeth looming before him. The body looked slimy and colourless, but thankfully it had shrunk from the spark.

He had fallen into a puddle of slimy water, and he frantically spun the flint wheel again and again, trying to keep up a continuous flashing of sparks. There was a scuttling and splashing from further away in the darkness, but thankfully there were no more *things* being illuminated in front of him.

'Must have been a wild dog.' Arn spoke this thought aloud, simply to take comfort from hearing his own voice. It didn't work. He sounded scared and his voice was about several octaves higher than normal.

Once more he spun the small wheel, another spark of light and this time a small red glow flashed back at him from the ground ahead. He scrambled forward, and felt around in the dark muck. His hand closed on a cylindar about three inches long, smooth, and strangely warm. He flicked the lighter again, and in the split second flash he saw the red glass-like rod.

'What the hell?' It was Fermilab's diamond. 'How did you get here? What's going on?' From some reason, Arn thought he'd be in real trouble now. He shoved the finger-length stone in his pocket, and wiped his hands on his shirt.

His constant flicking finally encouraged the last squeeze of gas to erupt in a tiny flame, and the bright light made him squint. In the seconds of light he had, he saw that the tunnel went on for miles, but he also saw that the small tongue of flame was bending – *a breeze.*

'Thank you God,' he whispered. 'If air is coming in, then I'm damn well going out.' Arn scrambled to his feet.

His thumb ached and he bet he had a blister forming, but he kept flicking the wheel. He moved as quickly through the damp tunnels as the debris would allow. He only slowed to glance over his shoulder when he heard a strange shuffling coming from behind him. It was impossible to see in the inky blackness, but he increased his speed, knowing that if the flint wore out on the lighter, he may never find a way out . . . and he had a feeling that the *thing* didn't need light to see *him.*

Arn had been changing hands to share the load on his thumbs, but after what felt like hours of trudging through the thick darkness, the wheel spun without sparking. No matter what he did, it refused to do anything more than spin uselessly. The little orange lighter had given up.

Orange?

He'd forgotten . . . it was orange. He didn't know how long he had been travelling underground, but he now also noticed that he could make out the dim shapes of the debris covering the floor. *Light,* he marvelled. He dropped the lighter and started to run, leaping over fallen rocks, decayed steel girders, and in one instance what he thought looked like a weird rib cage.

He eventually came to a shaft of blue light falling from the ceiling across a tumble of boulders blocking the tunnel.

He pulled in long ragged breaths, feeling the fatigue of the run and the heavy mental drain of wandering through pitch darkness with nothing but sparks of light, and some weird *things* for company.

The hole in the collapsed ceiling led to a shaft going straight upwards. No sky was visible, so the shaft must have twisted on its way to the surface. But there was definitely natural light coming from somewhere further up.

He didn't give it a second thought and pulled himself up into the hole. It was narrow – that was good; it allowed him to brace himself between the walls, and slowly inch himself higher. His muscles protested, and his back was scratched a thousand times over by the sharp walls, and felt sticky with blood.

He had to pause several times to work out how to traverse some difficult sections, and he wished he had have spent a little more time on the gym rope, or the rock-climbing wall at school. It didn't matter; he was going to get out, even if it meant his back was shredded.

What felt like hours later, he pulled himself up and out into the light. He rolled onto his back and sucked in a deep breath, wincing from the pain and waiting for his breathing to calm. He sniffed and frowned. The air smelled different, strange.

He opened his eyes and just as quickly had to shut them. They streamed with tears from the glare. After hours in the gloom, it would take a while for him to adjust to bright light again.

Sitting up, he cupped his hands around his eyes and squinted between his fingers, breathing slowly and allowing his vision to come back into focus.

What . . . ?

Chapter 5

The Wasteland

What happened? Where am I? Arn had assumed there'd been some sort of explosion and the Fermilab facility had collapsed, burying him inside. But now . . .

He blinked another few times and got slowly to his feet, still cupping his hands over his eyes against the glare. For as far as he could see, there was nothing – no modern facility with its strange, sagging sandwich building, no roads, no metal sculpture, nothing at all.

He turned in a circle. In fact, there were no trees, no grass, not even any hills. It was like a desert, but not quite as hot and dry. He looked at the sun, just up over the horizon – was it morning? A warm breeze blew past him; that was what he had found strange – it smelled like . . . nothing. The word *sterile* came to his mind.

There must have been a nuclear explosion, he thought. But when he knelt down and sifted through the sandy dirt, it ran freely through his fingers – no melted or fused glass or rock, no building debris, nothing but grains of bleached rock.

'But . . . what was that thing, then? A dog, a deformed dog . . . or maybe a giant rat.'

But it giggled – it was watching you, following you. It looked like a . . . He shook his head to clear the argument that was washing back and forth in his mind.

He licked his lips; he'd need something to drink soon.

Maybe he should wait here, otherwise when Dr. Harper or Mr. Beescomb came to look for him, they'd never find him. Arn looked back at the hole he had just climbed out of. It was just an open wound in the flat surface, like a dry sinkhole. He turned again, looking at the ground, and then the landscape – it had a wiped-clean look – like someone had dragged a giant beach towel across the sand, flattening all the features.

There was no one . . . There will be no one. That scornful voice in his head again, filling him with dread and pessimism:

Stay here and die.

The warm breeze wafted again, and he turned his face into it. He remembered a science class on weather, and the droning teacher telling them that wind usually blew from the coast – if that was true, then that'd be a pretty good place to head towards.

Arn looked back at the hole for a second. There was water down there; maybe he should . . .

Forget it. The thought of climbing back down into that labyrinth was both frightening and repellant. Instead, he used his foot to make an arrow in the sand.

'I went this way,' he said, to no one but the sterile breeze.

I'll head towards the coast, he thought – *see what sort of land this is. And if there are any rivers, that'll be where they'll empty.* Besides, if this was still home, then the coast was to the east – twenty-five miles; sure, a long way, but he was young and fit. He turned into the breeze and started to walk.

'Winds always blow from the coast, and the coast is east,' he repeated automatically.

Unless its winter, then breezes blow towards the coast, not from it – you're going the wrong way, dummy.

Arn groaned. *Heads you win, tails I lose,* he thought and kept walking into the breeze.

*****

No one spoke or moved for many minutes after Arn had vanished from the observation screens.

Edward was in shock, but excited – an idea forming in his mind. Becky closed her mouth, and pushed through the crowd of bewildered teenagers, scientists and administrators, to stand before one of the large screens.

'What happened? Where did he go?'

One of the technicians got to his feet. 'Vaporised.'

'Stop that sort of talk.' Dr. Harper frowned and took a step towards the screen.

Beescomb was still regaining his wits. 'Where . . . where's my student, Harper? What just happened here? Can we get someone down there?'

Harper ignored him and squinted at one screen, then the next. He barked some instructions to his team, and moved to a control panel, quickly ordering a lockdown of the facility. One of the screens began to flash, and Harper said to his senior scientist: 'All right, Takada, shut it down . . . All of it.'

Jim Takada nodded, rapidly tapping in the command sequence on his computer, before stopping and frowning, and then repeating his movements again, this time with more care. He swore under his breath and lifted his hands from the keys for a second, and then he tried it again.

Harper, dragging his eyes away from his screen, noticed Takada's frustration and turned to him. 'What's up? What's wrong?'

Takada shook his head. 'It's just . . .' He entered an alternative sequence into the computer, then shook his head again. He spoke out of the corner of his mouth, 'It's just not shutting down. In fact it's still running as if there's a high-speed, high-energy collision taking place – but that's impossible. The energy draw is phenomenal . . . and it's building.'

Harper looked back at the screen, and then brought one hand up to his face. 'Oh no, no, no – where's our diamond? What the hell happened to the acceleration lens?'

Takada spoke over his shoulder. 'The kid must have it. Maybe that's why we can't shut the track down; he's done something to the collision acceleration instrumentation.'

The rise and fall of a siren could now be heard in the corridor outside. Further along the room, a female technician in thick spectacles skidded along the floor on the wheels of her chair to a different position at a long wall of electronics. She flicked some switches, then read some numbers off one of the small screens – speaking loudly, trying to be heard over the raised voices, the pulsing beeps now coming from most of the control panels in the room.

'I've got radiation – something is bleeding high gamma down in the pipe room.'

Edward heard Harper swear, and then saw him rub his chin in nervous indecision. That concerned him more than anything he had seen – if Harper was worried, then so should they be.

Edward felt a rising panic, and looked back at the screens that had showed his friend disappearing only moments before. The more he stared, the more the image looked . . . wrong.

Harper also looked along the bank of screens, shaking his head slowly. He turned back to the bespectacled technician. 'I don't see anything. There can't be a leak . . . There should be nothing *to* leak.' He shook his head again. 'Doesn't make sense at all. Regardless, I'll have a team go in and shut it down manually.'

'Well, we'd better hurry; we've got an enormous power drain going on.' She turned back to her station; between her and the other technicians, the activity was now furious.

Edward took his glasses off and wiped them. Replacing them, he moved closer to the screen. He frowned, took his glasses off again, and rubbed them even harder on his shirt. This time after he put them back on his nose, he squinted and then spoke softly, 'Look.'

Even in all the confusion, Harper must have heard him, and turned to stare at Edward for a moment, his eyebrows shooting up in recognition, as though remembering the students were still in the control room.

'I need everyone cleared from this room – authorised personnel only.'

An electronic voice intoned from a speaker overhead, the phrase repeated in an emotionless repetition: *secure lockdown initiated – secure lockdown initiated . . .*

Harper turned to a small black-and-white screen showing sets of enormous doors sliding shut at several exits to the building, and larger, two-foot-thick blast doors moving into place in the deeper areas of the underground facility. Harper swore again and turned to the group, urgency now in his movements.

Edward spoke the word again, 'Look.'

Harper looked briefly at Edward and made motions to herd the teenagers from the room. 'Sorry all, but we're going to have to evacuate you immediately. Looks like we have some sort of, *ahh*, electronic or magnetic disturbance. Nothing to worry about, no danger. We'll find your friend. He's probably just managed to wander off into some section of the tunnel that isn't under surveillance.'

The school group started to move backwards towards the door. Edward stood his ground, and pointed to the screen that had once shown his friend. This time he yelled it: 'Look!'

Harper studied the screen, and then turned back to face Edward. 'There's nothing to see, son.'

Edward kept on pointing. 'That's just it. It's not what we *can* see ... it's what we *can't*.' He looked from Harper to Beescomb. Many of the technicians had swivelled in their chairs to listen to him. 'There's something missing from the room ... other than Arn, I mean. C'mon, look.' He pointed at the screen to where his friend had been standing.

The entire room had fallen silent, and every eye was following the line of his pointing finger. No one heard the pinging, beeps or sirens anymore.

Edward walked right up to the screen and jabbed his finger at it. 'Near the collision recording section – see? There's something missing ... like a small bite has been taken out of the machinery and background. But if the device was damaged, you'd know about it, right?'

Harper frowned, and leaned so close to the screen that his nose was almost touching the glass. He spoke over his shoulder. 'Takada, take a look at this. What do you make of it?'

Takada leapt to his feet and hurried over. He nodded and spoke softly to his boss. 'There's an anomaly there, all right. Might be a fault in the film recording, though.'

Harper pressed some buttons, causing the screens to switch to a different angle. The same golf-ball-sized section was missing from every angle, like something oily was masking a section of the room or distorting the air.

Harper rubbed his chin and whispered, 'I think I know where the boy went ... and our diamond.'

*****

Arn stumbled in the sand and fell to his knees. His lips were beginning to crack; when he swallowed, it felt like the dryness in his throat was caught halfway and refused to be pushed down any further unless accompanied by the reward of some water.

He blinked several times, and rubbed his eyes with the back of his hand – they felt gritty and dry. In the distance, he could make out a large boulder sticking up from the sand. He felt somewhat elated – at least there were *some* features other than an endless, baked earth. He could use it for shelter, or climb it to see if there was anything over the horizon. He plodded on, still feeling the breeze on his face.

Shielding his eyes, he looked up at the sun; it was no longer directly overhead. It must have been morning when he set out, and he bet it was some time past midday now.

He wiped his dry face – he had stopped perspiring long ago, and he knew this meant his body was starting to seriously dehydrate. He'd need a drink soon, or his mind would become foggy.

Foggier, the little voice sneered. It was constantly with him now, never letting him be for a second.

Along with the voice, there was the dull pain. His head throbbed – another sign of dehydration.

There's water inside you.

'Huh?'

You know what I mean.

'Oh no, no, no. No way.'

Did you know you could drink your own pee three times before it became toxic?

'Urk. Now I'm really losing it.'

Drink it – it'll keep you alive.

Arn laughed dismissively. 'And do you think that would improve my chances with Becky if she ever found out?'

I wont tell if you don't.

Arn ignored the voice, and looked up at the huge stone that loomed before him. He had wandered so far in his mind, he hadn't noticed how close he was to it now.

His dry mouth fell open. *This can't be real . . .*

It wasn't a boulder at all. It was a skull – gigantic, and bleached by a million sunshines. Just behind it, the tops of waist-thick bones stuck out of the ground for a good forty feet before they gradually sunk below the sand. *Huge ribs*, Arn thought.

He ran his hand along the skull, perhaps to see if it *was* real. It was warm and rough to his touch, and tilted slightly onto its side. He could see inside the mouth that it still had a few sharp teeth.

A dinosaur? No. A whale, maybe.

And that'll be you soon, if you don't find water.

Arn remembered why he came to the skull, and climbed up onto it. Still facing into the breeze, he squinted. In the distance, something gleamed.

Chapter 6

That's Not Supposed To Happen

The room had been cleared and Harper and his senior scientist huddled around one of the screens. Takada tapped the glass with his knuckle.

'I think we've got a topological paradox.' He folded his arms and peered at the blurred area on the screen.

'A wormhole?' Harper whispered, and ran his hands up through his thinning hair. 'Maybe; after all, we knew it was theoretically possible. But one that stays open – that's not supposed to happen . . . even on paper.'

'Well, the visual evidence sure points to something being there that wasn't there before. Or rather I should say, something *not* being there, that *was* before.'

Harper blinked a few times at the oily distortion. 'And the boy and our diamond fell through it, or were pulled through?'

'I know, I know, it's all crazy. But it could have all been a lot worse: if the collision had generated a black hole, even a miniature one, and it failed to evaporate in nanoseconds, it could have given off enough gamma radiation to fry the planet. So we should be thankful for that at least.'

Harper grunted. 'So, you think it's safe to go down there?'

Takada shrugged. 'None of the instruments are registering lethal gamma or X-rays anymore. The anomaly gave off just enough rads to cause the blast doors to activate, but not enough to harm anyone.'

'Yet.' Harper raised his eyebrows.

'And that's the problem, isn't it? The *non-mass* is somehow causing our systems to be drained of power, and refuse their shutdown orders on the collider. We somehow opened a wormhole, and now something is

38

causing it to be wedged open. It's drawing ever more power, and I don't know what'll happen when it reaches a tipping point.'

Harper leaned on his fists and looked hard at the screen, which had now been recalibrated to focus on the small area of blurred disturbance next to the collision point.

'Give me some options, people.'

Takeda sat forward. 'The collider is moving at a speed that has surpassed light. That's pretty cool.'

Harper turned to glare at him, and he swallowed and went on.

'But the fact is, the particles we have created are still accelerating. Don't know why, but each rotation in the chamber means more power is drawn, more speed is achieved, and more fragility enters the system. So . . .' He shrugged. 'We need to slow them down. We need a brake.'

Harper's eyebrows went up.

Takeda nodded as he spoke. 'We need to refire the laser. Derail or slow those particles down, and remove the paradox's energy source.'

'Perfect. Now if only we had a red diamond we could calibrate. Anyone got a year and ten million bucks?' Harper rubbed his forehead and sighed. 'Okay, so, we need to do something – at least get in to take a look at it. Before it reaches this unknown tipping point.' He leaned back. 'You know, it still may close by itself.'

Takada nodded. 'That's right; it may evaporate any second, or . . .'

'Or?'

'Or it could swell and absorb more of the facility, or all of the facility. Or maybe generate a nuclear meltdown, causing a chain reaction that could irradiate the rest of the planet.' Takada wiped his brow. 'Or it could do something else we can't even imagine.' His voice was rising. 'We've got to get in there.'

'Okay, that's enough,' Harper said. 'We're going in – as for what happens then, we'll cross that bridge when we come to it.'

Takada sucked in a deep breath, and visibly calmed himself. 'We're scientists; we'll do what we're supposed to – observe.'

'Observe,' Harper repeated, and then thought gloomily, *Perhaps observe the end of the world.*

Chapter 7

The Garden Of Eden

There was rain on his face, and he opened his mouth to let some of the drops fall onto his tongue. Memories floated back slowly: he remembered walking towards the shining object in the distance, and then seeing the mirage – a forest of tall trees, almost like it was fringing some unseen border.

He must have dozed again, for when he finally opened his eyes the rain had long stopped, and his clothes were dry. Arn groaned as he sat up, blinking to try to clear his vision.

The Garden of Eden, he thought. Every muscle ached, and he still felt dehydrated, but he couldn't help smiling. He had first woken in some dank cave of horrors deep below the earth, had crossed a sterile desert, and now he found himself on a green hillside dotted with trees that towered above him.

Where am I? he wondered. It looked a little bit like California . . . Maybe the Sequoia Forest. He looked up at the sky – it was a darkish blue tending to purple in the west as the sun was about to set. Above him, a tree that could have been a black oak spread its huge limbs in an enormous umbrella-shaped canopy.

A giant nut, like an acorn the size of a football, dangled heavily over his head. He saw that there were many more of them on most of the lower branches. As he examined them, the closest one wiggled.

Arn stood slowly, shaking off a moment of dizziness, and reached out to touch it. Just as his fingers brushed against the glossy brown casing, the head of a worm burst from somewhere underneath and lashed out at his hand. The finger-thick grub had a ring of fangs like daggers, and only

Arn's fear gave him the speed to avoid it. Missing his hand by inches, it bit deeply, digging furrows along the side of its own shell. He grimaced in disgust and backed away, wiping his hand and looking over his shoulder to examine his surroundings.

He breathed deeply, calming himself. The air tasted strange . . . Everything was slightly strange. He stood quietly; except for the hum of hidden insects, there was no sound. The hill he stood upon gave him a view over a shallow valley that ended in a small stream ringed by thick forests. Many of the trees were so thick and tall they resembled mighty redwoods, except their canopies spread more like oaks.

Arn turned slowly in a circle. Through the trees to the east he could make out the dry sands he had just trekked across. He shook his head in amazement at how far he had managed to walk into the forest without even realising it . . . *Without even being fully awake*, he thought. To the north, the land became more raised, and in the very far distance he could see snow-capped mountains pushing up like ragged purple teeth against the darkening sky.

Arn sucked in another breath. *No pollution*, he thought . . . *and no car exhausts, factory smells, asphalt warming in the afternoon sun, perfumes, cooking odours . . . nothing.* Now he knew: *that* was what he had found strange – the air was pure.

He felt his face, his chest, and looked down at his feet and legs – dusty sneakers, jeans ripped at the knees; in his pockets, some gum, a multi-tool pocketknife, wallet and antiseptic gel his mother made him take on the field trip – *door handles were smorgasbords for germs*, she always said to him. And lastly, a blood red diamond worth about ten million dollars. He felt guilty just handling it.

Everything was exactly where it had been when he left for the science trip that morning . . . when he had come out of the room Barkin had locked him in . . . when he had found himself left behind and then tried to get someone's attention on the camera. He frowned, trying to remember what happened next. He couldn't. Everything had got a little crazy and mixed up after that.

The sky had now turned a deeper purple; it was going to be night soon, and Arn didn't fancy sleeping out – if the cold didn't kill him, his parents sure would. *How did Barkin get him out here? Did he somehow fall off the bus on the way back home?* He knew that Fermilab was built on about ten square miles of land, and that they had preserved much of the grounds to be like a wilderness to demonstrate their commitment to both science and the environment. Perhaps he had been knocked out and left in some remote corner of the estate.

But the worm thing? Maybe Fermilab was giving off radiation and mutating some of the forest creatures.

He dismissed the idea. He'd read that the reforested land around the facility was now providing some of the best birdwatching in the state. *And no one had taken photographs of any two-headed birds . . . or vampire worms inside acorns*, he thought.

Arn looked up at the seed casing, just in time to see that the pod had worked its way along the branch towards him. It had also extended its long muscular body down from the shell by about a foot, fangs extended and rows of small hooked legs opened wide, poised to seize hold of his head.

Yecch. He ducked and rolled out of the way. Looking back, he could see that many of the other nuts in the tree had now managed to inch their way across the lower limbs, and had moved to hang from the limb that he had been standing underneath. *Not fruit at all*, he guessed – *more some sort of larvae casing for a carnivorous worm.*

He ran further out into the open, and stopped. *Where was he going?* He didn't even know where he was. *At least away from that tree*, he thought, moving further into the clearing. He was fortunate he had woken before those things had managed to reach him. He shuddered at the thought.

Arn sat down heavily. Twilight was now upon him and he tried to come up with a plan. Find shelter? Continue on . . . but to where? While he contemplated his next action, a number of small animals entered the edge of the clearing, obviously heading to the stream for an evening's drink. At first Arn thought they were large hares with their long ears and twitching noses, but as they cleared some of the longer grasses he saw that their legs didn't end in small pads like a normal rabbit, but were longer and ended in hooves.

Some small sound in the forest caused them to start, and in unison their ears flattened back against their heads and they bounded forward – straight towards him.

A moment later, they caught sight of him and most swerved away, but two had to leap completely over his head. He frowned, then smiled – weird, really weird. *What would Edward make of these strange things?* he wondered. *Rabbilopes,* he thought, and smiled again.

Thinking of his friend made him homesick. It also caused him to recall one of the last questions he remembered Edward asking Harper in the laboratory. Something about wormholes and space-time distortions.

Arn watched as a few of the strange rabbilope creatures worked up the courage to re-enter the clearing near the stream. Edward had been pestering Harper about the possibility of creating a doorway that could send you somewhere else . . . or some-when else. Arn remembered laughing at the time. But now?

Is that what happened? I'm either somewhere, or some-when else? His stomach rumbled and he looked again in the direction of the drinking rabbilopes. *Nah, too soon to go Robinson Crusoe just yet.*

Watching the drinking animals, two things jumped into his head from both his social studies and biology lessons – one: creatures came to drink in the evenings when they thought it was safe. So that meant there was also a time when it was unsafe – there were probably predators. And two: civilisations usually grew up along rivers – so if he followed the stream, he'd either find a city, or at least a coastline.

Arn stood, feeling slightly better now that he had mapped out a course of action. The sky had gone deep black purple, and just as he felt a creeping panic at the thought of wandering around in the dark, it suddenly began to lighten. Not to a sort of day brightness, but to more of a cool silver hue.

To the east, a gigantic moon was rising. It was so large, he could raise both arms wide apart and only just map out its edges. It hurt his eyes slightly to look at it, and he felt a small tingling buzz in the centre of his head.

Ignoring this, he studied the moon's surface. Comfortingly, he could even see recognisable details on its silvery skin – it was *his* moon after all. He could see the craters, dry lakes and oceans, and he remembered their names from his astronomy classes – the Sea of Tranquillity, the Tycho and Copernicus Craters. He frowned and squinted; at the edge of the Sea of Rains, a dark smudge stained its silvery exterior. There were veins running out from the stain's centre to smaller smudges. He shook his head, guessing at what it could be. *Impossible . . . A city?*

The buzzing in his skull persisted. He opened his arms and stretched his back and shoulders. The moon's bathing glow made him feel strange – a good feeling, powerful almost. Could the increased gravitational pull of the closer moon be affecting him? He flexed his arms. His fatigue had almost completely fallen away. It didn't matter; all that was important was he knew he was on Earth, and that only left him to find out the somewhenelse.

*****

Arn crossed the lower plains of the valley, and walked along the edge of the stream for many hours. Finally, when the huge moon was beginning to fall towards the horizon, he sat for a moment to rest.

The water burbled over rocks, and from time to time he saw flashes of silver being reflected back from the moonlight. *Fish* – his empty stomach growled loudly.

I can eat raw fish, he thought, *but with no rod, no reel, no bait? No chance.* He continued watching the silvery flashes, listening to the water tumble over the rocks – it was almost hypnotising.

So tired, he thought. *But I'm never going to be able to sleep in this weird place. I wonder if Beescomb is looking for me? I wonder where Becky and Edward think I've gone? I wonder if she misses me?* He watched the fish continue to dance and tumble in the crystal water. In another second, he was fast asleep.

*****

His face was warm.

Arn woke with a start. He sat bolt upright, getting his bearings. Warm sunlight glittered on the stream, and felt pleasant on his cheeks and shoulders. Now, in the full light of the morning, he could fully take in his surroundings. He had fallen asleep on the bank of the stream where it bent at a tumble of boulders. He was sheltered by this small wall of rock at the base of a hill. Knee-high plants with fleshy leaves and small red star-shaped flowers grew in bunches at the water's edge.

Arn followed the flow of the stream with his eyes and saw that it actually disappeared in among the rocks at the side of the hill. He hoped that it reappeared on the other side of the hill, so he could continue to follow it.

While he sat musing, his stomach growled again and this time actually hurt a little. Small yellow butterflies danced around his face and he blew

44

air at one that looked to be contemplating a quick landing on his nose.

'Shouldn't get too close to my mouth when I'm this hungry, little guy.'

While he continued to watch them, one alighted on his hand. He smiled, until he felt a sharp pain; he slapped at the butterfly, cursing, and flicked it into the water, where its small yellow body circled in a little eddy at the shoreline. He looked down at his hand and saw a puncture mark with a dot of blood welling up from it.

'Jeez, does anything not bite, sting or peck in this weird land?' He lifted his hand to his mouth to suck at the wound and ease the sting. There was a splash from the stream and he looked up in time to see a good-sized fish come in close to the shore to snatch the butterfly from the water's surface. His stomach rumbled again, and he lowered his hand, wondering at the possibility.

Arn swatted another couple of the large yellow butterflies. From a large bush, he dragged down a branch about four feet in length, broke it off and stripped away the smaller branches. Taking out his pocketknife, he sharpened one end of his makeshift spear.

Once finished, he admired his handiwork. He lifted the spear, weighed it in his hands, and looked down along its length as though checking a pool cue. Satisfied, he returned to the rocks by the stream.

He had only been gone a few minutes, but on returning he saw his butterfly bait was gone, and some of the fish from the stream were waddling back towards the water, propped up on stiff forefins. One still held one of the butterflies between its rubbery lips.

'You've got to be kidding me.'

On hearing him, the fish started to move a little faster towards the water. Arn leapt, spear held high.

*****

Arn threw the remains of the fish onto the ground and went to wash his hands.

He caught sight of himself at the water's edge. 'Like fishy, bony pork, and very nice.' He finished with a belch at his reflection.

The sun was climbing towards its zenith, and he decided to set off again – he'd climb the hill and then hopefully be able to pick up the stream when it reemerged on the other side. He felt better after his small meal, and now he knew that at least there was *some* food he could eat . . . and more importantly, catch.

He looked back at the remains of the fish. It was already covered in the yellow butterflies. He shook his head. *Carnivorous butterflies . . . What next – acid-spitting squirrels?* He laughed at the thought, and set off.

*****

Arn climbed to the top of the hill – a tough climb, as it turned out to be a lot higher and steeper than he expected. As he neared its summit, he smelled a coppery odour and something else unpleasant that he couldn't identify.

Once at the top, he stood and looked down into a bowl-shaped valley, and recoiled in disgust. Bodies were strewn everywhere; blood still oozed from vicious wounds.

He struggled to believe it was real. The dress of the fallen combatants made it seem more like some sort of dorky medieval battlefield recreation. But then the smell, blood and broken bodies, and what looked like large crows circling overhead – these proved otherwise.

He stared hard into the valley. Armoured warriors – like a cross between knights and Vikings – lay everywhere. But there was something about them that wasn't . . . right.

And not all of them were dead. Other knights knelt among the bodies, and Arn crouched for cover before they caught sight of him. Further up the other side of the valley, a knight on horseback emerged from the shade of a tree, his armour shining silver in the sunlight. Upon his head was a mighty helmet in the shape of a snarling dog or wolf – all silver rivets, wild eyes and fangs.

Arn felt a sudden urge to yell to them – let them know he was there. Perhaps he might even get some answers. But something in their shape held him back. At that moment, the mounted warrior lifted his hands to his head and removed his helmet.

Arn's breath caught in his chest. The shape of the helmet was no simple design of fancy. Instead, it looked as if it had been moulded to its owner's actual features; a silver grey wolf's head looked up to the sky, and the knight lifted one hand and ran it across his fur from snout to forehead. He opened his mouth in an anguished grimace, long teeth gleaming whitely in his long face.

Arn was frozen with fear and indecision. Given the dangers he had encountered to date, he fully expected these creatures to be carnivorous. The knight turned his head, and eyes like twin gun barrels fixed on Arn. Even from that great distance, Arn saw them momentarily widen in surprise. Those long teeth flashed again as the knight spoke to another, now standing at his shoulder. He pointed, and then the other armoured wolf also looked to where Arn was standing.

Arn wasn't going to wait for these creatures to come and fetch him for dinner, but as he turned to run back down the hill, he found himself face-to-face with a sinister, robed figure.

It was no more than four feet in height. From under the hood of its robe, eyes that were yellow slits embedded in night-dark orbs stared unblinkingly. Beneath a small, flattened snout, a wedge-shaped mouth hung open to reveal rows of needle-like teeth in black gums.

Arn thought he saw it smile as its furred hand, which was little more than a clump of wickedly curved hooks, snagged his shirt and dragged him forward. As he struggled to free himself, something hit him on the side of his head, and mercifully everything went black.

Chapter 8

I Come In Peace

Arn woke to feel a chill across his belly and chest, and pain across most of his upper body.

He tried to sit up but couldn't, and realised he was roped, spread-eagled, to a wooden frame. Worse still, he was naked. He leaned forward and saw that his clothes had been ripped to shreds and dumped in a pile. His wallet lay open, its contents also shredded, his sticks of gum scattered on the grass. Another piece lay chewed up in a small puddle of slimy goo, as though someone had tasted it and then spat it out.

Arn saw that his pocketknife lay unopened on a bench nearby, its stiff hinges obviously proving too much for the creature's clawed hands. But there was no diamond. A small sound made him whip his head around, and the frame squeaked underneath him.

Several more robed creatures, squatting nearby, heard the movement and got to their feet. All moved to stand beside the frame, staring for a moment, before talking in a whining singsong language to each other. One pointed to several bits of Arn's anatomy, this followed by more hissing and whining that grated on his already stretched nerves.

A hooked claw was pointed at his groin. The look of disgust on their flat features was plain to see – he was obviously as repugnant to them as they were to him.

There came a noise from behind the strange group that immediately quietened them, and then the frame was lowered until it lay at about his captives' chest level. *Feels like an operating table*, Arn thought as he watched the creatures, and teased the ropes at his wrists.

With their robed heads bowed, they parted to allow a grey-faced creature to approach. It moved immediately up to his head, and bent closer to examine him with an unblinking stare, its yellow slitted eyes never straying from his own. The gaze was so intense, Arn felt it was stripping him down to the bone.

Arn tried to return the stare, but found it hard to look into the hypnotic gaze for very long. Instead, he looked into its mouth, which hung open to reveal the same needle-like teeth the others had, but these were grey and decayed with age. The vile smell of its hot breath on his face made him turn away, gagging.

The creature held up its hand and between two claws sat the magnificent diamond from the laboratory.

Arn nodded. 'You can have it.'

The thing kept its eyes on Arn's face and motioned with one arm, hissing something to the small group behind it. They immediately carried over a wooden bench, on which they then placed a heavy stone jug and bowl.

The creature looked Arn up and down, as though deciding where he would begin. Arn felt his nerves were about to break.

'Can you understand me?'

The creature stopped and stared for few seconds, and then went back to pouring a stream of water from the jug into the bowl.

'I'm your friend,' Arn persisted. 'I mean you no harm.'

The creature ignored him. Instead, he dipped his small, clawed hands into the water and rubbed them together, holding them up and inspecting them as Arn had seen surgeons do before commencing an operation.

'Oh God, no. Listen, I come in peace.' He knew it was pointless, but fear was doing the talking now.

It reached up to his face, and Arn felt the sharp talons raking his skin for a second, before circling around his temple as if searching for the tenderest places to start.

'Please don't . . .'

Then it began. The pain was excruciating as all five of the sharp talons entered the soft skin of his temple. The face leaned forward to stare again, the breath reeking of carrion, rotting teeth, and a foulness that was both nauseating and frightening.

The hissing and whining commenced, and then stopped. Then came more probing and whining. Arn gritted his teeth. It made no difference –

the hissing and whining became ever more forceful, insistent, like an endlessly repeated question.

More probing, and then the voices lowered, punctuated by pauses and different inflections. The pain that he felt at his temple moved to the centre of his skull, and then . . .

'Ugly hairless creature; your shape disgusts me. All apes are long dead. From where do you come?'

Arn's first thought was that the pain had caused him to pass out and he was just dreaming. Or worse – that it had sent him insane. Perhaps that was it? Whatever happened in the acceleration room at Fermilab had rendered him insane, and this wasn't happening at all? He giggled deliriously at the creature's flattened face.

The thing started talking again, but this time its eyes were closed, and the words didn't seem meant for him.

'This one has travelled far. Strange mind, complex mind, toolmaker, war maker. Not fully grown yet – almost, but not yet.' It opened its eyes and leaned in close. 'Are you ape?' The claws sunk deeper. 'Where do you come from, ape? What do they call you?'

The pain in the centre of Arn's head turned to fire, and he felt blood stream from his nostrils.

The claws dug deeper, the questions repeated.

Arn screamed out his answer, 'I hear you, I hear you!' He grimaced and spoke through gritted teeth. 'Not an ape; I'm a man.'

'No!' The creature spat this into his face, and then turned and hissed the words, 'This ape is a liar'. It spun back and growled into Arn's face with such hatred, that he tried to shrink back into the frame that held him.

'Man is gone. Man is long dead.'

The creature once again held the diamond in front of Arn's face. 'What is the blood stone for?'

Arn nodded, summoning as much warmth as he could. 'It's for you . . . a gift.'

The creature snorted derisively, turned to drop the stone and snatched up Arn's pocketknife and held it in front of him, while keeping its other claws embedded in his temple. 'And what is this? Is this a weapon?'

Arn tried to shake his head. 'No, just a sort of . . . tool.'

'More lies. Make it work for us, ape.' The old creature pushed the knife into one of Arn's hands. Then he frowned and leaned forward to sniff him.

'I sense a kinship with the Wolfen on him.' The thing growled, and dug deeper with its claws – this time it seemed, just to inflict pain.

Arn cried out and tried to pull away. Tears were rolling down his face. 'Not lying . . . I don't know what a Wolfen is. I'm not an ape; my name is Arnold Singer, and I'm . . .'

The creature jerked upright. Arn suddenly felt like a door had been opened, and he was suddenly able to see back into the dark corridors of the creature's mind.

Arn flexed his thoughts, and saw the creature wince. The doorway to its mind had been opened a crack – he now kicked it wide. He saw an army of the small yellow-eyed creatures who had captured him; behind them were other terrifying beasts, similar in shape to the creatures, but many times larger. There were thousands of them – brutish and powerful, and thirsty for blood and war.

Shock was written momentarily on his interrogator's furred features, and Arn felt its claws withdraw, sliding out from beneath his skin. The slitted eyes were now wide, but not with hatred. Arn sensed something far more primal in them – perhaps even fear.

'Impossible. Not Sigarr. Not *the* Arnoddr-Sigarr.'

Arn felt blood trickle down the side of his face, and watched numbly as the other hooded creatures joined the old sorcerer. All were now highly animated by the mention of this name. Strangely, Arn could still understand them all. Whatever the vile thing had done to him, its effects seemed permanent.

One of the hooded creatures pointed at Arn. 'Make the link again – ask it when the war will come. If there be victory, will it be ours? If it truly is the Arnoddr, it will know.'

Arn closed his eyes. So they didn't know that somehow the link remained. A complex mind, the thing had said of him. *Perhaps more complex than you realise,* Arn thought.

He listened. They called themselves Panterran. And they had a hatred and distrust for almost everything – but none more so than for a race they called the Wolfen.

The old Panterran looked at Arn, its goblin-like features twisted into slyness.

'No more link; it hurts with this one. Not like Panterran or Wolfen mind. I will open the ape and read our future from its entrails.' It gave a small whining chuckle. 'We will save the extra meat for our giant friends.'

51

Arn gulped, and gripped the pocketknife in his fist, praying the pain from the last link had caused the old Panterran to overlook it.

Another Panterran burst in among the group, and after looking scornfully at Arn for a second while it caught its breath, spoke a single word: 'Wolfen.'

The old Panterran hissed. At its orders, the small, deformed-looking creatures began grabbing bows and arrows, and curved swords like scimitars.

'Take the Lygon, but be sure to bring me one of the Wolfen alive – all others are to be killed. Information and secrecy are our weapons now.' The old Panterran turned briefly to Arn and looked him up and down, its mouth twisting in disgust. It picked up some of Arn's shredded clothing and threw it across his face.

'Your hairless form is repulsive . . . but your face truly sickens me.'

You should talk, you ugly freak! Arn screamed the retort in his mind, but kept still and silent as he heard the old creature rush to join the others.

He fiddled with the knife in his hand, his sweaty palm making it difficult, but he needed to hurry. He didn't think *digging around in his entrails* sounded like something he wanted to hang around for. He tested his bonds. *Gotta get out of here. Now!*

Chapter 9

Fenrir Watches Us All

The four Wolfen, three adults and one youth, moved silently through the deeper parts of the forest, pausing from time to time to lift their heads in the air, or get down close to the ground to examine some minor disturbance to the soil or grass.

Isingarr, their senior warrior, held up one hand and remained stock-still. His ears were erect and pointing forward. The tip of one of them was missing, and a long scar ran down the side of his face, the result of a previous battle. The others held their ground and waited.

His eyes were unblinking as they scanned the forest ahead, and a low, almost imperceptible rumble came from deep in his chest. Immediately, his two adult companions joined him, drawing long silver blades that glinted in the shaded gloom.

Isingarr spoke over his shoulder. 'I fear we may be late in rejoining the Valkeryn pack this eve.' He drew his own blade as the stillness of the dense forest was broken. Their ears twitched at the soft hissing and whining that echoed both low to the ground and high in the trees – all around them.

Isingarr turned to one of the warriors. 'Ussen, you will escort our ward back to Valkeryn. Turok and I will give you some time – use it well.'

Ussen stared hard at Isingarr for a second, looking like he wanted to disobey the command to leave his leader, before nodding once. Behind him, the young Wolfen began to protest, and Ussen sheathed his sword, just as an arrow took him in the neck. He coughed hard and went to his knees, then fell forward to the ground and lay still.

Isingarr noted the accuracy of the fatal bolt, bared his teeth and roared his anger. Then he pulled the small warrior back behind himself and raised his sword. 'Slinkers. Visors down.'

With a clank, the warriors lowered their visors and raised their swords. More arrows flew out of the dark, bouncing off their armour. There was movement at the forest's edge, and more hissing and whining, then a roar that shook the trees all around them.

'Something else comes.' Isingarr gripped his sword so hard his hand began to shake.

The smaller Wolfen whimpered. Isingarr grabbed his forearm. 'Steady yourself, young one; it will be over soon. Remember who you are.'

He looked down and held the young Wolfen's gaze with his own. Then he banged one of his gauntleted fists against the raised wolf crest on the smaller warrior's chest. 'Fenrir watches us all.' After a moment, the smaller warrior nodded.

Isingarr grunted in approval and then turned back to the dark forest, yelling to the giant shadows bearing down on them, 'For Grimvaldr, and for Valkeryn!'

He heard the answering clang of fist on steel beside him, and the ferocious growls of the two remaining Wolfen preparing for battle. His own growls turned into a roar, and his fist tightened on his sword as he raised the mighty weapon.

Isingarr knew they would die this day, but their enemies would just as surely know that they had met Wolfen warriors in battle, and paid a heavy price for that misfortune.

Giant figures rose around them, and the three Wolfen leapt to meet them.

*****

Arn heard the commotion in the camp as the Panterran returned. Long yowls of triumph were accompanied by an eerie howling, like hundreds of cats singing at midnight.

Too soon, Arn thought. He still hadn't come close to freeing himself. He lay back and waited.

Something heavy was thrown onto the rack beside him, and it grunted as if in pain. Though his face was still covered with his shredded clothes, Arn smelled new odours – blood, fur, and something strangely like cinnamon. He also sensed something else, which, in an odd way, comforted him, reminded him of home.

He heard the voice of the old Panterran again – the new captive must have been undergoing the same sort of interrogation he'd had. The old creature asked its questions again and again, and though there were moments of silence when Arn felt the vile old thing was pulling its answers directly from the mind of the new captive, the other never spoke a word.

At last, there was a furious shaking of the rack as the body next to him must have begun jerking and straining against its bonds. There was a thumping blow, then silence and stillness – it seemed the Panterran had run out of patience.

Arn heard the vile old thing speak to its companions in its distinctive whining chuckle. 'The fools don't suspect we are so near, or aware of our pact with the Lygon. Time is still on our side.'

Arn could feel the moist, stinking breath on his bare shoulder once again. 'But we'll know our future for certain when this ape wakes.' Its voice grew fainter as it turned. 'Let me see the bodies; there is something we will need to collect for our emissary . . . before we give them to the Lygon. Our giant friends are developing a taste for Wolfen flesh.'

Wolfen? wondered Arn. *Is that what the new captives were?*

He waited for what seemed an eternity until he could detect no sound or impression of anything close by. Then he shook his head violently to shake the rags off his face, and immediately turned to the new captive, hoping to see another like himself.

He stayed staring for several seconds with his mouth hanging open, feeling his heart sink and his nerves jump at the same time. A large wolf-like creature was strung to the frame next to him. The creature was similar to those he had seen from the hilltop, but smaller, and he could see through the crusted blood much younger, finer features.

Through the shattered armour, he could see that the body was covered in fur, but did not possess the V-shaped chest of a dog. Instead, it was broad and flat like a human's chest, as were the shoulders, arms and waist. The bound paws were more like hands – long fingers ending in short and sharp claws. But further down, the anatomy of a canine returned in the legs with their knee joints turned backwards – but oddly, ending in human-like feet.

Arn craned his neck forward and frowned. He could see inside a tear in the chest plates the swell of human-like breasts – female, then. Arn looked back up at the head that lay turned towards him. He winced. Her face was cut, but it was hard to tell if the wounds were serious as there was so much blood matting the short silvery fur. Where the body looked like some weird type of hybrid dog-human, the face was still all wolf.

'*Wolfen* – amazing,' he breathed softly.

Her eyes opened. They were so luminous and light, they resembled slivers of pure silver blue ice. There was intelligence there – not the crafty, hate-filled slyness he had seen in the Panterran's eyes, but something very different. On seeing him, they widened momentarily, before they half closed and she turned her face away from him.

'Am I in the promised place?' The Wolfen tried to move, and groaned. 'No, there is too much pain.' She turned back to Arn. 'Are you Man-kind?'

Arn nodded.

'My father said you would come back one day.' She smiled weakly. 'We always believed . . . that you would return to us in our hour of need.' She grimaced, closed her eyes again. 'Death will come soon – the Slinkers will see to that. I just pray it is quick, and I can hold my tongue when the old sorcerer returns.'

Arn swallowed. He could not believe that only yesterday he was worried about a few taunts from the class idiot, and now he was in some nightmarish place, bound to a rack, and talking to a dying wolf-warrior woman.

He leaned forward. 'Hey, what's your name?'

Her eyes didn't open. 'I'm called Eilif.' She smiled. 'My father would have been proud of me this day.'

She turned her head again, the ice blue eyes drilling into him. 'Why don't you slay them all? You are one of the Old Ones – whose magic was so powerful it allowed them to fly away. You were the original rulers of this world.'

Arn shook his head. 'No, not me; I'm not from this place . . . or time. I'm just someone who is lost.'

She sighed, and looked disappointed. 'Why are you here?'

'I wish I knew – an accident, I think.' He craned his neck to look around. 'We need to get out of here. They said they were going to read my entrails; I certainly don't fancy being killed and then cut open.'

Next to him Eilif gave a soft, tired chuckle that ended in a cough that left blood on her lips. 'Then rest easy, Man-kind; they'll be cutting you open first, *then* killing you – the sorcerers like their entrails warm.'

'Great.' Arn gulped. 'Then we're definitely leaving.'

If the old sorcerer had forgotten the pocketknife in his hand, Arn certainly hadn't. But try as he might, he couldn't get it to open. Some things that seemed so simple with two hands – like doing up buttons or opening a pocket knife – were near impossible with just one. He dared not rush; if he dropped the knife, he didn't want to think about what would happen when the creatures returned – both to him and the young Wolfen.

Arn froze – he could hear thundering roars coming from further off in the dark forest, and knew that the throat that made these sounds was much larger than those belonging to the small vile creatures that had imprisoned him.

He turned to Eilif. 'What the hell are those things?'

She looked at him with fatigue in her eyes. 'What are they? We met them in battle and I still don't know. But they now stand with the Slinkers. They were able to bring down Isingarr, one of the king's mightiest warriors. I fear for the kingdom if there are many more of these creatures. They are something straight from Hellheim.'

Arn watched her face for a moment, and then shut his eyes to concentrate. He held the pocketknife between the tips of two of his fingers and opened the others wide for a few seconds to allow his sweat to dry, and afford him a better grip.

With his eyes shut, he pictured the knife in his mind, and worked through his plan for opening it. He turned it in his hand, and held it between his two outer fingers, wedging his thumbnail into the notch in the back of the blade. He had it nearly a quarter of the way out, but try as he might, he just couldn't work his fingers into a good position to get the leverage he needed. There was only one thing to do – he slid one of his fingers along the sharpened edge of the blade, to stop it retracting. He then pushed – it cut deep, but the knife opened at a right angle. It was enough – it would do – *it would have to.*

He immediately set about sawing at the rope binding his wrist, concentrating on his task, while also listening to the forest around him. He had to be careful, as already the blood from the cut in his hand made the pocketknife slippery.

There came the sound of something approaching – a Panterran, or Slinker as Eilif called them, pushed through the trees.

Arn stayed silent and still, and closed his eyes. He could sense it approach him, and lean over his face – perhaps interested in seeing his features up close now that the torn clothing had fallen away. Arn smelled its foul breath; sweat trickled down his cheek, and something like a wet rasp – a tongue – slid up his flesh, almost making him scream. *It was tasting him.*

He needed every bit of mental resolve to resist the urge to pull away, or gag, and the thing's face was so close, it must have been nearly pressing its short flat nose up against his own. He couldn't help it – he was going to have to open his eyes, going to have to see what it was doing . . .

'Disgusting vermin of the night – cowards, backstabbers, unblinkers, disease carriers.' It was Eilif, and Arn knew what she was doing.

The hot, greasy breath swung away from him. The Panterran leaned over Eilif, and drew from its robe a wicked-looking dagger. It whispered something into her ear; then, finding a place on Eilif's shoulder where the armour had been torn open, it dragged the blade across her furred flesh.

Eilif grunted from the pain, but didn't cry out. Instead, she spoke as evenly as she could manage. 'Mighty warrior . . . but only when I am bound.'

Arn knew she was drawing the Panterran's attention away from him, and continued to saw at his bonds until he felt the coarse threads part and fall away. He considered his options – he could reach across and saw through the ropes binding his other wrist, but the chance of his being de-tected was high with the Panterran so close. And with his feet still bound, it would only have to step back, and he'd end up a sitting duck – a trussed and sitting duck.

He looked down to his side; the old sorcerer's heavy water jug and bowl were still there, on the bench – within reach.

Eilif saw that Arn had released one of his hands, and she spoke again to her tormentor, the scorn heavy in her young voice. 'Be warned, vermin – Fenrir sees all cowardly acts.'

The Panterran hissed back at her, 'Then Fenrir can watch while the Canites are wiped from the face of the Earth . . . beginning with you.' It laughed cruelly, and then sniffed at her. 'Your very stink makes me un-well.' It lifted its blade again, this time to Eilif's face.

'Perhaps Fenrir sees, but soon *you* will not.' He brought the dagger close to one of Eilif's ice blue eyes, but she refused to blink or look away. Instead, she smiled.

Arn swung the heavy jug down onto the creature's head. The Panterran fell heavily, and Arn was momentarily confused; he didn't think he hit it that hard, or that these creatures were so fragile. But its crushed skull was evidence enough of the force he had used.

Eilif spoke quickly, 'Hurry, Man-kind; time now is against us.'

Arn finished cutting himself free, then stepped down to quickly rummage through his torn clothing and pull on his mangled jeans. Only one leg remained intact; the other had been ripped off at the knee. His shoes were gone.

He looked at Eilif and hesitated.

'Can I trust you?'

The Wolfen held Arn's gaze for a second before responding, 'Always.'

Arn cut through her bonds, and she immediately fell forward into his arms. He helped her to stand. She was lighter than he expected, even though she was still partially dressed in her armour.

'Can you walk?'

'Not far. I have lost much blood, and have no strength. I need to find some feninlang leaves – they'll help to numb the pain, and give me enough energy to travel. Once we get back to one of our outposts, they can treat my injuries properly.'

Arn held the Wolfen upright, and placed one of her arms over his own shoulder. 'Let's go . . . *Ahh*, which way?'

Eilif pointed with her long nose. 'East, and fast away from this Slinker encampment.' She groaned as they started off.

Arn could smell cinnamon again as she slumped against him.

'Man-kind, if they come, you must promise to leave me. You must get to Valkeryn to tell the king that the Slinkers are near our lands. This unholy alliance they have with the giants . . . We must be ready for them.'

Arn spoke quietly to the Wolfen without meeting her eye. 'Not a chance – no one is going to be left behind today.'

He felt her relax slightly. 'Yes – the Man-kind were said to be honourable. I still don't know your name. What are you called?'

'I'm called . . . I mean, I *am* Arnold Singer – Arn, to my friends.'

She nodded, as though expecting this. 'Of course; the Arnoddr-Sigarr – your name means *Bringer of victory.*'

No wonder the Panterran became excited at hearing my name, he thought. He looked down at her. 'Quiet now. Show me where this feninlang grows, and then let's put as much distance between us and these creatures as we can.'

'To the river, and then home, Arnoddr-Sigarr.'

'Arn, please call me Arn.'

'It would be my honour, Arn.' She gritted her teeth.

Arn felt something warm running down his side, and knew it was the young Wolfen's blood. The thought crossed his mind that he should check the wound, but seeing he had no real idea of first-aid for himself let alone for a hundred pound wolf-girl, he decided that they should keep moving.

Eilif's head fell forward, and he spoke to keep her conscious. 'What does this plant look like?'

'It grows on the banks of rivers. Some call it the blood-star flower. Its fat leaves are what we seek.'

Arn nodded. 'I know it.'

Eilif looked at him wearily. 'Of course you do. This is your world, after all.' She collapsed against him, and he lifted her in his arms and ran on, hoping he found the river soon.

Chapter 10

A Daemon On Earth

Twilight had caught up with them.

Arn easily found the river, and left Eilif leaning against a large rock, still warm from the late afternoon sun. Blood-star flowers lined the water's edge, and he pulled free several of the fat juicy leaves. He looked up the bank to the girl . . . He shook his head. He was starting to think of her as a normal girl, yet she was as strange to him as he probably was to her. She half dozed and her breath now fell in a shallow wheeze. He looked at the small pile of leaves in his hand, wondering if she would be able to tell him how to administer them – was she supposed to rub them on? Swallow them? Burn them and then inhale the smoke? He had no choice; he'd have to try to rouse her.

Arn was making his way back up the bank with a handful of leaves, when he noticed that Eilif was covered in the small, carnivorous yellow butterflies – they were fighting over her wounds. Disgusted, he ran forward kicking and swatting at them.

'Get outta here!'

They floated upwards in a yellow cloud, content to hover overhead – waiting. It seemed that the smell of blood attracted them like a school of gossamer-winged piranha.

Arn knelt beside Eilif. She was very still. Arn was thirsty, so he guessed she must have been severely dehydrated, given the amount of blood she had lost. He placed the leaves on the ground next to her, glanced up at the hovering butterflies, and then raced back down to the stream. He scooped some water into his hands, and ran back up the bank. Her nostrils twitched as he approached, and her eyes opened slightly. Arn had expected a long

61

tongue to dart from her mouth, and for her to start lapping at the water. Instead, she reached out to grab his hands and guided them to her mouth, sipping the water daintily. Swallowing, she gave a soft croak of thanks, and then lay back.

Arn leaned forward. 'I have the leaves – what should I do?'

Eilif lifted a hand, palm open, and Arn dropped some of the leaves into it. He noticed that a few of the butterflies were once again starting to flutter close to her head, and he swatted them. Looking at their broken bodies scattered in the dirt reminded him of the marching fish. His stomach rumbled.

'Back in a minute.' He grabbed the fallen butterflies and raced down to the stream. But when he returned a minute later carrying a couple of freshly caught fish, he was dismayed to see that she hadn't moved. Her head lolled to one side, and the leaves lay untouched in her open palm. He knelt beside her and shook her gently.

'Hey, wake up. You need to show me how to prepare the leaves.' He shook her again, and she mumbled groggily, but didn't open her eyes.

'Eilif, please. You need . . .' A deep trumpeting sound came from the forest behind them, and Arn swung around. He looked along the edges of the forest, now quite dark as the sun was nearly down. He held his breath . . . The forest beyond had grown ominously silent.

He heard it again – like a giant horn being blown, this time a little closer. *A hunting horn,* he thought. *We're being tracked.*

He looked down at the comatose Wolfen and shook his head. He wanted to run, and got to his feet. He couldn't think clearly. If the Panterran caught them again, there would definitely be no escape. His stomach lurched at the thought of that vile old sorcerer cutting him open. He was breathing fast and knew he was starting to panic. It took all his willpower to close his eyes and drag in a few deep, calming breaths.

He had more at stake than just his own safety. He needed to think of the girl – well, *wolf-girl.* He knew they couldn't stay out in the open; they needed a place to hide . . . and it certainly wasn't here.

Arn quickly gathered up the blood-star leaves from Eilif's hand, and stuffed them into his pocket. In his other pocket he managed to stuff one of the fish, but gave up on the other, leaving it to the butterflies.

He scooped her up in his arms. In the fading light, he could make out some cliffs just a few miles back from the river. *Gotta be some rocks or a cave we can hide in*, he thought, looking down at the unconscious warrior in his arms.

The horn blared again – still distant, but definitely working its way closer. With Eilif in his arms, Arn started to run.

The lengthening shadows merged into darkness, and as the giant moon had not yet risen, Arn knew there would be a period of utter blackness. He didn't break his stride, knowing that the Panterran would be worried little by the lack of light – he had the feeling they would probably prefer it.

He shook his head, not fully understanding how he managed to carry someone nearly as big as himself, and not fall over from fatigue. *Adrenaline,* he told himself, and increased his speed.

After another few minutes, he saw a cave in the distance and raced the last few hundred feet towards it. Pushing some overhanging brush out of the way, he stepped through its mouth and gagged. The smell was slightly like fish and ammonia, but the cave looked unoccupied. It didn't matter anyway as he was out of options. He just needed somewhere to hide until morning, and time to work out how to administer the plant medicine to his new friend.

Once his eyes had adjusted to the gloom, he noticed that the cave opened up into a larger cavern. Dagger-like stalactites hung from the roof overhead, and sticks crunched painfully beneath his bare feet. He carefully lifted Eilif to one side of the cave, away from the mouth, to give them better cover. He eased her down against a tumble of smooth boulders.

Arn pulled the leaves from his pocket, noticing many were now crushed, coating his hand in thick green fluid. They gave off an odour like cloves and mint, much more appealing than the smell of the cave. Once again he held them out to the Wolfen.

'Eilif, how do you take them? Do you . . .?'

It was no use – she was unconscious. Lifting her head, Arn squeezed the leaves over her open mouth. Their flesh gave up more of the thick green liquid.

Arn watched intently as the liquid first fell onto her tongue, and then slid down her throat. He waited, but nothing happened.

His injured hand had begun to sting like crazy now that the sap from the leaves had coated it. He turned it over, and as he watched, the pocket-knife wound fizzed and foamed, the skin around turning pink and closing together like a zipper.

Wow, I gotta take some of this back home to show Grandfather, he thought. Beside him, Eilif coughed.

'Have you got any water?' she croaked.

Arn smiled, and felt like hugging her. Instead, he settled for putting his hand on her shoulder. He shook his head. 'No, but I've got a fish.'

'*Yecch* – Slinker food.' She sat up, rubbing her forehead and blinking. Arn noticed her eyes shone luminously in the dark.

'Where are we?' she frowned, her nostrils twitching as she inhaled the smells of the cave. She grabbed his arm and her eyes widened. 'Thor's hammer; we're in a jormungandr hole!'

'A wha . . .?' Arn looked around. The moon must have risen, as a silvery glow washed in along the cave floor, and now he could see clearly what he had previously taken to be dry sticks underfoot as he had entered. *Bones.*

He glanced about warily and leaned in close to Eilif. 'What's a jormungandr?' He already guessed it wasn't going to be something pleasant. He pulled the Wolfen to her feet.

She kept her eyes on the back of the cave. 'It's the closest thing to a daemon on Earth, and something you don't want to meet without a company of strong warriors, or at least a sword of Wolfen steel . . . Arnoddr?'

'Yes?'

'Back up slowly.'

Arn noticed Eilif's ears were flicking back and forth to the multiple passages that branched away into the impenetrable darkness at the rear of the cavern. He shook his head – perhaps the blood-star leaves were making her hear things. Then there came a heavy sliding sound, and something else like giant knitting needles clicking, clacking together.

He looked back towards the mouth of the cave – he had dragged Eilif quite a way inside; at the time, he wondered whether it was going to be enough to hide them. Now he wished he had stayed near the entrance.

The heavy scuttling and clicking was getting nearer, and the stench of ammonia was becoming overpowering.

'I can smell it,' he whispered.

Eilif sniffed. 'All I can smell is that stinking fish – get rid of it.'

Arn reached into his pocket; pulling out the slimy fish, he threw it to the other side of the cave. It bounced once, but before it could come to rest, the tip of an enormous spiked leg speared it to the ground.

Arn's breath caught in his throat and he felt the hair on the back of his neck stiffen. The same feeling of dread had an even more pronounced effect on his companion, whose fur stood on end from the top of her head.

Arn was frozen in place as the enormous creature rose up over them. Glistening a deep red like oily blood, its segmented body resembled massive bulbs joined together, each sporting a pair of legs that ended in sharp, bristly points.

The largest segment was a bulging, tear-shaped head, gaping open to display fiercely curved mandibles that clacked open and closed like some sort of machine for grinding wood . . . or bone.

Arn watched in horror as the creature raised the fish to its mandibles and ground it into paste.

He couldn't see any eyes on the glistening head, only a pair of wrist-thick antennae waving in the air, perhaps tasting or sensing the surroundings. Arn was in no doubt that the thing was aware they were there.

He whispered to Eilif, 'It's blind – does it track by sound or movement?'

'Sound, smell, movement – it doesn't need eyes in the dark depths of Hellheim.' Eilif started to back up, then spoke without taking her eyes off the creature. 'Run.'

No sooner had she uttered the word then the thing swiftly positioned itself by the cave entrance; its huge teardrop head hung over them, mandibles dripping, almost daring them to try and pass underneath it.

Eilif's shoulders slumped and she turned to Arn. 'Both may not make it, but one might have a chance.' She put her hands together and twisted free a silver ring that was on her right middle finger. She held it up to kiss it, and Arn saw that on its surface was the raised face of a wolf, with red eyes. She grabbed his hand and pressed the ring into it.

'I cannot run far now, even if I escaped the cave. Already the effects of the fenninlang leaves are wearing off. But you must make it back to Valkeryn and warn the brother Wolfen.' She squeezed his hand. 'This is the seal of the house of Grimvaldr – it will open any doors to you, even royal ones.'

She turned wearily, searching the ground for a moment, then crouched to pick up a long, broken bone, and moved to place herself between Arn and the creature. He saw the weight of her fatigue pressing down on her, and felt a rush of anger. The thought of allowing her to sacrifice herself was so horrible, it made him grit his teeth.

She spoke quickly over her shoulder. 'Tell them I died with honour.'

She staggered under the weight of her injuries. But despite his own fatigue, Arn felt the same sensation of flowing power through his limbs that he had felt on the hillside. He raised his hands to his face, fingers flexing, and studied them in the moonlight.

The thought echoed in his mind: *the moonlight.*

He spoke softy to Eilif's back. 'You can tell them yourself.'

Reaching down to pick up a stone the size of his fist, Arn launched it at the creature. It struck one of the segmented sections behind its head, chipping off a large piece of its red-hued carapace.

Eilif's mouth dropped open. 'Odin's beard! That was a mighty throw, son of Man-kind. Only the heaviest blows can pierce the jormungandr's armour.' Eilif picked up a stone, and threw it as well, but it simply bounced away without any damage to the thing at all.

The jormungandr hissed. The greenish liquid that dripped from its mandibles foamed and sizzled on the dirt floor of the cave.

'Beware of its venom,' Eilif warned him. 'Its bite is poisonous.'

'Thanks. I wasn't worried until now.'

The massive creature's mandibles clicked together, and more of the caustic venom dripped to the ground. Eilif motioned towards it. 'While the cave mouth is open, we have a chance. But when it closes . . .' She let the words hang.

Arn frowned. 'Closes?' He turned to Eilif, who pointed again to the creature that was still hanging above the cave mouth.

'Watch.'

As they watched, white foam sprayed forth from the creature's head, sticking to the top of the cave mouth and hanging down in thick webbed strands. These stiffened and darkened on contact with the air. The jormungandr seemed to rest, but only for a few seconds. It swelled slightly, as if drawing a breath, and then spewed out still more web, sealing the cave mouth entirely.

No sooner was this done, than the jormungandr hissed and pounced at them. Arn pushed Eilif to one side, and dived to the other. He kept rolling and moving quickly, but the injured Wolfen was slower. The effects of the drug were obviously starting to wear off.

The thing dragged more of its segments up from the bowels of the cave, and where the first dozen or so had been the size of a small table, the ones now appearing were as large as a line of small cars linked together. Arn wondered briefly about the size of this thing that still coiled away into the cave's depths, and he had a mental image of a giant hermit crab, using the entire mountain as its shell.

The jormungandr had sensed that Eilif was its easiest prey and focused its attack on her. The massive body was already looming over her, its tusk-like mandibles drawn wide. Arn only had seconds more before she would be engulfed by the horrible monster from the Wolfen's own version of hell.

His instincts took over. Snatching up a heavy thigh bone lying near his feet, he ran hard at the beast and leapt upon it, bringing his makeshift club down on the back of its shell with a sickening crunch.

Cracks and fissures crazed away from the wound in its back, which immediately started to ooze black blood. The jormungandr swung away from Eilif and coiled around on itself, whipping back and forth and throwing Arn to the ground. Hissing with rage, it raised the front part of its broad body high into the air.

Arn set his feet, preparing to leap the opposite way to whichever angle the creature came at him. Instead, its enormous body began to vibrate. He heard Eilif's cry of warning a few seconds too late to understand what she was trying to tell him.

A globule of green slime flew from the mouth of the beast and struck Arn in the face. His eyes burned; tears streamed down his cheeks, and his vision dimmed to a shadowy blur. The head of the creature swam before him, now seeming to fill his entire world.

This is gonna hurt, he thought, and closed his eyes.

Arn was struck hard from the side, and cried out in fear – until he realised it wasn't the clacking mandibles that had engulfed him, but his friend leaping and pulling him out of the way. Wrapping him in her arms, she dragged him behind some rocks.

He murmured, 'I can't see.'

She whispered urgently into his ear, 'The poison of the jormungandr is paralysing, and blinding when sprayed into the eyes.' She hugged him close. 'It was a pleasure knowing you, Arnoddr – if only for a while.'

The huge head of the jormungandr now loomed above both of them, but as Arn buried his face in the warm fur of the strange creature that held him, he felt her stiffen and turn her head.

Eilif let out a long and eerie call. Then she paused, listening. The jormungandr was now so close, Arn could feel the air moving as its huge body hovered over them.

She lifted her head and howled again, letting the notes echo and stretch inside the cave, and beyond. This time, there was an answer. And not one voice, but many. Arn could hear the sound of approaching hooves, then a huge crash as the webbing over the mouth of the cave was hacked to pieces.

The jormungandr swung away from them, and even with his weakened eyes, Arn could see the Wolfen who first stepped through the mouth of the cave was twice the size of Eilif. Dressed in his armour, the warrior looked like an enormous medieval statue that had come to life. In his hand he held a sword as long as Arn himself.

'Mighty Strom!' Arn could hear the elation in Eilif's voice.

The Wolfen warrior let out a roar of anger, charging at the jormungandr with his enormous sword raised. He leapt in the air, sailing towards the gaping mandibles, and burying his blade to the hilt in the thrashing, tear-shaped head.

Roars and cries of battle filled the dark cavern, and for Arn, in his semi-lucid and half-blind state, the rest unfolded in a frenzy of blurred movement and frightening, chaotic noise. The poison of the jormungandr must have been seeping into his brain, for he thought he could feel the mandibles of the beast closing around him, and lashed out with his arm. He felt the impact of his hand on steel, and heard a corresponding yelp of pain.

'No, Arn,' said Eilif, holding him tightly. 'It's my brother Wolfen. We are saved.'

The pain from the poison was now so great, Arn could only guess that he was dying. He could see her – Becky Matthews, her long hair flowing as she turned to smile at him. But then her face began to change – her nose grew long, fur grew on her features, and her eyes became a silver ice blue.

The images exploded into darkness, and Arn slumped against Eilif's chest.

*****

Strom spread wide his arms and roared – it was both a victory cry and a warning to the monster as it slithered away. He watched it disappear, then spun to yell commands to the other warriors who had fanned out in the cave, or stood at the entrance to keep watch on the surrounding countryside.

He knelt beside Eilif and placed one large gauntleted hand on her shoulder. 'Is there any trouble you cannot find, little one?'

She placed her hand over his. 'How can there ever be trouble while you exist, my big friend?' She smiled, then winced in pain.

'Easy there.' Strom called over his shoulder to one of his warriors, who ran to his side carrying a satchel, from which he extracted several bottles and pouches. He set about treating Eilif's wounds.

She pushed his hands away. 'No, treat the Man-kind first.'

'He can wait. Goran . . .' Strom motioned to his warrior to continue working on Eilif.

'No!'

Strom growled with annoyance and looked at Arn. His nostrils flared as he took in his scent. 'It is as the king said, a Man-kind . . . and not very nice to look at, all hairless like that. I suppose we can cover him up.'

Eilif felt her anger rising. 'He has a noble spirit, and he saved my life.' She looked down at the unconscious Arn, and brushed his long dark hair from his face. 'And I think he's beautiful.'

Strom grunted and nodded to the warrior, still poised with the medicinal salves in his hands.

Goran pulled back each of Arn's eyelids. He shook his head and spoke softly. 'Not the same as a Canite eye – the medicine might restore his eyesight, or he might lose what little vision he has left.'

Eilif spoke without hesitation. 'Do it anyway. Without any treatment, he'll end up as blind as a ground-worm.'

She held Arn's head tightly as Goran again lifted his eyelids, and poured a thick, milky liquid into each eye. He let the lids close, and then rubbed the eyes for a second or two. Then he bandaged Arn's head.

'There is nothing more we can do. It is in Odin's hands now.'

Strom motioned for Arn to be taken outside while Goran tended Eilif's wounds.

69

'What of the others? What of brother Isingarr?'

Eilif gave no response other than a small shake of her head.

Strom grunted. 'It is as we expected. We must leave now; there are Slinkers everywhere. We've never seen them in such numbers, and working so closely together – almost like a pack.'

Eilif grabbed his arm. 'Yes, Slinkers – and others like nothing I have ever seen before. You must get me back to Valkeryn; I have important news for the king.' She got to her feet. 'Truly we face an enemy like no other.'

Chapter 11

Behold, Valkeryn

Arn held onto the strange saddle and bounced in time with the jerking gallop of the horse. His back hurt, his thighs were chafed, and his butt cheeks felt like a thousand mules had kicked him. He'd never ridden a horse before, and after this he'd make sure he never did again.

He wanted to reach up and touch his bandaged eyes. They itched terribly, but the pain in the centre of his head had subsided, and he hoped that was a good sign. Blindness was not something he relished, especially in a land where monsters really existed.

The horse swerved suddenly, and he gripped the saddle tighter. Someone else held the reins of his horse – leading him, he expected, back to their homeland. A branch whipped over his head – they were travelling quickly, and he assumed the danger was still close by.

Strange birdcalls, and the hum of insects gave the impression of mid morning. He could feel its warmth on his skin, and was aware of the strange scents of flowering plants, the many Wolfen around him, the horses, and the slight smell of fish that still permeated his jeans pocket.

They slowed a little, and he felt another horse bump up against his. A small hand grabbed hold of his arm, and Eilif asked him gently, 'How do you travel, Arnoddr-Sigarr? Are you well?'

'Like I said, just call me Arn. I'm well – but uncomfortable. I don't usually ride horses. Well, I don't *at all* actually. Are we far from your home?'

'We'll arrive by high sun. I wish you could behold Valkeryn. The turrets and towers touch the sky, and its mighty granite walls are so polished that they shine golden in the afternoon sunlight. Never have they been breached in all its history. You will like it there.'

71

'What happens then? I mean, what happens to me?' An image of being locked in a cage as some sort of Wolfen carnival freak leapt into Arn's mind.

'You are my friend. You will always be safe, Arnoddr . . . Arn. You may even get to meet the king. He's nice, but a bit stern. I know he'll like you.' There was silence for a moment as if she was thinking. 'Well, I think he will, anyway.'

Chapter 12

At Last A Worthy Foe

Grimvaldr sat at his long table, with a circle of his most trusted warriors gathered close around him. Spread before him were the recovered remnants of the massacre of his warriors – smashed armour, torn chain mail, a punctured shield. It came as no surprise to him that Ragnar, brave and impetuous by nature, was first to break the silence.

'We must hunt them down, sire. The Wolfen pack must have been ambushed and overwhelmed. Give me one hundred warriors and I guarantee I'll bring you back the heads of these Panterran assassins.'

Grimvaldr looked at the faces of the Wolfen surrounding him – all tall, strong, and scarred many times over – the greatest warriors in his kingdom. They had never known defeat in battle, and now hungered for revenge. *Blind revenge*, he thought.

'Brave Ragnar, I know you would fight to the very gates of Hellheim for your Wolfen brothers, but sometimes it is better to know your enemy first. You will have your justice – we all will. But we need to know who it is that has declared war on us.'

The king rose slowly to his feet. 'I want six of our best scouts and hunters to track our enemy back into the dark forests. A group large enough to bring down so many of our best fighters must be either large or extremely formidable. And no matter how stealthy, they must have left a trail that can be followed.'

'My lord, there is talk that they are wraiths, and . . .'

'Silence those words, Bergborr!' The king pounded the table, his stentorian voice echoing around the stone room. He threw the punctured shield to the floor at the gathered warriors' feet.

'Could a wraith do that? No, the attackers were real. And if real, they can bleed . . . and die.'

Bergborr dropped to one knee. 'Forgive me.'

Grimvaldr looked down at the warrior. 'Rise. The unknown is our enemy now. There will be no talk of wraiths, or werenbeasts, or monsters from the darkness. What we seek will be made of flesh and blood and bone. It will be brought down by Wolfen steel, like all those who have made war on us in the past. But first we must know who or what it is we fight.'

The king motioned to the large double doors of the chamber. 'Let us hear from the sciences. Bring them forth to show us what they have learned from the print we found at the battle site.'

The king sat back down as the massive oak doors swung wide and a broad, low cart was slowly hauled before him. Standing on the cart, a tall figure, draped with a heavy cloth, towered over the Wolfens' heads as it was dragged past them, towards the king's throne.

Shuffling up next to it, an elderly Canite in flowing robes bowed deeply. The king motioned for him to rise. He looked up at the cloaked figure.

'So, Balthazar, it seems you have been busy.'

The other nodded. 'We thought at first you gave us only a little to work with, but it turned out to be more than we needed, my king. The print was of the Panterran line – its shape is unmistakable. We have all the biological information we need on Slinkers, and know that a Slinker print of a certain size will determine the height and weight of the one who made it. The average size of one of their adult warriors is roughly a little over half as tall as a Wolfen, and their weight about fifty pounds, give or take.'

Turning, Balthazar reached towards the figure, then grabbed the sheet and tugged. It fell away, and the king's eyes widened. The assembled warriors either cursed or gasped at the strange sight.

The king couldn't help baring his teeth, and his strong fingers curled around the arms of his throne, splintering the hard wood.

The decloaked figure had been crafted from clay, and stood about nine feet in height. It was similar in shape to a Panterran, but had a heavily muscled torso, leading up to a head that was both terrifying and ferocious.

The king spoke slowly. 'The head and fangs; how could you know this detail, just from the single print in the mud?'

Balthazar looked from the figure back to the king. 'Not from the print, sire, but from other clues in the remains of the armour before you.'

Grimvaldr gazed from the punctured shield up to the giant creature's fangs. He felt a moment of dread, but he knew he could not show it. Any display of fear or indecision on his part would sow seeds of doubt and despair among his warriors.

He stood and grinned at his assembled Wolfen.

'So, mighty warriors, it looks like we may at last have a worthy foe to fight. We now know their shape, but we need to know their mind. Send the scouts immediately – they are to report back in two days. In the meantime, to all my generals, I command you to assemble your Wolfen warriors, and be ready to march after we have learned a little more from the field.'

The Wolfen bowed and banged their fists against their chests, and then headed for the large double doors that had been thrown open – each of them glaring at the clay giant as they passed by it.

Grimvaldr called softly to the last of them, 'Karnak, wait a moment.'

The tall, heavily scarred warrior stopped and turned. The king strode around the table and took his friend's arm. He nodded up towards the snarling figure. 'What say you, son of the House of Karnak – could they be real?'

Karnak grunted. 'I have heard talk of a race of terrible creatures from the far dark lands. Things that look like Slinkers, but are more powerful and brutish, and a hundred times more deadly. Do I think they are real? Who else could bring down our warriors so easily?'

The king sighed and stared off into the distance. 'I have also heard those tales of the dark and unknown lands of the giants. I thought . . . I had hoped they were little more than legends . . . just like the rumoured sightings of the Old Ones every few generations. But we saw one, didn't we, my friend?'

Karnak raised his eyebrows. 'Two myths, seeming to take flesh at the same time, and the Panterran hordes pushing into our lands – do you believe there could be a connection?'

'The Old Ones reappearing at the time of our greatest need? It is the oldest of our prophesies.' He stared up into the clay figure's snarling face. 'And we have faced monsters before. Valkeryn has stood for a thousand years, and it will it stand for a thousand more.' He turned back to Karnak. 'I do not fear these giants . . . and I do not fear the Panterran hordes . . . but I pray that the two are not in league with each other.'

Chapter 13

I Also Like Sandwiches

Arn woke with a jolt. Everything was blackness; reaching up, he felt the bandages still over his eyes. He called out. 'Hello?'

There was no answer. He waited a few moments, and then called out again – still silence.

He patted the soft bedding around him. He felt refreshed, and as the air was cool on his face he guessed he had slept for many hours, or perhaps he was deep inside some large building, away from the sunlight.

His hand went once again to his bandages; just as he began to tug at them, he heard the grating of steel on wood, and the sound of a heavy door creaking open. Footsteps. 'Eilif?'

He continued to pull at his bandages.

A hand stopped him. 'Be still. I am Morag, and with me is Birna. We've been sent to get you cleaned up, and to bring you food.'

The hand travelled down his arm and took his hand, placing it on a tray on his lap. Arn's hunger flared in the pit of his stomach, and his fingers immediately felt around a plate what he hoped was food. 'Thank you . . . *Ah*, what is it?'

Morag spoke again, 'Meat, fruit, and even some raw fish that Eilif said you liked.' He felt hands checking his hair, feeling its texture, or perhaps looking for any passengers he might have picked up,

'Thank you.' He lifted a slice of meat and sniffed it – it smelled like dried beef and he pushed it into his mouth, already watering in anticipation. It was delicious. 'Yum. I also like sandwiches.'

There was silence, and Arn guessed the word probably made no sense to them, or they called it something completely different. 'You know; it's where you put the meat inside some bread.' He waited – still nothing. He thought he understood why. 'Okay, bread is where you get the tiny seeds of wheat and crush them to powder . . . *Err,* wheat is like a long type of grass . . . Anyway, then you mix in some water, salt and oil, until it's a soft doughy paste.' The hands left his head, and he waited in silence for a few moments more. For all he knew, they were probably all carnivores anyway; what would they know about bread? 'Well, you bake it before you eat it – it's really nice.'

He tucked more food into his mouth, and decided to change the subject. 'Where's Eilif?'

This time it was Birna who spoke. 'She is bathing and getting dressed. She must meet with the king . . . and you have also been granted an audience. So you will need to be bathed and dressed also.' The hands returned to his head.

Arn kept chewing, thinking over what he had just been told. *Bathed?* His hand went to his waist. His jeans, or what was left of them, had been removed, and he was naked under the sheets.

'*Ah,* my pants?' He felt about on top of the bedding that was, thank heavens, still covering him.

Birna laughed. 'They were rags, sir . . . in pieces. We've kept all the items you carried, and while you slept we had your sizings taken, and sent to the tailor. New clothes will be here shortly.' There was more laughing, and then, 'Do you get cold?'

'Huh, cold?' Arn turned in the direction of the question.

'I mean, without fur.'

Arn laughed. 'No, not really – not with clothes anyway. So, no, we humans don't need fur.'

Birna was persistent. 'But . . . you still have patches of fur on your head, and we saw, lower down, that . . .'

Arn pulled his blankets higher as Birna finished inspecting his scalp. 'Clean – good. We can never be too careful after coming into contact with those dirty Slinkers; they're covered in all sorts of horrible vermin.'

He felt Morag's breath against his ear as she leaned near to him. 'I've never actually seen one, a Slinker. Are they as ugly as they say?'

Arn remembered the flat face, the needle-like teeth, and yellow slitted eyes. And then the claws digging into his flesh. 'Yes, both inside and out, I'm afraid. They're not very nice . . . creatures.'

He sat in silence, thinking for a moment, then felt a weight on the bed next to him. It was Birna, he decided, as she took the plate from his hand. A piece of fruit was held to his lips. He bit into it, and raised his eyebrows – it was soft like melon, but tasted like apple and banana all in one.

'Wow, that's nice.' He took the bowl. 'I can do that, but thank you anyway.' *If they know of fruit, then maybe they aren't total carnivores after all.* He was relieved at the thought.

'Yes sir, but you must eat.' The weight lifted from the bed. 'We'll be back shortly to take you to your bath.'

'Okay. And it's Arn. Call me Arn.'

*****

A short time later, Arn was led down a cool corridor. He could smell stone, burning candles, and the floor under his bare feet felt cool and cobbled. He was desperate now to pull off his bandages, as there was so much that was fantastically new. Not being able to see it made him more impatient and anxious by the minute.

On leaving the bedroom, he had draped one of the blankets over his shoulder and wrapped it around his waist, Roman toga style, out of modesty. Even though physically they were quite different animals, and he thought he shouldn't really care, he couldn't help feeling awkward at being naked in front of them. Maybe he was worried he'd freak them out . . . or that they'd make fun of him.

After all, he still remembered the way Morag and Birna – and Eilif before them – had scrutinised him. He pulled the blanket tighter as it started to slip. The intelligence in Eilif's eyes, her humour and vulnerability; he found it hard to think of her as not being just like him.

Suddenly he smelled her familiar cinnamon scent, and detected the soft padding footsteps of her approach. He felt her take his arm.

'Enjoy your food?' she asked. 'It wasn't easy getting the fish – no one here even likes the smell.'

Arn turned to her and smiled. 'Yes, thank you. But you'll be pleased to know that fish is not part of my everyday diet.'

'Good. I'd hate to think you were part Slinker. I mean, your face is flat enough.' She squeezed his arm, and he felt, rather than heard, her laughing. There was silence for a few seconds as they walked, and even though he couldn't see her, he knew she was looking at him.

At last she spoke. 'With that small nose, how do you smell?'

'Excellent – but I'll smell even better after my bath.' He grinned, but he guessed she must have missed his joke. He felt her hand on his head, stroking his hair.

'You have beautiful fur . . . What you have of it.'

Morag made a sound like a giggle, and Eilif growled back at her.

'*Err*, thank you.' Arn blushed. She touched one of his ears.

'Amazing that you can hear at all with these little half circles . . . And you can't turn them at all? You are a thing of wonders, Arnoddr.' She stroked his hair one last time. 'Enjoy your bath, Man-kind. The tailor has made you some fine clothing – you've got to look your best when you are presented to the king.'

'The king? When?'

Arn heard Eilif's footsteps fading down the corridor. She called back to him.

'Soon . . . This evening. Don't worry, brave warrior, I'll be there to protect you.' She laughed, but it was faint – she must have disappeared around a bend in the corridor.

*****

The bath was a gigantic wooden tub filled with warm water that was soapy, scented with something like cloves, and felt magnificent. He had soaked for what seemed like ages, letting the water ease the knots in his overworked muscles and spine. Even his multitude of cuts and abrasions had ceased to sting the longer he had relaxed.

On Birna and Morag's insistence, he had finally climbed out, and he had needed to be just as insistent himself to keep his two attendants – or nurses, as he was starting to think of them – from drying him off and dressing him.

He took the rough towel that was offered and eventually managed to shoo them both away, their good humour reminding him of home and his family.

Arn heard the heavy door close behind them, and sat down, alone in his own personal darkness. In the silence of the bathing room, it occurred to him that everything he had known was probably dust a million times over; his family, his friends, Becky Matthews, even that ass Steve Barkin were now nothing but memories living in his head. It was such a miserable thought that, for the first time in years, he began to cry.

He had no idea how long he sat there, but when there came a knock on the bathing room door, he realised he was cold and dry. He turned in the direction of the doorway, expecting it to be one of his attendants, but instead a deeper, male voice addressed him.

'I am the court physician,' said the voice, Arn heard the door open, and felt a slight breeze as someone entered. 'I've come to look at your eyes.'

Large hands gripped his head and the bandages were lifted away. Arn blinked, but immediately scrunched his eyes shut again – even in the muted candlelight, the glare was agony for him.

He pressed the heels of his hands into his eyes, wiping away tears of pain. Then he opened them again. Images swam slowly into focus, and though he should have expected it, he was startled to see an enormous wolf's face staring hard into one of his eyes, then the other.

The physician used a glass lens to peer into each of Arn's pupils. He grunted his approval.

'Good. No permanent damage.' He held up one clawed finger and moved it back and forth in front of Arn's nose, expecting him to follow it. Arn found it hard not to look at the large, furred face, but did his best.

'You are very lucky, young Man-kind. Not many have their sight return after having their eyes bathed by the venom of the jormungandr. It is a terrible creature.'

Arn shuddered in spite of himself. 'Yes, it was one of the worst things I've ever seen. Are there many creatures like that here?'

'Not so many in our lands. But in the dark lands . . . there are even worse things.'

'Worse things?'

The old physician patted Arn's shoulder and turned away.

'Wait . . .'

The physician stopped, half turned.

'How . . .' Arn wasn't sure how to frame his question. 'How did you . . . come to be? The Wolfen – *err,* Canites, I mean.'

The physician considered Arn thoughtfully, as if trying to determine the nature of the question – or, as Arn hoped, the best place to begin.

Clearing his throat, he grasped the edges of his robe, like a lawyer in a courtroom.

'We have always *been*, young Man-kind. Our pack, the Canites, have been here since the dawn of all things. The almighty Fenrir led us from the forests and taught us how to work together, how to live together, how to fight for our land and our race. The king is his descendant – only he knows more of our history, as it is passed down along his noble line.'

'Fenrir. I've heard that name a lot. Who was he – your leader?'

'Fenrir, may his name be blessed, is all things – our father, our spiritual leader, our teacher and our warlord.'

Arn nodded. 'Did he teach you to talk? I mean, how did you learn to speak? And the Panterran – did he lead them from the forests as well? Where did they spring from?'

The physician's lips curled slightly at the mention of that hated name. 'The Panterran crawled out of the dark. They are our opposites. They would destroy us and Valkeryn and everything it stands for if they could. If not for our Wolfen warriors, they would have overrun us a thousand years ago.

The more Arn learned, the more questions came to his mind. 'You are Canites. And the Wolfen, they're Canites too? Your warriors, right?'

'Yes. A Canite trains for many years to become a Wolfen warrior. They are the elite guard of Valkeryn, and join the king's army. The very best are picked to serve as the king's personal bodyguard, or perhaps even become his champion, like Strom, son of Stromgarde.'

'I've met Strom.' Arn frowned. 'Are there any other . . . types of, ah, *races*, other than Canites and Panterran in this world?'

The old physician folded his arms. 'Not in these lands, but there are stories of other races beyond the dark borders.' He sat down next to Arn and stared at the ceiling, thinking over his earlier question. 'The great libraries talk of the time of the *great fire*, and how the many tribes and races were born within it. But how did we learn to speak? We have always spoken.' He turned to Arn with a half smile. 'Perhaps only now can we be heard, Man-kind.'

'Man-kind – and what happened to Man-kind?'

'There are a hundred different legends about them . . . *about you*. There are an unenlightened few who refuse to believe you ever existed, that perhaps you are nothing but a myth.' The old Canite snorted softly. 'So much for that story. But the most pervasive theory is that the Old Ones left this world long ago, and left it in our care.'

'They left? But how . . . how did they leave?'

The physician shrugged. 'Just stories and legends. In some tales, it is said they all flew away on ships of the sky. Others talk of them simply ascending to Asgaard as spirits. Still more tell that their spirits were released in the great fire. But in all, it is promised that there would be a return of the ancients one day, when we need them most. As I said, it's all myth and legend, and though our explorers have found artefacts in certain deep caves, we cannot truly confirm whether these belonged to Man-kind, or some other race.'

'I might be able to help. Could you take me to these caves?'

'They are in the dark lands or lost. There may be maps, but the archives are so vast that you'd need another map just to find them . . .' Balthazaar stopped and his brows knitted together. '. . . Unless . . .'

'What? Unless what?'

'Unless old Vidarr is still the archivist. He's probably the oldest Canite in all of Valkeryn. No one has seen him for years, but . . .' He slapped his thigh. 'But enough of your questions. I am Balthazar, physician and chief scientist in King Grimvaldr's court.' He looked at Arn steadily with a twinkle in his eye. 'I have seen many strange things in my lifetime, but I never expected to see . . . *you*. Now it's my turn to ask some questions, Arnoddr-Sigarr. Where exactly did *you* spring from, and are you alone?'

Arn held his gaze for a few moments, trying to decide what to tell him. How to tell him? The castle, the Canites' clothing, weaponry . . . everything was ancient, almost medieval. How could he describe being sucked into a black hole and thrown, he guessed, into some distant future? It would seem like magic or witchcraft.

Magic or witchcraft – the thought gave him an idea.

'Do you believe in magic, Balthazar?'

'I believe in the sciences, and also the mystical arts – light and dark.'

Good, thought Arn. This gave him some leeway to explain the inexplicable.

'You asked where I sprang from? Well, I sprang from right here. Perhaps a million generations ago, or . . . or *some* long time ago anyway. But it was in the time of all Man-kind. Our people were testing a machine to . . . *uhh*, give us energy to power our lights and fires, and instead it opened a magical doorway, which I accidently fell through.'

82

Balthazar leaned forward, his eyes wide and his mouth agape. 'Can it be opened again? Could I go through it, or at least see through it, to your time?'

Arn shook his head. 'I don't think so. I can't be sure, but I think it closed after I arrived, and I'm not sure anyone can open it again . . . at least not from this side.' His brow furrowed. 'I hope that someone is trying to open it again, so I can get home.'

'I would give anything for one glimpse of your time – the legends have it that it was a paradise. Is it true that in the time of Man-kind, there was no war? That there was no disease and no famine, and that everyone lived a long and full life of happiness?'

Arn thought for a moment that he was joking. 'No, not in my time. There was still war and hardship. And like here, there was good *and* evil.'

'And the Canites? Were they friends of Man-kind? Were Man-kind and Canite brothers?'

'*Ahh*, yes . . . Yes, of course you were there. You were . . . man's best friend.'

Balthazar nodded, pleased. 'I knew it would be so.'

Arn shivered, and for the first time noticed the clothes and boots stacked beside him on the bench. There were soft fabrics with gilt edges, silver buttons and shining leather – it looked almost regal. There was even a scabbard for a sword . . .

Balthazar got to his feet. 'I'm sorry. Of course, you are cold and I am keeping you. It must be terrible not to have fur. But we must talk more later; there is so much I wish to know.'

'You and me both, Balthazar.'

'I shall see you in the eve.' He bowed and headed for the door.

Arn started pulling on his clothes. 'I have to meet with the king. Will you be there?'

'Of course, young Man-kind.' Smiling, Balthazar moved to close the large door behind him as Morag and Birna, who had obviously been waiting outside, pushed their way past. He nodded to them and disappeared.

Together they circled Arn, tightening straps, straightening robes, and showing him where the sword scabbard should hang.

Arn grabbed it and pointed. 'There's something missing.'

Morag laughed. 'Soon enough. A stranger doesn't enter the king's court when he is armed. Wait until he sees if you are a friend.'

Birna leaned closer. 'But we already know you are. We've been told.'

'How? Who told you that?'

She placed her finger on a small silver crest sewn into his vest. It depicted a snarling wolf with red eyes.

'You have friends in high places, Arnoddr-Sigarr.'

Chapter 14

In The Hall Of The King

Arn sat on a wooden bench in the long, cold corridor. On either side of an enormous wooden door, a guard stood in full armour, enormous steel axes cradled in their arms. Both treated Arn as though he didn't exist. Morag and Birna sat across the corridor on another bench, talking quietly together, occasionally turning to nod and smile, as if to reassure him. It didn't work. He shivered again, and felt slightly sick.

What could possibly go wrong? he thought. *I'm about to have a meeting with a pack of giant upright wolves.*

Through the door, he could hear many voices. Some were raised in argument, but comfortingly there was also laughter – he hoped that whatever was going on inside was just a friendly gathering. He'd just have to pop in, say hello, then he'd be ushered back out again – *no problem.*

He studied the corridor; it was old – very old – but in magnificent condition. The flagstones had been polished by generations of footsteps, and the walls' and ceiling's ancient granite blocks were smooth and seamless. There were carved corbels and ornate arches, and every twenty feet or so, small alcoves contained a single portrait. Some looked contemporary and of the type of Wolfen he had already encountered, and others looked far older, the creatures more primitive, more like . . . large dogs standing upright. Everything gave the impression of ancient power, and a sense of . . . permanence.

Morag gave him a little wave to catch his eye. She smiled and nodded towards the large double doors. He noticed that both hers and Birna's ears were pointed towards them, as was their gaze. He gulped. Moments later, the doors were pulled smoothly inwards, and a large warrior stood staring down at him, motioning with one arm for him to enter. The guards on either side of the door stood back and finally acknowledged his existence – both had turned to glare.

Arn stood slowly, his knees shaking, and looked desperately towards his two nurses, hoping they were also preparing to enter the imposing room. They smiled and nodded, but held their ground. At last, Birna pointed inside and said, 'Only you are invited, Arnoddr-Sigarr; it is a great honour.'

Nodding, he walked stiff-legged through the doorway. He felt exactly the same when he won the history award and had been asked to address the entire school on prize-giving day – except this time he was walking into a room full of non-humans, in some other, weird time zone, after fighting and then being blinded by a monster in a cave. *Yep, exactly the same* – he felt sick again.

Arn drew in a long, shuddering breath and stepped inside. His first impression was of warmth and light – lots of light, from the golden blaze of burning torches lining the walls, standing on the tables, and in huge burning cauldrons hanging from the ceiling.

There were many warriors, though few in armour, with some preferring clothes similar to the ones he had been given – boots, jerkins and vests with differing crests sewn over the heart. None he could see were like his, with the red-eyed wolf.

The Wolfen who had bade him enter the room kept one huge hand on Arn's shoulder as he guided him towards the front of the room; the crowd parted around them. There were both males and females, and all looked at him with a mixture of awe and suspicion, and perhaps just a little fear. He heard a soft word spoken from the far end of the hall; there, one figure was seated, and others stood – six of them, three on each side of the huge Wolfen throne.

Arn was so nervous that he almost felt disconnected from his body – as if he were somehow watching the strange events from just above his own head. He tried to calm himself, but the unblinking gaze of the seated wolf terrified him. He was older than most around him, and huge. He was dressed in crimson robes pressed with knotted leather, sewn crests, and silver. There were no jewels, exotic fur trimming or garish displays of wealth; instead, this looked to be the cloak and vestments of a warrior king.

Arn looked at the face: the eyes were like silver blue gun barrels – he had seen those eyes before somewhere, but his mind refused to give up any clues. They seemed to stare right through him, right into his very soul.

The king's nose twitched, and a small smile played at the corner of his lips, just under the long, silvering snout. This was enough to break the spell, and enable Arn to pull his gaze away and look at the other Wolfen standing by the throne.

On one side stood a female, tall and fine featured. She seemed roughly about the same age as the king, and rested one of her hands on his shoulder.

The queen, he thought.

Just behind her were stood two smaller figures. One, he immediately recognised – it was Eilif, secretly waving with the hand on her hip. Just beside her, staring wide eyed in wonder, was an even younger wolf.

The eyes, thought Arn. *I recognise them.* The young Wolfen ducked back behind Eilif and Arn turned his attention to the other side of the throne. There stood several warriors, all powerful-looking and fearsome; the largest, easily a head taller than the rest, was the one he knew as Strom – he remembered what Balthazar had told him – the king's champion, and the one who had saved them in the jormungandr cave.

All three had their hands on the hilt of their swords, which were half as long as Arn was. He had no doubt that if he made one threatening move, they would have cut him down faster than he could blink.

There were murmurs now coming from all sides, but the king just sat and studied him. Even Eilif had her eyes on the king – watching, waiting for something, some sign or gesture from him.

It was becoming unbearable. Arn had no idea of protocol, of what was expected. *Magic tricks?* He wondered.

'Greetings, sire,' he said at last. 'My name is Arnold Singer.' He bowed slightly.

The young wolf beside Eilif drew in a breath, and his eyes widened even further, if that was possible. Arn heard him whisper to Eilif, 'He *can* talk.'

The king smiled and nodded, as though the simple words and introduction were enough.

If it was a test, then it was an easy one, Arn thought.

'You're not as tall as I expected, Man-kind. What is your age?'

'*Ahh*, seventeen years . . . and nine months, your high-nesty . . . I mean, majesty.' Arn cleared his throat, his nerves making it and his chest feel tight.

The king sat forward. 'Son of Man-kind then . . . and to what age do your people live?'

Arn shrugged. 'Depends. But it could be anywhere from eighty to a hundred years.'

There were gasps from the assembled crowd, and the king raised a hand to quiet them.

'That is longer than the oldest Wolfen by many years. But you are not a speck of that oldness – in fact, I believe you are not fully grown at all yet, *young* Man-kind.'

He motioned over his shoulder to Strom. As the giant Wolfen stepped forward, Arn saw him up close for the first time – and this time without the burning poison of the jormungandr to blur his vision. The king's champion was even bigger than he remembered. Arn guessed he stood close to seven feet tall, and even without armour his shoulders were as wide as any linebacker Arn had seen on television back home. His face showed scars old and new, and the fur looked like it struggled to regrow over some of the rents in his flesh.

The king pointed to his champion. 'Will you grow as tall as Strom?'

Arn looked up the Wolfen warrior, and an image of his father leapt to his mind, making him momentarily homesick. He drew in a breath and tried to focus on the question.

'My father is . . . was a tall man. And there are some men who are as tall as Strom. But me? No, I won't grow as tall – I'm pretty average height . . . for a Man-kind, I guess.'

While the king thought this over, Arn looked around and spotted Balthazar, who had been scribbling notes or sketching while they had been talking. The scientist looked up and caught his eye. He nodded. Arn returned the greeting and felt more confident – perhaps it was the thought of having some friendly faces in the room, or maybe it was due to the slow rise of the moon, its glow flooding in through the high windows.

He resolved to speak further, and turned back to the king. 'My name is Arnold Singer. I have arrived in your land by accident, and I am a long way . . . and I believe a long time, from home.' He waited. No one said a word, so he hurriedly added, 'I come here as your friend.' The seconds stretched.

'I know you are our friend, Arnoddr.' It was Eilif, but immediately the king raised one large hand in front of her, and she fell silent.

The king spoke again. 'I have been told of your escape from the Panter-ran, *and* of the encounter in the jormungandr hole. It seems you have a knack for finding this world's worst elements, young Man-kind.' He turned briefly to Eilif and smiled. 'But without you, perhaps my daughter would not be here today. For that, you have my thanks.'

The king's daughter! thought Arn, and gulped.

The king rose to his feet. 'I am Grimvaldr, son of Grimkell, and blood-line of the mighty Fenrir himself.' He glanced again at his daughter. 'And I think we are all prone to being overly quick to speak our minds. But we are also a good judge of noble character, and we see that in you, young Man-kind.'

His expression grew dark. 'I saw you days ago on the ridge above the killing fields. I thought you were a vision at first, an omen. Your name itself, Arnoddr-Sigarr, means *bringer of victory* to us.'

The king sat back down, and continued to study his guest. 'And perhaps you *are* an omen. I shall grant you shelter among us, but know that soon all of Valkeryn may be called upon to fight.' He looked hard at Arn. 'Will you fight with us, Arnoddr-Sigarr?'

Arn wanted to say *yes* immediately, but the closest he had ever come to fighting was arguing in the canteen line with Edward over the last piece of pie. In Valkeryn, fighting meant something frighteningly real – something bloody, brutal and deadly.

'I'm not sure how to fight . . . but I'd be happy to help in any way I can.' It was the best he could offer.

Eilif stepped up beside the king and whispered to him. He snorted, then nodded. She walked quickly towards Arn, reaching into the folds of her cloak, and removed a small silver dagger, which she offered to him.

'We can teach you to fight, Arnoddr, but it helps to have a weapon.'

'It's beautiful,' Arn said – and it was. Just under a foot in length and of highly polished silver, the familiar snarling wolf with its red eyes was moulded into the pommel. Arn slid it into his empty scabbard and leaned towards her to whisper, 'Guess I'm not a risk anymore.'

'You never were to me.' She smiled and dipped her head, looking up at him from under her ash silver brows. Turning, she bowed to Grimvaldr, and then stepped back up behind him.

Grimvaldr leaned forward in his large throne, the wood creaking under his weight.

'Good – all help is needed in these dark times. But for one who says he cannot fight, I have been told you seem to have a mighty arm. Perhaps it just needs to be trained, *eh,* Andrejk?'

Across the hall, a Wolfen stepped forward, grinning. Part of his forehead was shaved, and stitches zippered a long wound. Under his arm he carried his helmet, and he lifted it, and looked at it briefly, before turning it around for the king and Arn to see.

'There were more dangers in the jormungandr hole than we expected.' The warrior's grin broadened.

Arn saw the huge dent in the steel, matching the position of the scar on the warrior's head. He remembered lashing out in the cave, when he thought he was being attacked. *Oh crap,* he thought.

'I saw stars for two days.' Andrejk didn't seem angry with him at all.

The other Wolfen laughed, and one next to Andrejk slapped him on the shoulder.

'There was nothing inside that thick skull to damage.' He slapped Andrejk's shoulder again.

The king turned back to Arn. 'With such an arm, perhaps we should be grateful that you have chosen to help us.' He stood and waved towards the far end of the room. 'Come, dine with us. I'm sure you have more questions . . . as do we. In this kingdom, food and conversation always go hand in hand.'

The doors at the end of the hall were thrown open and the small crowd moved towards it. Arn stood watching for a moment, unsure what he should do, until he felt a tug on his arm. Looking down, he saw the young Wolfen who had been standing just slightly behind Eilif and the queen. His eyes were still very round.

'You can talk. I thought you were only a story made up by my father and Balthazar.' He let go of Arn's forearm and banged a small fist on his chest. 'I'm Grimson, son of Grimvaldr.'

Arn laughed and sank to one knee, to look him in the eye. He held out his hand.

'And I am Arnold Singer . . . *ah*, son of Johnson Singer. My friends call me Arn.'

The young Wolfen looked at the hand for a second or two, seeming unsure what to do with it. Arn decided to help and reached out to grab Grimson's hand and shake it.

'Nice to meet you, Grimson.' Arn shook the small hand some more. 'And this is how *my* people greet each other.'

Grimson smiled and kept pumping Arn's hand up and down, looking back and forth from it, to Arn, with great amusement. After a moment, he stopped and turned Arn's hand over in his, to study it.

'You aren't totally hairless, are you? I can feel some hairs there.' He looked up. 'Will they get thicker as you get older?'

Arn shrugged. 'Yes, but not ever as thick as your magnificent fur. In fact, as I get older, I may lose some of the hair on my head.'

Grimson looked at the top of Arn's head and pulled a face. 'Yuck.'

Arn laughed again. 'Thank heavens for hats.'

'Your eyes are so black. Are they hard to see out of?'

The queen called to her son. Grimson let go of Arn's hand, and on his jacket Arn noticed the same silver, snarling wolf crest. It was also the same image pressed onto the ring that Eilif had given him. He felt his pocket – it was still there. He'd return it later, when he saw her again.

As Arn walked beside the youth, he pointed to the crest. 'What does this mean? Is it your . . . *ahh*, house badge?'

Grimson looked shocked. 'Of course – it is the crest of the house of Grimvaldr. The royal crest.'

Arn nodded. *You have friends in high places*, he remembered Birna telling him.

Grimson stopped and pointed to Arn's chest. 'You wear it because you saved Eilif's life. And for that, you are under Grimvaldr's protection.'

He motioned Arn closer, who leaned down expecting the young Wolfen to whisper something to him. Instead, Grimson reached up and touched his cheek, then his nose, pinching it.

'*Ouch!*'

Grimson ignored him and lifted Arn's upper lip to peer at his teeth.

'Loki's beard! Everything is so small. How do you fit food in there?'

Arn laughed. 'We cut it into small pieces first.'

Grimson looked shocked at the concept. 'I can't wait to see that . . . Arn. You can be seated next to me. Let's go; I starve.' He took Arn's forearm again, and led him towards the open double doors.

Chapter 15

Not All Wolfen Were Honourable

Orcalion watched the execution with pitiless eyes. The Panterran soldiers who had allowed the prisoners to escape were quickly beheaded, and the bodies would be dragged deep into the forest for the night beasts to tear to shreds. Incompetence was not tolerated among Panterran warriors.

Time was growing short, and the Lygon were becoming harder to control. Their common ancestry bound them to the Panterran – but only loosely. The monstrous brutes were unpredictable, and could easily turn against them if their lust for carnage wasn't sated.

He looked down at the bloody bag at his feet. The Wolfen scouts they captured had refused to talk – not a single word or scream of pain. He knew he had hurt them; he had taken his time. He narrowed his yellow eyes as if willing it to speak, to reveal the hated creatures' secrets. It worried him that these Wolfen had such strong hearts, their honour a shield against his torture. The bag held only the trophies he had removed from them. He grinned, baring his needle-like teeth. Others' agony was satisfying and information was vital for the coming war – torture worked on some, but not all. Other sources were needed. Not all Wolfen were honourable. You just needed to find the right ones, and use the right methods.

The Panterran slung the bag over his shoulder and walked back to the camp. His spies had already found out that the Man-kind had made it to Valkeryn, and King Grimvaldr was calling it an omen for the Wolfen. There was no doubt: the Man-kind arriving, at this of all times, was a sign – but for whom, and of what?

Orcalion cursed the executed Panterran again for allowing the hairless creature to escape before he had a chance to interrogate him personally. He needed the information the creature held – in its mind, or in its guts – either would do. And he meant to get it.

It was time to pay the Wolfen a visit.

Chapter 16

Sterkest Slag

Arn sat at one end of an enormous horseshoe-shaped wooden table. Close to fifty Canites sat around it with Grimvaldr and Freya – as he had learned the queen was named – at its centre. Eilif sat next to her, requested that Arn be seated nearer as well, but the queen quickly overruled her. It seemed that order of nobility determined where one sat. *At least I have Grimson close by*, Arn thought. The young Wolfen now saw himself as a Man-kind expert, and had appointed himself Arn's tutor and cultural guide. Perhaps as an heir to the throne, he could choose wherever he wanted to sit, or he just wanted to be further from his mother's watchful eye.

Arn watched as dozens of attendants brought huge platters of food. He could see now why the table had its shape – the attendants were able to supply food and drink from the front, without having to reach over any shoulders.

Grimson kept up his high-pitched commentary, pointing to different male and female Wolfen and telling Arn who they were and what role they played in the kingdom. As a bonus, Arn also got to hear who had bad breath, who cheated at cards, and who was rumoured to love-chase someone other than his or her life mate.

Arn noticed that the other guests took the opportunity to sneak glances at him, but most looked away quickly when Arn caught their eye. Most, but not all: there was one older Wolfen – an advisor to the king, said Grimson – who went by the name of Vulpernix, who held his gaze. Grimson called him *White-eye* due to his having one milky, dead eye, and his stare made Arn feel a little creeped out. After a few moments, it was Arn who had to look away.

Arn decided to see if he could find other, friendlier faces along the table. Eilif was seated next to the king and queen, and immediately waved to him when she saw him glance in her direction. She then pointed to the different plates of food on the table, then back at Arn – he guessed she was trying to give him her opinion on which he'd most enjoy . . . Or was it the ones better avoided? *I'll soon find out,* he thought.

At last, the king raised his enormous tankard, and the table fell silent. Even the attendants froze, as if they were automatons suddenly powered off. Grimvaldr looked first down one length of the long table, and then the next. He nodded to each of his guests, and also to Grimson and Arn when he reached them.

Arn noticed Grimson nod in return, and he quickly did the same. The king then lifted his tankard even higher, and spoke to the group in a deep and strong voice that carried to every corner of the large room.

'In the beginning, there was the light – and from it came Fenrir and the Guardians. May they look over us, and all our charges, until the end of all time.'

As one, the crowd responded, 'Until the end of all time. Long live the king.'

Cups were raised, emptied, and then slammed down. Only then did the guests reach for the food.

Grimson grabbed several huge chunks of meat and dropped them onto his plate. He then paused to watch Arn, obviously intrigued as to what he would choose.

Arn looked at each of the platters – meat, meat, and more meat. Great slabs of what had to be pork, beef, lamb, and poultry – the selection was enormous. Thankfully, it was all cooked, but though he was far from being a vegetarian, he knew for his own health he needed some sort of fruit or vegetables. Looking down the table, he spied a large bowl that was filled with what he could only describe as lawn clippings.

He nudged Grimson and turned in time to see him stuff a fist-sized chunk of red meat into his mouth. Arn grimaced at the blatant reminder that these things were not people like him at all. He pointed at the grass-filled bowl down the table. 'What's that?'

Grimson half stood and looked down the table. He waved an attendant over to request the bowl be brought nearer. Once it was set down, he grabbed a pinch and pushed it into one corner of his already full mouth. He spoke while chewing. 'Gronus shoots – they're for digestion, stomach complaints . . . and also act as an expungent.'

He pushed the bowl towards Arn.

Expungent? Oookay, I think I know what that means . . . An image of a dog vomiting up grass onto the carpet leapt into his mind. *Erk . . .*

Arn pushed the bowl back. 'So, meat it is, then.'

He slipped the silver dagger from its scabbard, and used it to spear a piece of the red meat Grimson was enjoying. He put it on his plate, and sliced the chunk into smaller pieces. Spearing one of the slices, he put it in his mouth. It was delicious – tender and slightly salty. He couldn't quite place it – a little like fillet steak and bacon all in one. He speared another piece, holding it aloft while he chewed.

He noticed a quiet had fallen over the table – no sounds of talking, eating, plates being rattled, or even tankards slamming down onto the wood. He looked around. All eyes were on him – or rather, the piece of meat speared on his knife.

Arn guessed everyone had been waiting to see exactly how he ate . . . especially with his small-sized teeth and mouth.

Feeling self-conscious, Arn raised his free hand, made an 'O' with his thumb and forefinger, and said, 'Delicious.'

The king nodded and repeated the gesture back to Arn. Eilif had pulled her blade, and sat next to the queen holding aloft a speared chunk of meat.

Arn smiled and waved to her, but the queen reached across to make her lower her dagger. Arn guessed, judging by the expression of displeasure on the queen's face, that Eilif was also receiving a scolding. Beside him, Grimson was also spearing his meat.

Arn smiled. *Hey, I'm making an impression already*, he thought.

Having piled the table high with food, the attendants returned with all manner of boxes, pipes, stringed objects and what looked like shallow drums. Sitting on the floor in the middle of the table area, they began to play music. Arn winced; to his ears, the music was strange, with discordant notes that usually ended with one or several of the musicians lifting his or her head, and emitting a long, mournful howl.

Arn laughed behind his hand. *Guess some things never change*, he thought.

The remaining attendants brought around large earthenware jugs containing a dark liquid that smelled like herbs in ale. Arn poured himself half a mug.

He lifted it and sniffed. The soft curl of warm spices tickled his nose. He shrugged. *When in Rome*, he thought.

He lifted the mug to his lips – nearly gagged, and had to secretly let the liquid dribble back into the cup, trying hard not to allow the contents of his stomach to follow. It was so bitter and so vile, he wondered briefly whether it was supposed to be some sort of cleaning fluid. Arn quickly pushed another small piece of meat into his mouth to try and remove the lingering taste – it didn't work.

Beside him, Grimson kept up a constant stream of questions: about his home, his family, his weapon of choice – to which Arn simply answered, *hockey stick*, to the youth's bewilderment. His curiosity then turned to how fast Arn could run, climb, or jump over things. It seemed the young Wolfen was competitive; it wasn't long before his questions morphed into his boasting to Arn about his *own* physical capabilities.

Arn looked around the long table. Everything was so strange, yet so familiar. The Wolfen slumped in their seats, belching loudly, slapping each other's shoulders and laughing – perhaps ruminating over the day's events, or those still to come. Though the scene looked medieval, it was so . . . normal. It was easy to forget that these beings were wolves, or at least descended from them.

Arn also leaned back in his chair. *Ape*, the vile Panterran had called him. Was he so different, then? Perhaps what he was seeing was not so fantastic after all.

He looked up at one of the hall's high windows just as the moon appeared from behind the clouds. The night made him feel good, the moon even better. *Guess, I'm a night person now*, he thought, just as the king raised his hand to silence his guests.

'Young Man-kind, it is said you have a mighty arm, even though you yourself have professed to not being of warrior stock. Is this a truth?'

Arn cautiously nodded, not sure exactly what he was being asked. He looked to Eilif, who mouthed something to him. Was it an encouragement . . . or a warning?

The king must have sensed his uncertainty, and added, 'To make war on a jormungandr by oneself, let alone to crack its hide, usually takes

Wolfen steel and a mighty arm – or many mighty arms. But I have been told that you managed to do both with little more than a length of bone. How is this possible, Arnoddr-Sigarr?'

Arn felt the moon's glow on the back of his neck, the energy it gave him. Was his unnatural strength due to the silver orb being so close to the Earth now? Was its gravity somehow affecting him? How could he explain it, when he didn't understand it himself? He didn't try.

'Ahh, baseball . . . and a lot of luck, I guess.' Arn shrugged. There was silence as the crowd obviously expected more from him than just some obscure and alien term that no one in the room understood. 'It's a game we play, where we throw a ball really hard to another player who has a bat – *ahh*, a long piece of wood . . . Anyway, it's his job to hit the ball. Gives you strength.'

Grimson whispered, 'I could try that, if you show me.'

The king leaned forward. 'And this baseball teaches you how to put so much power into a blow, it can put crushing dents into the armour of the strongest beast in this land?' He looked along the table to where Andrejk sat with his stitched forehead. 'And also bash in a Wolfen helmet . . . and head, as well.'

The guests laughed at the king's jibe. Andrejk joined in, and lifted his mug in a toast.

The king's face suddenly became serious. He motioned with one arm for Arn to stand.

Arn rose slowly to his feet. 'Baseball teaches you to throw straight, but as for cracking the creature's armour, I just think I must have been lucky enough to hit it in a weak spot.'

'A weak spot? *Hmm*.' The king turned to Strom and nodded. In response, the giant warrior stood, pushing back his chair, its feet grating loudly in the now silent room. He walked slowly around the table, his eyes fixed on Arn.

Grimson nudged Arn and whispered, 'He wants to fight you.'

'What?' Arn hadn't taken his eyes off the enormous warrior as he approached.

Strom stood in front of him, fists planted on his hips, his deep voice ringing out strongly, 'There are no weak spots on the jormungandr, young Man-kind. I saw the rents in the thing's skin – there were several. Several times lucky? I think not even once.'

Arn was still on his feet, but his legs shook and demanded that he sit back down. He started to sink, and looked from Strom to the king, and then to Eilif, who appeared as worried as he felt.

Strom boomed again, 'Man-kind, it is honourable for a warrior to be modest. It is not, if one is concealing something.' He raised one of his huge arms, motioning for Arn to join him at the centre of the room.

Arn swallowed. 'I'm not concealing anything.' His voice sounded squeaky, even to himself. *I am definitely not fighting this guy, today or any day,* he thought.

'Approach, Man-kind; I do not bite.' He grinned, his sharp teeth suggesting otherwise.

Arn still didn't budge.

Strom looked to the king, awaiting a sign. The king smiled, lifted his tankard and drank, looking down into its depths for a second or two. He spoke softly.

'*Sterkest slag.*'

A roar went up around the table, and the Wolfen started to bang their mugs on the wood and chant. *Sterkest slag – sterkest slag – sterkest slag . . .*

Grimson gripped Arn's forearm, 'Sterkest slag!' Looking down at the youth, Arn could see the young Wolfen's eyes were alight with anticipation.

'What's . . .?'

There was a distant rhythmic sound of creaking wheels as the attendants returned. This time, there were no musical instruments, food, or beer brought forth. Instead, a trolley containing two tree stumps was dragged to the centre of the room. Both were about three feet in height, extremely solid and freshly cut.

A bench was also carried through by four more attendants, and laid close by. On the bench lay a pair of large, single-bladed axes. They looked heavy; even the four-foot handles appeared to be made of iron. Many of the Wolfen cheered and clapped, and started to chant Strom's name. Some raised their hands and looked to the king, as if asking for something, or vying for his attention.

'*Sterkest slag* – strongest blow,' Grimson explained. 'Go.' He pushed Arn forward.

Ah crap; what the hell have I got myself into? Arn stepped out from behind the table and slowly walked to the centre of the room, feeling the weight of the dozens of eyes upon him. *Strongest blow* – he felt he had walked into some jock's football test, except instead of facing the high-school quarterback, he knew he was about to be asked to challenge a creature more than a head taller than he was, and probably twice as wide.

He heard a voice above the chanting crowd – not calling Strom's name, but his own. It was Eilif. She cheered and made a small fist in the air.

'Strongest blow.' Grimson appeared at his side and looked at Strom with admiration. 'Strom always wins; no one is stronger in the kingdom.'

Arn bent down slightly, and whispered, 'What am I supposed to do?'

Grimson pointed to the tree stumps. 'You need to sink the axe deep into the wood – the winner is whoever has buried their axe head the deepest.'

'That's it?' Arn straightened, feeling safer now that he knew he didn't have to try to swing the huge weapon at the giant Strom . . . or worse, having the king's champion swing an axe at *him*.

Grimson looked at Arn's arms and shoulders. 'I like you, Arnoddr, but I don't think you'll win today.'

'I don't really think I'm supposed to. But hey, who cares?' Arn shrugged, now willing to play along.

'You might care. The winner is sometimes allowed to pick another challenge. Strom usually likes the punching contest.'

'Oh great, that sounds like fun as well.' Arn shook his head. 'I wish I could at least see it done first, so I don't *totally* humiliate myself.'

Grimson nodded and looked to the king. 'Demonstration, father?'

Eilif seconded the request. 'Yes, a demonstration of the art of *sterkest slag* by one of the elite!' There were mutters around the able, and Eilif added loudly, 'A dozen sølvs on the Arnoddr.'

For a moment, there was silence, then a burst of activity as bets were shouted from one end of the table to the other. Arn could hear they were nearly all for Strom, with a few extremely small wagers on him . . . and only because the odds against him winning were so great.

A young warrior with almost jet black fur spoke up loudly above the excited babbling of the crowd, 'A thousand sølvs on the king's champion.'

The bet's effect was instantaneous – silence, followed by a roar of applause.

Even Grimvaldr shook his head. 'A fortune, Bergborr, and one that no one will dare to claim.'

'I'll take that bet.'

Like a beast with many heads, the crowd turned as one to gaze in the direction of the voice. It was Balthazar. The old Wolfen looked first at Bergborr, then at Arn. His wise old eyes had a look of understanding that made Arn think he knew more than he was letting on.

'Done.' Bergborr banged his tankard down, his expression now as dark as his fur. Arn wondered whether he had expected no takers for his huge bet. But now he would make or lose a fortune this day.

The king banged a fist down onto the table, making the remaining plates and cups rattle and jump. The crowd settled and turned towards him.

Grimvaldr looked up and down the table, taking in each of his diners' faces. 'I *will* allow Arnoddr a demonstration. We must give the Man-kind some time to gather his strength, seeing there is so much coin riding on it.'

He continued to scan the assembled faces, stopping at a large young warrior. He nodded to him. 'Sorenson, stand and show us your arm.'

The young warrior whooped and stood up from the table. He raced around behind all the other seated Wolfen, occasionally patting one on the shoulder, or pushing a head forward good naturedly. Arn liked him already.

Sorenson was tall, but still many inches shorter than Strom, and as he approached the centre of the room, the king's champion threw back his head, and laughed heartily.

'You, little brother? I should have known.' He and Strom punched knuckles in a gesture that was eerily familiar to Arn, and reminded him of the camaraderie displayed at a million sporting events he had seen back home.

Strom bowed theatrically and motioned with his hand towards the axes – the first choice was to be the challenger's. Sorenson nodded and walked to the bench. He selected an axe, and judging by the way he dragged it from the table, Arn could tell it must have been extremely heavy.

Sorenson walked back towards Arn, and slapped him on the shoulder.

'Use the force of the swing, and never ease your grip,' he said, his sharp eyes examining Arn's face. 'And beware the impact; it has broken many a strong Wolfen's arm, whose hand was loose.'

He walked away before Arn could thank him, and positioned himself in front of one of the stumps. Spreading his legs, he allowed the axe to lean

101

against his thigh for a moment as he wiped his hands up the length of his pants. His fingers flexed and closed around the steel, getting a feel for it. Cheers and jeers came from the crowd, and Grimvaldr sat back smiling, his arms folded.

Sorenson looked to the king, who nodded once. The young Wolfen started inhaling and exhaling – slowly at first, then faster and deeper. Then he let out a mighty yell and swung the axe in an arc from the floor, over his head, and then down onto the centre of the stump. The strike echoed around the stone room, and was only drowned out by the cheers of the seated Wolfen.

Arn had expected the wood to be cleaved in two, but it must have been like the toughest ironbark, as the axe only penetrated to about a third of the way. Sorenson raised both hands in the air, obviously satisfied with his swing. Strom raised his eyebrows, showing he was impressed with his younger brother's arm.

Then came the chant: *Strom – Strom – Strom* . . . The king's champion bowed and walked purposefully towards the bench, taking up the other axe and swinging it back and forth one handed, the heavy weapon some- how looking smaller and lighter in the giant Wolfen's grip. He rolled his shoulders and looked to the king, waiting.

The king nodded. Strom turned to the stump and started to growl low and deep. The crowd fell silent. Even among his kinsmen, he was a fear- some sight. When he roared, it made Arn cringe slightly. He lifted the axe and swung it.

The blade buried itself more than two thirds of the way down into the iron-hard wood. Arn had felt a shudder from the impact as it travelled from the axe to the stump, and then down through the heavy stone floor.

There were gasps, then cheers and applause. Strom released the handle and turned to the king, first bowing to him, and then to his opponent. As he straightened, he held out his hand. Sorenson laughed and grabbed the forearm of the large Wolfen. Strom in turn gripped the shoulder of his younger brother, and spoke with a smile. 'Next time.'

Sorenson nodded and spoke softly, 'Probably not until you are an old Wolfen, I think.' He returned to his seat, getting slapped on the back by many of the seated warriors as he passed by them.

The two stumps were left side by side – Sorenson's axe buried about a third of the way down, and Strom's more than double that.

The familiar creak of wheels from behind Arn heralded the arrival of another two stumps and axes. Grimson nudged him. 'Your turn, Arnoddr. Just use your baseball magic again.' He gave Arn a gentle shove.

Reluctantly, Arn stepped forward. As he stood by Strom's side, there was another furious round of betting. Arn guessed that the sight of him, next to the massive bulk of the king's champion, inspired renewed confidence in those who were betting against him. He could also see that Bergborr now had a smug look of satisfaction on his face.

Arn turned to Strom, who bowed to him. As before, the giant motioned towards the axes. Arn looked to Eilif who had her hands clasped together in front of her chin, looking like she was ready to start praying. She mouthed something he couldn't understand.

Arn flashed her a tight smile, drew in a deep breath and walked like a condemned man to the bench. He examined the enormous weapons laid out there; to his eye, there was no difference between them, and he placed his hand on the closest.

His heart raced in his chest, as he picked up the axe. Surprisingly, it was light . . . in fact, *much* lighter than he expected. He knew it shouldn't have been; he had seen Sorenson, and even Strom, straining to lift it. Was he once again under the influence of the strange energy the giant moon seemed to be affording him? The thick blade was carved with runes, and its polished surface threw back a distorted image of his face. *I look sick,* he thought.

Arn turned and walked back to the stumps. He carried his axe in one hand, and even managed to spin it slightly in his grip. Strom raised an eyebrow and stepped back to give him room. He placed his hands on his hips, and a smile broke across his face. He looked like he was enjoying the challenge.

Arn rested the axe head on top of the stump, and took a few deep breaths. Sorenson's words drifted back into his head: *use the force of the swing . . . and beware the impact.*

He felt calm; he was ready. He looked to the king.

Grimvaldr was smiling, and Eilif now stood behind him, her hand gripping his shoulder in anticipation. The king nodded once.

Arn turned back to the stump. In his mind, he saw himself lifting the axe and swinging it with all the strength he could muster. It would be just like being at a carnival and swinging the wooden mallet to try to drive the puck all the way to the bell at the top of the pole.

I can do this, he thought. *I can ring the bell.*

He raised the axe over his head, and swung.

It passed cleanly through the stump and buried itself deep in the floor beneath it. The clang of steel on stone was startlingly loud, and many of the warriors leapt to their feet to obtain a better view.

The two halves of the large stump teetered, then toppled over.

Arn let go of the axe handle and stepped back, as surprised as anyone else. No one said a word; perhaps they were waiting to see how Strom would react to being beaten, and by a creature much smaller than himself.

A single pair of hands applauded him – it was Eilif. Arn felt a small hand on his forearm, and looked down to see Grimson staring wide eyed up at him.

'I knew you could do it. You must teach me this baseball magic, Arnoddr.'

A huge hand grabbed his other arm and raised it into the air. Strom turned him to the king and roared, 'A mighty arm on this one indeed!'

Strom felt the muscles up and down Arn's arm and shoulder, as if searching for some secret, some hidden muscles. He gave up and leaned forward. 'And you must teach me as well, Man-kind.'

At last the crowd found their voice, and one by one the Wolfen got to their feet and clapped. Many rounded the table to speak to Arn, or to Strom, or simply to see the axe embedded in the stone floor.

Grimvaldr also nodded his approval, and the queen hung onto Eilif to ensure she didn't run over in a manner that might have been undignified for a daughter of royalty.

But there was one Wolfen who remained seated. The dark-furred Bergborr looked sullenly over his mug. It had been a mighty blow to the stump, but a mighty blow to his purse as well.

Strom still hadn't released Arn's arm, and gave it one last tug, almost lifting the other off his feet. He slapped Arn on the shoulder and said to the room, 'Imagine if we could get this Man-kind to wield a sword?'

Eilif, at last breaking away from her mother, shouted, 'He would be a mighty warrior in the defence of Valkeryn!'

The king scratched his chin. '*Hmm,* just so. What say you, Arnoddr-Sigarr; would you wish to learn more about the Wolfen ways – learn to become a brother warrior?'

The room fell silent again. Everyone waited for Arn's response.

'I'm not sure – I mean, I guess. I'm not really a fighter. I might just get in the way . . .'

The king raised his hands. 'We are born with two strong arms, fang and claw, and more importantly with honour and courage. But what good are they, if they are never used to defend your home, your kin, or your Wolfen pack? We all must fight – the safety of the realm depends on it.'

Arn nodded, and the king stood up. 'Then it's settled; we will teach you our ways, and in return you will teach us yours.'

Arn watched as the attendants dragged away the axes and stumps, and three of them leaned on the handle of his buried axe, finally levering it free after several attempts. *Teach them my ways? What could I possibly teach them here and now?* he wondered.

Eilif skipped around the outside of the huge table, clapping as she skipped, and stopped beside him, grabbing his hand. Arn felt something cold and wet press against his cheek, and turned to see her pulling her head back. The inside of her ears had gone pink, and she looked away with a shy smile.

'You are already a champion, Arnoddr-Sigarr – king of the Man-kind.'

Arn smiled at her, but before he could thank her for the compliment, the queen dragged both her and Grimson from the room. As they left, Eilif looked back at him, mouthing something he couldn't understand.

A mug of the vile ale was thrust into his hand, and he raised it in a toast, but only pretended to drink. Throwing up might not have been a good look at that moment. He now felt welcome among the Canite Wolfen – well, among most of them, anyway. The older Wolfen, Vulpernix – the milky-eyed one – sat staring stonily at him.

Arn stared back into the milky eye. *So maybe not everyone's a fan of baseball,* he thought.

Chapter 17

Under The White Flag

Orcalion listened as the tall, hooded figure spoke softly from the shadows. The Panterran only interrupted him from time to time to ask a question, but for the most part he was struck silent by the recent occurrences in the Canite castle.

It seemed the Man-kind was growing in influence and support with each passing day, and once more Orcalion cursed the guards for allowing it to escape. He wished they were still alive, so he could torture and execute them all over again.

The tall figure stopped speaking, and waited. Orcalion could feel the other searching his face, perhaps looking for signs of deceit or treachery.

'Remember our bargain, Orcalion – when the time comes to pass, I alone am to rule Valkeryn, with the Princess Eilif at my side.'

The old Panterran stared off into the distance. In turn, the tall figure reached out a hand, on which he wore a silver ring depicting a snarling wolf with emerald eyes. Quick as lightning, Orcalion turned on him, holding a wickedly curved blade up to his throat.

'Never try to touch me again. I hear your words, and I remember our bargain well. You would open the deep gates and deliver up Grimvaldr to us. In return, we would give you his throne, and ensure all rivals for your new . . . queen, are gone. Just make sure you remain alive to claim them.'

He lowered the blade and glided a few steps away. 'There is more work for you to do. The Man-kind makes things more . . . complicated. My queen wants this creature alive.' He turned back to the hooded figure. 'And you will assist in making that happen.'

'That was not our bargain. Beware, little no-blinker, my desire for the throne does not make me your thrall, to be ordered about at will.'

The Panterran bared his needle-like teeth. 'Since the Man-kind and the young female Wolfen escaped, the entire kingdom must now know of the approach of the Lygon.' He rubbed his chin, his large yellow eyes slitted in contemplation. 'Perhaps it is time to pay a visit, give them a reason to hand over the Man-kind . . . willingly.' He laughed in an oily, wheezing fashion. 'See that the Man-kind is not in the throne room when I arrive.'

Orcalion turned away then, but added over his shoulder, 'This night passes, but I will be back soon . . . travelling under a white flag.' He threw back his head and laughed.

Chapter 18

Fenrir's Gift

Early the next morning, Sorenson led Arn out into one of the castle's enclosed forecourts, where they were met by a large and enormously over-weight Wolfen with a huge, soft leather roll at his feet.

'Olaf.' Sorenson bowed his head in acknowledgment.

The round Wolfen grunted and looked Arn up and down with a critical eye. He walked around him, prodding and poking, and tsk-tsking every few seconds – his chubby face bearing an expression as if he had just seen a spider on his piece of lunch-cake.

From his pocket, he produced a length of string knotted every inch or so along its length, and held it across Arn's shoulders, ran it down his arm to his wrist, the length of his leg, and then wound it around his head.

Arn tried to keep still, but found it extremely unsettling when Olaf brought his long snout in close to Arn's face, studying his features from one angle, then the next. Olaf shook his head and muttered something, probably about the dimensions of Arn's head – or more likely, lack of them.

He stood back and nodded to Sorenson.

'Good.' Sorenson clapped his hands together and motioned with his head to the chubby Wolfen. 'Olaf is the royal armourer and ironmonger. He'll make some war armour for you. Today, we'll just get a feel for the basic skills.'

'Okay,' Arn said, and Sorenson turned to the heavy Wolfen and spoke a few soft words that sounded like, *korte sverd*. Olaf knelt and un-fastened the leather roll, laying it out to reveal a variety of swords and clubs – all wooden.

Arn stooped to pick up the biggest sword he could find. Before his fingers closed around its hilt, Olaf grabbed his hand, turned it over, and stuck a medium-sized sword into it. The ironmonger handed another to Sorenson. It seemed the choice of weapons had already been made.

Sorenson swished his sword back and forth in the air a few times, before turning to Arn. 'The lesson for today is a simple one – don't get hit.'

He pointed his sword at Arn's throat. 'A Wolfen must know how to strike well. But there is much more to fighting than that. What good is a strike, if you too are hit in a vital area? Even Strom might find it difficult to fight with the thinnest sword piercing his heart.'

Sorenson reached forward and grabbed Arn's arm. 'Having the strength to split a stump is a magnificent asset – especially when battling the likes of a jormungandr, werenbeasts, or even thylakines. But against a couple of small, fast-moving Panterran, you'd be so full of holes, you'd leak like a fugl net.'

Sorenson placed his own sword under his arm so he could check Arn's grip on the wooden weapon. He stood back and smiled.

'Strength, endurance, skill and finesse – these are the things that bring a Wolfen home safely from battle. Any time the kingdom gets attacked by invading tree stumps, you're the one I want next to me.' He laughed and touched Arn's sword with his own. 'But in a real duel, against real foes, and to the death? We'll see.'

He swished his sword through the air again. This time, Arn did the same, testing its weight, and how it felt in his grip. Following his triumphant splitting of the tree stump, he was feeling confident, certain he had the strength and speed to win. He liked Sorenson, so decided he'd take it easy on him and try not to embarrass the youthful warrior too much on this first session.

Sorenson saluted, touching the blade of his sword to his brow. In turn, Arn adopted a fencer's pose, as he had seen a hundred times on television – side-on, legs apart, his sword pointed at the Wolfen warrior. His other arm was arched up above his head.

Sorenson laughed. 'What is this? Do you wish to dance first, young Man-kind?'

With that, the Wolfen lunged at him, and Arn moved out of the way, bringing his sword around to where he expected Sorenson's blade to be . . . Instead, he felt it crack across the backs of his knees, his legs buckling under him.

Arn blinked, his eyes focusing on the point of Sorenson's blade, which was now under his chin. It was strange; the electrifying strength he had felt the evening before was not running through his body anymore. The Wolfen warrior lowered his sword, and held out his hand.

'Maybe we should start with something a little simpler? Like how to balance while holding a sword.'

Arn grabbed the outstretched hand. 'I can get this. Let's do it again.'

Sorenson heaved him to his feet. 'Good spirit. I like that.'

They set themselves again. This time, Arn took the initiative, feinting to one side, but then shifting his weight and attacking from the other. But still the Wolfen seemed to know what he was planning to do, even before he did it.

Like before, Arn's sword found only thin air, the flat of his opponent's blade striking him across the back of his head, and knocking him forward. Arn spun on his heels, gritting his teeth.

Sorenson was trying hard not to laugh. 'Just as well the fur on your head is thick, Man-kind.'

Arn swore, and ran hard at the Wolfen – swinging and slashing his sword through the air. Sorenson parried each blow, but had to dive sideways to avoid a vicious swipe to his chest. Arn came at him again, and again Sorenson dived and rolled, yelling back over his shoulder as he bounced to his feet, 'Good speed, and good endurance . . . but still no finesse!'

Arn manoeuvred the Wolfen warrior up against a wall – or so he thought. When Sorenson had his shoulders pressed against the brickwork, Arn grabbed his sword arm. In turn, Sorenson did the same to him. Now they were locked together. Arn was gasping, while the Wolfen still seemed to be breathing easily.

Sorenson tilted his head. 'And what now, Man-kind?'

With his sword arm pinned, and not daring to release the Wolfen's, it seemed to Arn that they had reached a stalemate. But just as he was about to call it a draw, Sorenson bared his teeth – the huge fangs just inches from Arn's nose.

'These are the weapons all Wolfen are born with. They are Fenrir's gift to us. Of all the creatures I have seen on this world, your fangs are perhaps the least impressive . . . except maybe for the small fluffpeans leaping on the grassy plains.' His gaze, too, was locked with Arn's. 'Be wary of close fighting with any of the creatures of Valkeryn – use your speed, and strength, and endurance, but never let any foe get close to your throat.'

Sorenson pushed him back and raised his sword. 'Again.'

Chapter 19

There'll Be Luck This Day

Grimson stayed as still as the mossy stones by which he crouched, in among the bushes. His three attendants had stopped as well, keeping well back to allow the princeling some space to complete his hunt.

The young Wolfen's hunting ground was the edges of the lush forest close to the castle, still in sight of the tall ramparts that towered on the hill, but just deep enough and wild enough to provide some small game. His ears twitched as he listened intently to the sounds of the forest – something was close, he could sense it. In another instant, a cloud of creatures burst out from the brush into the air – small furred animals with membranous wings and long leathery tails, their screeches gratingly shrill as they fled the approaching danger.

Grimson drew back the elastic on his slingshot, took aim, and let loose the small round stone in its leather pouch. It flew faster than the eye could follow, and a squeal in midair immediately announced his success. One of the small flying creatures fell from the sky not fifty paces from where he knelt.

'I told you there'll be luck this day,' he yelled over his shoulder as he broke cover and ran to where the thing lay, his keen sense of smell locating it in some thicker bushes.

Grimson lifted it and weighed it in his hand – *not a bad size.* He'd show Arn when he got back, maybe get the cooks to prepare it for them. But of course, he'd keep the head for himself – that was always the best bit. The young Wolfen spread out the membranous wings, wondering what the Man-kind would make of this ugly little flygen-gnager. He smiled, imagining the expression on Arn's strange, hairless face.

112

He was growing fond of Arn. Grimson didn't have any real friends in the castle, and the strange Man-kind was fast becoming the closest one he'd ever had. He had a way with his words and humour that made Grimson laugh nearly every time they spoke.

He chuckled to himself. Maybe he'd sneak the gnager's tail into Arn's garments to give him a scare. *Now that would be fun*, he thought, and chuckled again.

Grimson turned, expecting to see his ever-present attendants, but found himself alone.

He called to one, and then another. There was no reply.

Grimson stood quietly in among the dark foliage. From where he stood, the castle towers now seemed a long way distant. It was strange – too silent. He concentrated; there was noise – almost imperceptible.

Breathing.

He couldn't help the tiny whimper that stole from the back of his throat; the brace of flygen-gnager had been startled into breaking cover when he wasn't even close to them – they'd been startled by something . . . but not him. In the moment it took him to pull his small dagger from its scabbard, a strong hand wrapped around his muzzle and bound it with a leather strap.

The last thing he saw before a bag was pulled over his head was that the hand belonged to a Wolfen.

*****

The runner burst into the throne room and went down on one knee to deliver his message, his voice echoing in the vast space.

'A Panterran emissary, my lord . . . He comes alone, and under the flag of peace.'

'Peace,' snorted Grimvaldr. He rose to his feet. 'Assemble my generals, and have the Panterran wait at the gates until we are ready.'

The Wolfen runner nodded and hurried away. Grimvaldr walked slowly to the window to look out over the castle grounds, and beyond to the green lands of the kingdom. Most Wolfen had heightened senses – they could *feel* when the ground was going to shake, even before it did. Some could even sense an intention before it was acted upon. But Grimvaldr was of the royal bloodline, descended from Fenrir himself; as

113

he gazed out the window, he felt a dark sense of foreboding deep in his chest, as if a great calamity or storm hung over Valkeryn and all his people . . . and he could do nothing to avert it.

He shook his head to clear away the disturbing thoughts, and sat down heavily in his chair just as his war party entered. As always, it was Strom first, in full armour, his brother Sorenson, followed by Karnak, Ragnar, and all his other generals, advisors and trusted senior warriors. Grimvaldr didn't believe for a minute that the vile creature would be on a mission of peace.

Any news of Panterran travelled swiftly, and already the group knew of the approaching emissary, and that it came from their most hated of foes. On entering, the Wolfen simply nodded to Grimvaldr and filed to his left and right as he sat forward in the large oak chair in the centre of the room.

The king turned to Sorenson first. 'Show our emissary and bearer of good news into the hall.' Grimvaldr smiled and added, 'And try not to bite his head off, young Sorenson.'

'The taste would sicken me, sire.' Sorenson bowed and walked quickly over to the double doors, pushing them open and allowing the smaller, hooded creature to enter.

The Panterran glided fluidly into the room, immediately reminding the king why they were called Slinkers. It halted after a few paces to look at each of the assembled Wolfen. There was no bow or nod – just a look of contempt on the flattened features.

'Greetings, ruler of the Canites. Greetings from Queen Mogahr, ruler of the Panterran – may her name be blessed above all others.'

There was a stirring in the Wolfen ranks as they listened to the praising of another ruler in the hall of the great Wolfen kings. Grimvaldr simply nodded and raised his hand for order.

'You travel here under a white flag of peace, and we will honour it. But you are not our guest, not our friend, and your race has been making war on us since before the dawn of remembered time. State your business quickly and go on your way.'

The small flat-faced creature grinned, his small tongue licking black lips.

'As you say . . . Canite king. I am Orcalion, and I have been tasked with bringing a message of true peace, lasting peace. If you would only accept it.' He paused and again let his amused gaze slide over the Wolfen generals and advisors. 'There is much danger in the forests and the outlands, and this danger comes even here to Valkeryn. You know the Lygon have entered the kingdom?'

Strom took a half step forward. 'Brought by you, vile eater of vermin.'

Orcalion grinned once more. '*Ah*, of course, the mighty Strom – the king's champion and strong right arm. It is true we sought to meet with the Lygon, only to find out their intent. After all, this is our land also. But they will not listen to reason. They say they come to make war on *you*, Canite king.'

Grimvaldr waved his hand in the air. 'We have met greater foes before, and have stood. We will meet any challenge to Valkeryn.'

'Of course you have. But a thousand Lygon, each half as tall again as your own Strom . . . This will be an interesting war for a king to fight in his olding years.'

Grimvaldr knew that the Panterran was trying to prickle him with his words. 'Is there anything else? Anything we do not already know?'

'Mighty Grimvaldr, honourable Grimvaldr. It is true our races have been at war for nearly all time, but even we cannot condone the atrocities that will be inflicted on you by the Lygon – the atrocities that are *being* inflicted at this very moment.'

Orcalion reached under his robe and pulled forth a leather satchel. Several of the Wolfen moved quickly to stand in front of the king, forming a shield, and Sorenson put his hand on the hilt of his sword.

Orcalion unwound the leather thong around the top, and pulled free a grisly necklace, tossing it onto the floor. It was made up of many Wolfen ears threaded together, one with a familiar notch missing from the top.

Ragnar bent and picked them up, rubbing the notched ear with his fingers.

'Isingarr, bravest of warriors . . .' He turned his gaze to the Panterran, baring his teeth as a growl rumbled deep in his chest.

Orcalion nodded and spoke quickly, the grin still not leaving his lips, 'The Lygon are no respecters of the dead . . .'

He reached into the sack once more and pulled forth a tattered and bloody scrap of cloth. It bore the image of a silver, snarling wolf with red eyes – the house of Grimvaldr – the patch of material having been torn from a small tunic. The colour, the crest, Grimvaldr recognised it in an instant.

Orcalion tossed it to the floor. '. . . Or age.'

The king burst from his chair, gripping the Panterran around the throat and lifting him from the ground with one hand. Even then, the yellow eyes stared back defiantly, a suggestion of wheezing laughter in the strangled voice:

'Brave king, righteous king, so noble, so large and powerful. You could crush me like a morning bug . . . but you will not. Your laws of safe passage deny it . . . and a Wolfen never strikes at an . . . unarmed foe. The war is coming, old king. It will be your last. Maybe I can save your young Wolfen son . . . maybe I cannot. Or perhaps the key to saving him rests with you this very moment . . . if you will but listen.'

Grimvaldr threw back his head and roared, and drew the creature so close, his breath moistened the fur on the Panterran's flattened face.

Orcalion hissed, 'You have something that Queen Mogahr wants, something that you can . . . trade to buy our help.' His grin finally twisted into a grimace of pain as the grip on his throat intensified. 'The Man-kind – give him to us, and she will intercede . . . personally . . . with the Lygon.'

Grimvaldr threw the Panterran from him, and roared his frustration to the high ceiling. Orcalion got to his feet and laughed softly. Around him, the other Wolfen had curled their hands into fists and snarled in their barely contained fury. Pulling forth a scrap of white cloth and holding it above his head, the Panterran edged towards the door, intoning the words for safe passage as he went. In the doorway he stopped. 'You must give your answer by three eves hence. After that, the son of Grimvaldr may either be out of the kingdom . . .' He sidled round the doorframe. '. . . Or out of his skin.'

With that he was gone.

Grimvaldr sat down slowly, his shoulders slumped, and stared off into the distance. Strom was by his side in an instant.

'Give me a dozen Wolfen elite and some trackers – I'll bring you Grimson, and the head of that creature, and anyone else who was involved in his capture.'

The other Wolfen were yelling their approval, and willingness to be in the first group to charge out after the king's son. Only one stayed silent and brooding. The older Wolfen turned his one good eye on the king, waiting.

The king brought his fist down hard on the arm of his chair, silencing the others.

'Speak Vulpernix. All voices are to be heard this day.'

Vulpernix nodded. 'I suggest another option we must consider.' He paused and walked forward. 'We must think hard about handing them the Arnoddr-Sigarr.'

'Never!' shouted Sorenson. 'The Panterran would kill the Man-kind, and then make war on us regardless. They can never be trusted.' He banged his fist to his chest. 'A Canite protects the pack, and the pack protects the Canite. He has already proved himself, proved he would fight for us . . . for your very bloodline, sire. Now we must prove the same.'

Vulpernix turned on him quickly. 'He is not one of us! He is not a Canite, and he does not belong here. If he were truly one of the prophesised Old Ones, he would never have allowed the young prince to be taken. Where is his legendary magic of science? Where are his machines of war to protect us? By his own admission, he is here by accident . . . and all alone.'

He turned back to the king, his voice softening. 'My king, I too like the Man-kind, but I would think hard about whether an idle friendship is worth the life of Grimson, and potentially every Wolfen and youngling in this mighty kingdom.' He shuffled forward and went down on one knee before the king, taking his hand. 'There is no other way, sire.'

Grimvaldr rose from his chair. 'This kingdom has stood for a thousand years, and will stand for a thousand more. Many have tried to bring down these walls, and their bones now litter our battlefields.' He scanned the assembled Wolfen.

'Who here fears the Lygon? Who would run from the Panterran? Who would flee the kingdom of Valkeryn and hand it to these vile vermin eaters?' The roars from the room were deafening; fists struck chests, and yells of fealty echoed around the stone chamber. Grimvaldr nodded. 'And neither would I. Ambushing a few Wolfen in the dark is one thing, but they will find that facing an entire Wolfen army is another matter. Prepare yourselves and your garrisons. Every Wolfen, male and female, must be readied to fight. If these creatures from the dark lands want war, we'll give them one until they choke on their own blood.'

Grimvaldr searched out Sorenson. 'You are right, young warrior. They cannot be trusted, but we must consider all our options to save the heir to the Valkeryn throne. Go,' he commanded them; 'have the ironmongers work from this dawn to the next, turning out Wolfen steel. Have them roll the metals until they are hard enough to slice through Lygon bone. Go!'

The roar of assent resounded around the room, and the group began to leave. Grimvaldr raised his arm and gestured to Strom and Vulpernix. 'A moment.'

As the last sounds of the disappearing Wolfen generals and counsellors echoed away down the long, stone corridors, the three Wolfen stood alone together in the great hall.

'Strom, trusted champion of Valkeryn,' said the king. 'I feel this time we'll need the mightiest Wolfen army that has ever stood. Bring me the maps of war, and then send word to the far edges of the kingdom. Assemble all the scattered Canite tribes, ready them and equip them. If we can hold back the first wave of the Lygon, and perhaps even damage them, then the Panterran will be easily repelled. Now is the time, my friend.'

Strom knelt and took the king's hand, pressing it to his brow. 'In seven days I will have them assembled; in eight, equipped and ready to fight. Or they'll answer to me personally.'

Grimvaldr put his hand on the giant's shoulder. 'Thank you, my friend.'

Strom stood and banged his fist on his chest. 'Long live Grimvaldr, and Valkeryn.' He turned quickly and strode from the hall.

Grimvaldr watched him go, then said softly to Vulpernix, 'Valkeryn has stood for centuries because we are strong. But a kingdom must also be smart . . . and so too its king.' He looked into the old counsellor's eyes. 'Tell me, Vulpernix – you of all of my Canite advisers have spent your life studying the Panterran and other creatures of Valkeryn. Do you really believe these Slinkers can be trusted to secure Grimson's release?'

The older advisor frowned. 'It's true that I have spent a lifetime studying these creatures. But their minds are so different to ours. They can scarcely stay loyal to each other for very long, and they have a history of deception. But I have heard Mogahr desperately wants the son of the humans . . . perhaps just as a pet. It would be in her nature to want to humble the old rulers of this world.' Vulpernix paced as he spoke. 'Maybe we can pretend to hand them the Arnoddr-Sigarr, and retake him at a later time. I'm sure he'll be kept safe enough until the queen tires of him.'

He stopped pacing and turned back to the king. 'It would at least buy us several more days to draft in and equip our scattered troops, and more importantly, learn more about the Lygon numbers, their strengths and, I'm sure, their weaknesses.'

Grimvaldr grunted, and after a moment he nodded slowly but continued to stare at the ground. 'Send for Queen Freya. I must tell her of the capture of her son.' Grimvaldr looked into the one good eye of his advisor. 'Is there anything else you can recommend, Vulpernix?'

Vulpernix pondered the question. 'Events are moving quickly; so much is still . . . unclear. But I do know that Queen Mogahr likes to be close when she smells a vulnerable king – if we could capture her, there may be no war at all.'

'Think how we could make this happen, Vulpernix.'

So saying, Grimvaldr turned to leave. Vulpernix bowed, just as the king stopped and half turned. 'Wait . . .'

'Yes, my Lord?'

'Valkeryn will not fall, of this I am sure . . . But I would be further comforted if our old, and very young, were taken up to the high garrisons at the far ends of the kingdom. If there is a siege, it would be better if they were . . . out of harm's way.'

'Very wise, sire. It will allow the Wolfen to focus on the battle.'

Vulpernix stayed bowed until the king had left the room. When he stood, a small smile played on his lips.

Chapter 20

A Girl – And What Is That?

Days passed, and Arn spent most of his time out in the field in front of the main gate of Valkeryn, practising his sword skills, the techniques that Sorenson had shown him. His Wolfen instructor and mentor had been urging him on without actually telling him why. It was as if there was a test coming, and Arn was being forced to cram for it.

Eilif had joined him this particular morning, carrying with her an enormous cloth bag, which Arn assumed was food for a small picnic. She sat on a low stone wall, keeping up a running commentary on his footwork, his length of thrust, or any tiny fault she spotted in his style.

Today, Sorenson had kitted him out in some armour to get him used to moving with the extra weight, and after working for over an hour, he was feeling the heat of the steel across his back and shoulders. Even though Eilif laughed from time to time when he seemed about to lose his balance, he felt that he was improving quickly.

'Keep it up, mighty warrior. The next time the jormungandr strikes, it won't be a sword of bone he'll have to face. He should tremble in fear, when the Arnoddr approaches.' She clapped as he thrust his wooden sword at the air.

Arn danced lightly with the blade, leaping up onto the wall, and then back down. He spun one way then the other, and finally brought his blade down on the thin branches of a tree, cutting away a good several feet of wood.

'*Ooh*, once again the Arnoddr-Sigarr makes war on the peaceful plant folk of Valkeryn. No tree stump, twig or leaf is safe from his wrath.' She laughed and clapped again as his face reddened.

Arn pointed his sword playfully at her throat. 'Better than a girl could do.'

Eilif reached up slowly and pushed the wooden tip of the sword away, smiling as she did. There was a mischievous gleam in her eye.

'A *girl* – and what is that?'

'A female.'

She laughed. 'And the female warriors are inferior in the land of Man-kind?

'No, but—'

She cut him off. 'All Wolfen, male or female, fight in the Valkeryn kingdom. I have been personally trained by the mighty Strom himself.' She knelt beside the cloth bag she had brought, smiling at him as she reached into it and pulled forth two steel swords and two small shields.

It seemed to Arn that she had come prepared . . . for more than just a picnic.

'Let's see what you can really do, son of Man-kind.' She handed him one of the swords, and he watched as she threaded her arm through the handle on one of the shields. 'My weapon of choice is the longbow – I'm one of the best archers in all of Valkeryn, but . . .' Eilif swung the sword in a loop, familiarising her arm with its weight, and then keeping her back to him, went through some practised moves, thrusts and blocks. '. . . This will do.'

She turned to him and bowed. 'Time to take the training up to the next level, mighty Arnoddr.'

Arn swung the sword in his hand. It was only slightly heavier than the wooden practice weapon, but the blade's edge was as sharp as a razor. He was immediately worried – he might really hurt her if he accidentally . . .

'Ha!' She lunged at him, and he only just managed to parry her thrust with his sword. 'Keep your shield up. It's used as much as a weapon as it is for defence.'

Arn was amazed; she was at least as fast as Sorenson, but with a light-ness on her feet that was half dancer, half sword master. Suddenly his worrying about hurting *her* seemed just plain stupid.

He tried to apply the manoeuvres Sorenson had taught him, even man-aging to force her back a few steps.

'Not bad,' she said. 'One day, you may even make a good Wolfen warrior.'

She came at him again, raising her sword high above her head, but when he lifted his own sword to parry her attack, she had already danced away, ducking under his guard and sweeping her blade, back-handed, lightly across his throat. It nicked him, and it hurt.

'Ow!'

'Pay attention,' she scolded him. 'I could have taken your leg if I wished. Don't watch my blade; watch my shoulder and my eyes. Anticipate my moves. Come on, you're better than this. I've been watching you practise.'

'I don't want to hurt you,' Arn protested.

She scoffed, 'Hurt me? I'll have you in pieces, small nose.' She spun and caught him again on the cheek.

After another five minutes, Arn could feel blood running down both his legs, both cheeks and his throat, into his armour. It made him feel sticky and even hotter. He wished it was evening, so he could feel the surge of energy brought about by the moon. Here and now, she was making him feel and look like a slow, stupid child.

Her angry words started to become taunts.

'Pathetic. Maybe it would have been better if a female warrior had come to visit us from your time.'

He gritted his teeth.

'Or maybe if you were older, more a full-grown?'

Defeated, Arn dropped his sword and stared at the ground between them. Then he tilted his head, as if catching sight of something. Eilif followed the line of his gaze for only a moment – but it was enough. Lunging forward, he smashed his shield into hers, knocking her onto her back. He leapt and landed on top of her.

'I could have taken your leg off, young Wolfen. You're better than that.'

Touché, he thought.

She was breathing hard, and looked deeply into his eyes. 'Like two dark, mysterious pools.' She smiled and raised an eyebrow. 'Feel that?'

He did. Arn looked down slowly; in her hand she held a small dagger, pressed into his groin.

She laughed and licked his nose.

Blerk. He stuck out his tongue and rolled away, also laughing.

Eilif sat up. 'You have potential, Arn. And your strength and cunning will give you an advantage. Are all Man-kind like you?'

Arn started stripping off his armour. 'We're all the same, and we're all different, I guess.' He used his undershirt to wipe his brow, and then stared off into the distance.

Eilif watched his face for a moment. 'You miss someone?'

He shrugged. 'Sure, I miss my family. I miss my home. I miss . . .'

She moved a little closer, and nudged him with her foot. 'Miss . . . who? Do you have someone back home? Someone special who . . . cares for you? Who you care for?'

Arn continued to stare into the distance. He shrugged again. 'Not really. Well, I'm sure she cares *about* me, but I don't think she cares *for* me.'

She nudged him again with her toe, and he grabbed her foot and lifted it, tipping her onto her back. She laughed and rolled onto her stomach, coyly fiddling with a blade of grass. She spoke without looking back at him. 'I would care about you – and for you, Arnoddr-Sigarr.'

Arn smiled at her. 'Thanks. You're a good friend, Eilif.'

She turned her head for a moment, and he saw what he thought was a look of disappointment on her face. He also saw that her ears had gone pink again. It suddenly occurred to him that this might be the Wolfen version of a blush. She looked back at the grass, continuing to examine it as if it was the most interesting thing she had ever seen.

'I saw you in a vision many years ago,' she murmured. 'I knew you would come for me.'

'What was that?'

She sat up. 'I said, I brought some food for you. Remember how you told Morag and Birna that you liked sam-widges? Well, we made you some. We could only find grass seeds, but . . .' She reached into her bag and lifted out what looked to be a small plate wrapped in cloth. She unwrapped it and handed it to him.

'Heey, not bad.' The bread looked to be the flat, unleavened kind – a little hard and overcooked, but when he lifted it to his nose, it smelled wonderful.

'Don't worry, it's okay to eat. I tested it on one of the servants, and they're still fine. I also tasted it myself . . . but I didn't really like the brett.' She waved both her hands at him, as though she was trying to shoo it into his mouth. 'But you try it.'

'It's *bread* . . . and it looks great. But no more taste tests on the servants, okay?' She nodded and watched him carefully as he raised the sandwich to his lips.

Arn bit down, hard. The bread was as tough as it looked, and had a slight acidic taste to it. Eilif had filled the sandwich with thin slices of beef, which was salty and tender. He chewed and swallowed and closed his eyes, and then sat still for a moment.

'What's the matter? Is it okay?' Eilif placed her hand on his forearm.

Arn opened his eyes and smiled. 'It's good . . . No. No, it's better than that – it's great.'

'Yes!' She threw both her arms around his neck – then quickly let go, and looked over either shoulder as if to make sure no one had seen them. She leaned in close to him. 'I knew you'd like it.'

Arn broke the sandwich in half. 'It's too much for me; here, you have some too.'

'No, Arn. This is your private meal.'

'I insist.' He saw she was about to object again. 'Where I come from, being asked to share someone's lunch is a great honour.' He looked at her solemnly.

Eilif looked at him, then the sandwich, and nodded. 'Then I would be truly honoured to share your sam-widge.' He handed her one of the halves, and noticed that she pulled out the meat, leaving the bread on the grass beside her. She nibbled at it daintily, obviously trying to mimic his slower style of eating.

He turned to her. 'I've been asked to attend a meeting with the king to-night. Will you be there?'

She stopped chewing and frowned at him. 'I know nothing of it. My father is very busy at the moment, as is my mother. Even Grimson I haven't seen for days. I *have* heard that my father sent runners out to the far corners of the kingdom, to bring in all the scattered warrior tribes . . .' She frowned and looked off into the distance, then turned back quickly, smiling. 'Maybe he has a special task for you?'

Arn ignored her flattering, and thought instead of the Wolfen tribes being summoned back to Valkeryn. 'Do you think there'll be a war?'

She jumped to her feet. 'I hope so. It'll be my first chance to fight in battle, now that I'm old enough. We Wolfen are good fighters . . . and have *never* lost a war.' She offered him her hand. 'And with the mighty Arnoddr-Sigarr by our side, we'll be victorious yet again.'

From a window of the castle, a dark-furred Wolfen watched, his lips curling back in disgust at their familiarity with each other.

Chapter 21

It Must Be Fun To Play God

Jim Takada paced the floor of the command room, his arms folded and his face pulled into a frown. He stopped and turned. 'But if it's still open, then what's to stop more . . . objects falling through?'

Albert Harper shrugged. 'What's to stop them falling back? Might be a revolving door, rather than a one-way exit only.'

'Do you think the boy could return with the diamond, or at least be retrieved?

'Good question. I hope so, but from where? He might be as close as tomorrow, but in a different dimensional slice of the universe. He could also be standing in a Cretaceous swamp – we can't know from here. But I think we should try and find out, don't you?'

Takada nodded. 'Gets my vote.'

There was a buzz from the communication panel beside Harper's hand, and he looked down at the flashing light. 'Front gate,' he grunted, flicking a switch. 'Harper here.'

'Dr. Harper, it's the girl, Rebecca Matthews. I guess she's come to check on our progress again.'

Harper sighed and looked at the security monitor for the front gate, where the girl stood beside a car, in which sat a middle-aged man and woman – probably her parents.

'Tell her I'm not . . .' He thought for a moment. *If we're going to find Singer, we first need to understand him . . . and she could help.* He shrugged. *Couldn't do any more harm,* he thought.

A news blackout, and a selective misinformation leak had thrown the press off for now. Most of the scientists and technicians required on the emergency project were flown in and out by helicopter, and stayed on the Fermilab grounds.

'Sure, Bob, let her through. I'll send a cart to pick her up. Just make sure one of the guards checks to make sure she doesn't have a pocket camera . . . And get her to turn her phone off immediately.'

Harper flicked off the communication feed, but continued to watch as the gates slid back and the girl was waved through. Bob Menzies leaned in through the car window and spoke to the parents for a minute, then stood back to wave as the car backed away.

The gate slid closed, and Bob chatted with the girl until another guard appeared, walking beside a dog that was unleashed. He spoke a few words to the animal and it immediately circled the girl, sniffing intently, and then froze to stare into her face. It held that position, simply starring into the girl's eyes.

What do they see when they do that? Harper wondered.

After a few seconds more, the animal returned to sit by the guard.

The guard and the dog wandered away, leaving Bob to chat with the girl for a few more moments until a golf cart pulled up beside them. She climbed in for the several mile trip to the head office, where the rescue attempt was being coordinated.

Harper looked at his watch. He had a few minutes until she arrived, so he turned to the bank of screens, now focused permanently on the sealed acceleration chamber. The small dot of instability hovered in the air like a smudge on each monitor – like something that needed no more than a quick wipe with a damp cloth to make it disappear. But it was much more than that; it was a continuing distortion in their universe – not opening any further, but not closing either. A distortion that one young person had already fallen through, taking with him the only thing that may be able to close it.

That the distortion refused to evaporate and disappear worried the lead scientist immensely. He was right to call the work now being undertaken a *rescue attempt*. And though he had said it was for Arnold Singer, secretly he knew the young man was insignificant – that the actual rescue might be for the laboratory and its grounds, or perhaps even the entire world.

Dark matter and black holes were insatiably hungry creatures, and the Tevatron continued to suck power at a geometrically increasing rate. They had to succeed.

*****

Becky sat in the cart as it passed under the huge three-legged, metal structure on their way towards the administration building – 'an optical illusion', Arn had said to her only a few weeks ago. She smiled at his dumb humour. Already talking to him seemed like a distant dream.

She couldn't stop accusing herself, and still didn't know if she was feeling guilty about her treatment of him, or whether she really cared for the nerd. Arn's parents had suddenly left town, which seemed strange to her, and the college acted like he was not even enrolled there anymore. Mr. Beescomb had asked her to leave it up to *the powers that be*, but she and Edward had refused to drop it, and while he banged away searching the internet for clues, she kept an eye on Dr. Harper. She felt she needed to know every day what they were doing to bring Arn home.

She tried to relax her face – once again, it had pulled into a frown without her realising. She reached up and touched the skin between her eyes, feeling the crease that was beginning to form there. *Damn you, Arnold Singer, you're giving me wrinkles.*

Becky looked across to where the dogs were housed. The white-domed buildings looked more like landed spaceships than regular kennels. The huge animals sat silently and watched her as she passed. From within the domes came the sound of barking – sort of. She saw that the dogs outside the kennels swung their heads at the weird noise. It was like a dog barking, but the cadences were different, almost like . . .

The driver, who noticed her confusion, chuckled. 'Sounds like talking, doesn't it? The lab boys have been genetically engineering the animals for size and intelligence. Even strengthened their cell structures to deal with high doses of ionising radiation. I think it's some sort of sponsored military sub-project.'

Becky frowned at him, and he chuckled again. He took her look of distaste to be a sign to carry on talking.

'Hey, you think *they're* smart? You should see the new dog, Fen. That's him you can hear making all the racket. The keepers say he can actually understand them.' He looked at her, taking his eyes off the narrow road. 'I mean *really* understand them. It's true! Weird, huh?'

The driver slowed as they neared the entrance to the Administration Centre.

127

'Okay miss, here we are, and right there waiting is Dr. Harper. I'll be back to take you to the front gates when you're ready.'

Becky craned her neck to look back to the kennels. The dogs were returning to the kennels by themselves as if they'd all been summoned. She turned to the driver. 'Why did you do it? Train them to try and talk, I mean.'

The driver looked quickly over to the kennels, and then back to her. He hesitated.

'But we didn't. They taught themselves to do that all on their own.'

It must be fun to play God, she thought, now feeling even more unsettled by the weird animals.

Climbing out of the cart, Becky headed over to the waiting scientist. She noticed that in the last few weeks he had aged considerably – he looked more beaten down and weary. *Things cannot be going well,* she thought, and felt immediately depressed.

'Hello Dr. Harper. I'm sorry to bother you again, but I had a dream . . .' She let her voice trail off, not really wanting to go into any more details.

Harper grabbed her hand and shook it. 'You're welcome any time, Rebecca. As long as you understand that anything you see or hear must be kept confidential.' He smiled and kept shaking her hand, pressing it for emphasis. Then he turned and waved her inside.

Becky noticed that there were now dozens of guards in every corridor of the facility, and many of the personnel wandered around in varying types of contamination suit.

'Is there more radiation?'

Harper walked to the large elevator doors at the far end of the reception area. He shook his head. 'Not really. The anomaly has stabilised, and is giving off mild gamma radiation and traces of X-rays, but nothing that needs any more than normal shielding.'

Becky looked back at the spacesuits and raised her eyebrows. Harper avoided her stare.

She followed him along the sterile corridor to the observation room – a room that she was growing to loathe. There were significantly more military personnel, scientists and equipment than last time. *Things are finally happening,* she thought.

From somewhere below them there was an irritating grinding, which sounded like a giant getting some dental work. Harper pushed open the observation room's door, and Becky entered, nodding and mouthing *hello* to the technicians and scientists she recognised.

The sound of the grinding was muffled inside the room, but she was still aware of it, and could even feel the mechanical vibrations beneath her feet.

Harper motioned to two chairs set up in front of a bank of screens. One was focused on the accelerator's particle collision point; through a cloud of concrete dust, the next screen showed a wall into which a machine was drilling a hole five feet in diameter. Its movements mirrored the vibrations.

Harper motioned with his head. 'That's what you can feel beneath your feet. We can't wait for something to happen anymore, when there is a real and imminent threat from the anomaly.'

He looked at her with sad eyes. 'To be candid, if we could simply close the distortion hole, we would. If we thought we could pour a thousand tons of concrete over it, we would. Neither option is possible. You see, one of the reasons we think the anomaly will not close is due to the theory of universal balance. Matter cannot be destroyed; it can only be transferred into a different state – solid to liquid, liquid to gas. Even ripping and shredding particles like we do here only creates different types of particles. What we think has happened is that Mr. Singer has been ejected from our dimension. To where or when, we don't know. But because he no longer exists in *our* universe, there was an imbalance created . . . and the anomaly wouldn't close until that balance had been restored.'

Becky searched his face. 'So you need to bring him back? You *have* to bring him back?'

Harper shook his head. 'Maybe if we brought him back within the first few seconds he disappeared. But now, the more matter that passes through, even if that matter is dust or even particles of light, the less chance of ever correcting the imbalance. Instead we believe we need to refire the laser . . . but first we need to find the laser acceleration diamond and we think Mr Singer has it with him. We just need to find him first.'

He examined her face. 'Tell me. If Arn found himself in a strange place, maybe somewhere totally alien, what do you think he'd do?'

Becky snorted. 'He'd go exploring.'

Harper exhaled wearily. 'Oh great; so the sooner we find him the better.' He pointed at the screen. 'The acceleration chamber has become magnetically sealed by the disturbance, so we're cutting our way in – right through eight feet of reinforced concrete. Once that's done, we'll fire a probe into the hole and try to take some readings.'

'Can I be here when you do?'

Again, Harper looked at her sadly. 'I'm sorry, Rebecca, but that's something that will be restricted.'

Becky's mouth dropped open in surprise. 'Are you kidding? I need to be here! I'm his friend . . .' She reached into her pocket and switched on her phone.

Harper had already turned away. 'It's because you're his friend that you can't be here. We must face the fact that where he went might be an airless vacuum, or hotter than hell, or have a crushing gravity . . . For all we know, Arnold Singer may have been dead for weeks.'

Chapter 22

Wait . . . It's Arrived

Harper watched the test with bated breath.

The bicycle-wheel-sized craft lifted from the ground on four rotational fans, like a miniature hovercraft – noiseless and sleek. The aerial mobile camera was modelled on deep-sea technology, except its housing didn't need to be armour-plated against water pressure, so strength and durability could be traded off for mobility and speed.

Harper almost applauded as the machine remained suspended about six feet from the ground.

The four near-silent fan-blades were recessed in a broad, flat housing that made it look like a bulbous stingray. Gyroscopic assistance gave it incredible stability – it could hover motionless, even in a near hurricane, and bank and fly as swiftly as a bird of prey . . . well, a very fast pigeon, anyway. The front housed a large glass lens behind which sat the camera with an illuminated ring around it. It looked like a floating eye, in which a bottomless glass pupil was ringed by an iris of light.

Its miniaturised battery pack contained enough energy to run a small building, and allow the craft to run for at least forty-eight hours. It also powered the digital image feed and recorders. There was no guarantee anything at all would be delivered back to them, or for that matter that the device would survive the trip, but they didn't have a lot of options. This would have to do.

Harper grunted his approval. 'Ready as we'll ever be. Okay, let's take her in.'

The pilot ran his hand over his keyboard, giving each of the fans some extra thrust, and the craft lifted higher into the air. He turned one of the twin joysticks slightly and it spun slowly to line up with the freshly cut hole in the wall, now a dark tunnel leading to a lighter exit. Another technician focused the camera, and the image zoomed to the far end of the small tunnel. The craft entered, navigating the space with ease, emerging to hover just beside the smudge that hung in the air like steam over an air vent.

'On your order, sir.'

Harper rubbed his hands together and leaned forward on the desk. 'Proceed, four knots.'

The small craft glided to within an inch of the smudge of nothingness. Harper held his breath. A slight push on the joystick . . . and the craft leapt forward, as if being snatched up and swallowed. The data screens showed the device was still moving at a leisurely four knots, but the image feed indicated acceleration that was beyond comprehension.

Harper found it hard to continue watching the screen, as vertigo was making him feel giddy and nauseous. He turned to yell over his shoulder, 'Distance?'

'*Ah*, you're not going to believe this, but: three feet – it's barely moved. Theoretically, it's still in the tunnel.'

'What?' Harper shook his head. 'It must have malfunctioned. Can we turn it around?'

'Wait . . . It's arrived.'

As if a brake had been applied, the sensation of speed dissolved, and the camera light came on automatically as it detected low light. Harper blinked in confusion, and his mouth dropped open. He got to his feet.

'Oh my God.'

Chapter 23

Dark Times

Arn was shown into the main hall by one of the castle's hundreds of attendants. The servant didn't enter the hall, but merely opened the door and motioned with his arm towards the darkened interior. Arn stepped through, and paused to allow his eyes to adjust.

A single candle burned on the far side of the room, and he made his way towards it. The silence was unsettling. Even his cautious footsteps sounded heavy as he crossed from the polished stones onto woven rugs.

Arn slowed when he saw that someone was seated in a massive chair, their head resting on one of their hands. Another empty chair stood close by. The figure lifted his head, silver eyes shining in the dark.

'Dark times, young Man-kind.' Grimvaldr sat back and studied Arn carefully. 'Dark times that require dark deeds.' He sighed. 'What would you do to save someone you loved?'

Arn stepped a little closer. 'Anything . . . *Everything.*'

Grimvaldr nodded. 'Yes, I too.' He opened his hand and showed Arn the scrap of material bearing the crest of the silver wolf with red eyes. 'Grimson has been taken by the Panterran.'

Arn felt a sudden surge of anger, and fear for the youth. The thought of the old sorcerer's talons digging into Grimson's flesh made him want to scream with rage. 'Is he a hostage? Do they want a ransom?' He stepped closer. 'Can we get him back?'

The king nodded slowly. 'I hope so. There is a ransom, but they want something that is not mine to give.'

Arn grabbed the king's forearm. 'Then you must get it, and do everything in your power to save your son. How can I help?'

The king stared at the floor, but his eyes were focused on something much further away. At last he looked up, the weight of all his years dragging his features down.

'They want *you*, Arnoddr-Sigarr.'

Arn frowned, momentarily confused as he tried to make sense of the words. He stepped back, feeling his legs bump against the empty chair, and he sat down heavily.

'They . . . They want me?' Arn's mind jumped back to being tied to the rack, the hooked claws piercing the flesh of his face, and the invasion of his mind. He also remembered the creature wanting to read the future in his entrails. It made his legs weak, and he shuddered and felt cold all over. 'If they get me, will they . . . release Grimson unharmed?'

'Perhaps they will.' The king stared hard at him.

'And did they say what they wanted me for?'

Grimvaldr shrugged his heavy shoulders. 'Perhaps to be a pet for their queen.' He paused. 'Or it could be something . . . else.'

Arn felt a lump of fear in the back of his throat. In the short time he had known the Wolfen, he had found them to be the noblest race he had ever met. Eilif, Sorenson, Strom; they wouldn't hesitate . . . He rose to his feet.

'Then you must do anything you can to get your son back. And I will do everything I can to make sure it happens.'

The king stood and placed his huge hands on Arn's shoulders, pulling the other towards him in a crushing embrace.

He stepped back. 'Putting yourself in harm's way for a friend is a noble thing.'

Arn nodded. He remembered Mr. Jefferson, the bus driver, saying the same thing. The lump in his throat grew bigger as he suddenly longed for his old life back. He nodded again, but still couldn't speak.

'Our races are very similar, Arn. It's no wonder the legends talk of our enduring kinship.' He walked over to a long table on which lay something covered with a soft cloth. He motioned for Arn to join him. 'You asked me whether the Slinkers would release my son unharmed. I said, *perhaps*. But truly, I think not. I also think your fate will be far more unpleasant than to be some curio for the queen.'

Arn thought once again of the claws in his face. 'I'll still do it.'

The king lifted the cloth. Beneath lay two small cages side by side – one slightly longer than the other. He used a knuckle to tap the top of the larger cage, causing its occupant to fall from the side where it had been hanging, close to its mate. The creature looked like a beetle, but was the size of his fist, with its abdomen blazing like a light bulb. In the other cage, its mate was smaller, and emerald green in colour.

'Fleet beetles.' Grimvaldr pointed to the larger one. 'The female fluoresces when close to the male. They mate for life, and even if you separated them by a thousand longs, she would still find him. The closer she is, the brighter she glows.'

Arn leaned over the cages. 'How does she find him?'

'By smell – the male fleet beetle gives off a unique odour that the female tracks. Only she can smell it, and once paired, the perfume he makes is designed to be just for her.'

'I think I see.' Arn saw the king's plan in his head. 'So, I hide the male beetle on myself, and then you use the female beetle's homing light to come and find me.'

'Yes . . . But the Panterran will most likely search you.' The king smiled ruefully. 'You will need to swallow him. The female will still be able to track him when he's inside your gut.'

Arn grimaced, and looked hard at the smaller beetle. *Smaller*, but still the size of his thumb, and with six spindly, sharp-looking legs. *Ugh.* 'When?'

'Not yet. Just before we hand you over. It will take three days for the beetle to pass through your system, which should be time enough.'

Arn nodded slowly, still feeling queasy at the thought of something that large, alive in his stomach. 'And then the Wolfen army will find me, and when they do, hopefully I'll be at the same place where the Slinkers have taken Grimson.'

The king lifted the smaller cage, and shook it slightly as he peered through the tiny bars. 'That's what we hope. But I'm afraid there will be no army. The Panterran scouts would alert them to a large force approaching long before it got anywhere near you. No, it will need to be a small party.'

This did nothing for Arn's confidence. 'So, *ahh*, fifty Wolfen elite?'

The king shook his head.

'Twenty? Ten?'

Grimvaldr just shook his head again.

'So how many?'

The king held up two fingers.

'Two? Just two? Oh, great . . .'

'Do not fear, Man-kind – I will send Strom and Sorenson. They are an army in themselves, and the best warriors and trackers this land has seen in many generations. They will find you . . . and bring you both to safety.'

Arn knew the king was right about the size of the force needed – the Panterran could probably hear a blade of grass bending in the darkest forest, so would certainly know if even a small force of Wolfen were making their way towards them. *Besides,* he thought, *the king won't risk perhaps his only chance to rescue his son.*

'Good as it gets, I suppose – when can I expect to go?'

'Tomorrow eve. Say nothing of this to anyone, young Man-kind. Even in the court of the king, there are those – a very few, thank Odin – who prefer the reward of riches to the brotherhood of the pack.'

'Traitors . . . Spies? Is that why we're meeting in private? Do you have any idea who they are?'

The king draped the cloth back over the cages. 'We have suspicions, but nothing we can prove. Just the same, we must be cautious. If the Panterran discovered our plan, they would remove the beetle – with a blade.'

This didn't do much for Arn's confidence either.

*****

Vulpernix had travelled alone through the dark forest for many hours. He sought out a secret passage only he knew – a cave that led under the fields and open spaces, emerging in a small valley at the very edge of Valkeryn.

Even as he approached, he could sense the being waiting just inside the hidden mouth of the cave. His nose twitched at the familiar, unpleasant smell.

'Vulpernix, betrayer of the Canites, friend to the Panterran.' Orcalion glided from the dark hole and sat with his hood pulled up over his head, his yellow eyes glowing.

Vulpernix turned away for a moment, to throw off the look of distaste that had spread across his features. He smiled indifferently at the Panterran. 'Greetings, wise Orcalion – and please, not a betrayer, but a saviour of the Canites. I bring good news: the king has agreed to hand over the Man-kind.'

Orcalion got to his feet. 'Good news for the king, I think. What else, brave Wolfen?'

Vulpernix frowned at the other's indifference to news he had thought critical to the queen of the Panterran. 'He has sent word to the far garrisons to bring in the scattered Wolfen tribes – in ten days their numbers will be powerful indeed. I suggest any attack takes place before then. The kingdom will be yours.'

The old sorcerer's soft, rasping laugh was like a hiss of steam. 'Yes, attack early. But I have also heard the scattered Wolfen are being recalled not in ten days . . . More like five. That doesn't give us much time at all, does it, trusted friend Vulpernix?'

Orcalion glided closer. 'It seems the information you bring is a little . . . *stale*. I have also learned that the king plans to send his young and old Canites away from the castle.' The yellow eyes glared with an intensity that seemed to burn into the old Wolfen's brain. 'We will need them. It is a long journey back to the dark lands, and the Lygon will need plenty of food . . . live food.' Again, there was the hiss of laughter.

Vulpernix recoiled in disgust. 'You go too far, Orcalion. I'll gladly sell you information, but I'll not see the young ones taken captive . . . for food. That was never part of the deal.'

In the blink of an eye, Orcalion had a curved dagger up under the old Wolfen's chin. 'Small, young ones, soon grow to be big ones. We cannot have another army of Wolfen coming down from the far lands after the Lygon have gone home. Best if the Panterran solve all their problems at once – besides, as soon as you took our wealth, you became one of us . . . brother Vulpernix.' He lowered the dagger and turned his back, stepping once more into the shadows of the small cave. 'Make sure next time you bring us *new* information. You told me nothing that I didn't already know, vile betrayer of your kind.'

A small leather bag hit the ground at Vulpernix's feet. When he looked up again, he was alone.

Chapter 24

The King's Mission

The evening was coming too soon for Arn.

Late into the afternoon, Eilif wanted to continue practising their sword skills, but he couldn't find any enthusiasm for it. His stomach was knotted in fear, and no matter how she joked, or cajoled him, he felt like a zombie.

In the end she gave up and wished him good morrow. Arn reached out to take her hand, shook it, but then held it a little longer than usual.

She smiled at first, and then frowned. 'What is it?'

He released her hand. 'It's nothing. It's just that you've been a good friend to me.' He turned away, not seeing her face fall at the use of the word *friend* again.

'I can tell something is wrong, Arnoddr. You don't look me in the eye when you wish to conceal something. Did you know there is a Wolfen saying that goes: *the eyes allow one's sáál to reveal its true self.*'

'Huh, a what?'

She took his hand and placed it in the centre of her chest. 'It's something in here. Not the heart or the breathers, but something that cannot be seen that is the core of every righteous being. You have one too . . . and I think it's a good one.'

Arn laughed and nodded. 'Yes, I do. We call it, *the soul*. We have a similar saying – *the eyes are the windows to the soul*. So I guess you're right; our races are more alike than we think.'

She placed her hand on the centre of his chest. 'Yes, I believe I can feel it inside you – your *soul*. And do you know what else I believe? Inside, you're really a Wolfen.' She smiled and grabbed his vest and pulled him closer. 'So, Man-kind . . . or maybe, Man-Wolfen, now that I look through the windows to your soul-sáál, what is troubling you? No untruths.'

Arn knew he couldn't tell her. She still didn't even know that Grimson had been taken; she had been told that he was in some sort of training school for young warriors.

'Tomorrow. Okay?'

'You'll tell me tomorrow?'

He looked at her solemnly. 'Tomorrow, you'll know . . . Promise.'

*****

Eilif watched him walk away, kicking small stones out of his path. He was the strangest being she had ever known – and easily the most interesting, and . . . *what?* She didn't know what he meant to her really. He confused her more than any other male.

She laughed at what she had called him – *Man-Wolfen*. Though there was no such thing, she really did believe he had the face of a man, but the heart and sáál of one of her own kind. She felt safe with him, felt . . . nice, when he was near.

She drew her sword, and practised swinging and lunging at shadows as the sun began to go down. There was a soft footfall behind her, and she spun around, a smile on her face and her sword raised, expecting Arn to have returned.

'I knew you'd . . .' She lowered her sword, just managing to drop the vestige of the smile on her face. 'You should not sneak up on someone brandishing a sword, young warrior. Even the best Wolfen may find themselves missing an arm.'

Bergborr bowed deeply, with one arm crossed in front of his waist and one behind. When he straightened, he brought his arm out from behind his back, revealing a handful of wildflowers.

Eilif looked at them and tilted her head. 'So I bring a sword, and you bring flowers. Things seem to be the wrong way around, wouldn't you say, friend Bergborr?'

The dark Wolfen laughed and pushed the flowers into her hand. 'Forgive me, I'm a fool in the presence of such beauty.'

Eilif's ears blushed pink; she relished the compliment, even though she knew it was flattery. She also knew of his ambitions, and although he would be considered a fine warrior mate, she had never been sure if it was *she*, or her father's throne, that most attracted him.

Like magic, from his other hand he presented her with a dagger in a scabbard of the most finely detailed silver, encrusted with fiery green stones. She reached for it, her fingers closing around the hilt . . .

She let her hand fall, empty. 'I am far too young to be receiving gifts from such a fine warrior as yourself. Perhaps there are more deserving ladies of the court, on whom you might lavish your attentions.'

'Would you at least walk with me tonight after I have attended to my duties in the king's court? Pay me that honour, at least.'

Eilif frowned slightly. Arn had an audience with the king that eve – Bergborr also? Strange things were happening.

She smiled innocently. 'We'll see. It has been a long day and I'm tired. Perhaps you can call on me in the morning?'

He drew in a deep breath of frustration, and bowed again. 'I will not give up, young princess. Tomorrow morning it is.'

Eilif watched him leave, and then opened her hand to let the flowers fall to the ground.

*****

Arn stood alone in the small chamber. On the table beside him stood a cup of water, a pot of honey, and a small box. The king had told him that now was the time to swallow the male fleet beetle, and with a shaking hand he opened the box. He squeezed his eyes shut for a second, and then reopened one of them; it was probably just his imagination, but the bug looked even bigger than when he had seen it in its cage.

He put his ear to the door – he could hear raised voices outside. He'd be called soon, and nowhere else to hide the beetle if he changed his mind. He thought again of Grimson and snatched up the box again, upending it. The glossy beetle fell into his hand and lay there, unmoving. He looked hard at the creature, half wishing it was dead. Instead, he could see that all of its legs had been tied with a sort of fine, waxy string. The king had told him that his stomach acids would not harm the shell of the fleet beetle, but he guessed the string would eventually be dissolved. He studied the small claws on the tips of its bound, spindly legs. It gave a whole new meaning to the expression, *butterflies in the stomach.*

He groaned, remembering his instructions. *Here goes nothing*, he thought. Dipping the bug into the honey, he squeezed his eyes shut, then placed it at the back of his tongue. He grabbed up the mug of water and began gulping furiously. He started gagging and gulped the water harder, painfully swallowing both the bug and, with it, some bile that was rushing up to try to escape.

Yecch! He doubled over, coughing, and his eyes watered. There was an acidic, almond taste in his mouth. He leaned over the table, breathing hard.

'I will never complain about brussel sprouts again, I promise.' He dipped his fingers into the honey, licking more of the sweet sticky nectar to mask the aftertaste of the bug.

There was a thump on the door. He wiped the tears from his eyes.

'I'm ready.'

*****

Eilif slowly leaned out, far over the stone balcony, and peered down into the closed courtyard. It appeared to be a small party of hooded Panterran, flanked by a larger group of Wolfen. Some of the guards were snarling, but the Slinkers sat as still as stones, ignoring them.

They weren't prisoners – had they come to the castle under a flag of truce? Something secret was happening, something her father hadn't told her. *But why?* she wondered? *Why wouldn't he tell me?*

The doorway outside which they waited led to the main hall – where Arn was supposed to be meeting with the king that very eve . . .

*****

Arn entered the throne room. It was already half filled with the Wolfen generals, trusted warriors and counsellors. The king sat on his throne, and flanking him were Sorenson and Strom. Sorenson looked Arn in the eye and gave him an almost imperceptible nod. Strom just continued to look along the lines of assembled warriors and advisors.

Arn heard the heavy doors close behind him as he walked slowly to the centre of the room. He tried hard not to let his chin quiver, or his knees buckle as he neared the Wolfen.

141

The Wolfen warriors dipped their heads as Arn passed them, and the king rose from his throne. He held a huge broadsword by its hilt, its blade sheathed in a heavily patterned scabbard, its tip touching the stones at his feet. He lifted it, then brought it down onto the ground three times. The room immediately fell silent.

He looked across the assembled warriors, and then to Arn. 'An honour has been bestowed upon you, young Man-kind – to sacrifice your liberty for that of the young child of the crown, Grimson, first-born prince of Valkeryn. Will you accept this honour?'

Arn could feel the wall of silence pressing in around him, as every eye was trained on his face, his eyes, his lips, waiting for them to form the words:

'I will.'

The king's shoulders slumped with relief. 'The kingdom thanks you. Know that whatever occurs, we owe you a debt.' He gave a small bow, and drew in a deep breath. His face grew stern. 'Bring in the Panterran emissary.'

The crowd of Wolfen warriors fanned out, looking back towards the doorway as the heavy wooden doors were pushed open. The small familiar figure of Orcalion glided in, grinning.

He bowed deeply to the king, then looked across at Arn. The excitement was plain on his flat features. 'You are to be our guest again, Man-kind. But fear not, we wish to be friends with you, and any previous misunderstandings will be quickly forgotten.' He glanced at Arn's hands. 'Bind him . . . for his own safety.'

Arn's wrists were tied together with a strip of leather, a further length of which trailed at least six feet from the knots – a lead. Orcalion picked it up, and pulled Arn a few stumbling steps closer.

'Please let me know if the binding is too tight; I do not wish you . . . discomfort.' He let out a small wheezing laugh, and tugged again on the tether, obviously relishing the moment.

'Two days.' The king watched the small creature with barely controlled fury on his face. His eyes went to Arn, and then back to Orcalion, who shrugged.

'Yes, two or three days. When we are back safely at our encampment, we will release the young princeling. No . . . accidents must befall us – you must guarantee our safe passage.'

The king nodded, once. His head remained bowed.

Oraclion began to drag Arn from the room, and Sorenson moved quickly to stand at the hall's huge double doors. As Arn passed and he looked him in the eye, there was just the hint of a wink, a small smile on his lips. Arn tried to smile in return, but his face was frozen, as he felt more like a condemned man heading to the gallows.

Once outside, a small band of Wolfen escorted them down the stone steps and across the lower entrance hall. Orcalion spoke to Arn over his shoulder, 'Have you anything concealed that I should know about, Man-kind?'

Arn felt a jolt of fear run through him. The king had said that there were spies in the castle; if they had learned of the fleet beetle inside him, then the rescue plan would fail even before it started. The Panterran stopped and looked briefly over his shoulder.

Arn shook his head.

Orcalion yanked the leash again. 'It matters not; we will search you, once we have reached the forest. But for now . . . lean forward.' Orcalion reached inside his cloak as Arn stooped slightly. The Panterran pulled a bag over Arn's head. 'Some say you have the strength of ten Panterran, and can see even better in the dark. Best to ensure you have as few advantages as possible, then. Be warned: there'll be a sword at the back of your neck the entire journey.'

Arn could soon feel the cool night air on his skin. After another few hundred paces, he guessed they were at the castle walls. A few of the Wolfen escorting them called out words of encouragement, and then there came a slamming of heavy wood, and he knew he was alone, with the Panterran, in the dark.

*****

From her vantage point on the stone balcony, Eilif watched as the small party led its captive towards the outer walls. The prisoner was taller than his Panterran captor, but shorter than the Wolfen escort, who kept their distance. As they neared the walls, the moon broke through the clouds, and by its light she could just make out the prisoner's pale, tied hands – they were hairless.

The breath caught in her throat, and she had to jam a knuckle into her mouth to stifle her scream of outrage. First Grimson disappearing, and now Arn being secretly spirited away . . . Her teeth came together with a snap.

She'd need to move quickly. Darting back into her room, she set to work fastening her night armour. She knew the Panterran; if they had Arn, it wasn't because they just wanted to talk to him.

Anger flared in her chest, and again she bared her teeth in the dark.

Chapter 25

It's Another World

'Is that a tunnel? I mean, *our* tunnel?'

Albert Harper felt his heart thumping in his chest as he strained to take in the detail that was just visible from the probe's camera feed. Data ran up the side of the screen – atmosphere: 78.09% nitrogen, 20.95% oxygen, 0.93% argon, 0.039% carbon dioxide, .0003 methane . . . *A little high on the methane*, he thought. Ambient temperature: 73 degrees, water vapour content, air pressure, and on it ran. All fairly normal.

Jim Takada leaned closer to the large screen. 'It's in ruins . . . and not just burned or blown apart. That's antiquated ruination. So if it *is* ours, then when the hell is this happening?'

'Good question. Swivel 360 degrees; I want to see what's around us, and also what we just came through. Is the sound on?'

The technician keyed in some commands, and then carefully thumbed one of the twin joysticks. 'Sound on, swivelling.' The image slowly panned to the right.

A soft mewling came from somewhere in the dark.

Takada flinched. 'What was that?'

'Forget about it. We're recording, so we can play it all back and analyse it later. For now, we need to get our bearings and see if we can find the kid.'

The camera continued to pan around until it was facing back towards their entry point.

'There's nothing there.' Takada bit his knuckle in agitation.

He was right – there was no magic dark hole, or glowing doorway – just a damp, debris-filled tunnel.

Harper shook his head. 'Gotta be, otherwise the signal would have no path back to us. We'll find it. Focus – micro-matrix – analyse section by section.'

A mesh-like grid appeared across the screen, and each square was enlarged and briefly scanned in turn. Harper banged his fist into his hand.

'Bingo.'

In the centre of the final quadrant, there was a slight swimming of the dark atmosphere, like steam rising over a hot bath.

'That's it. Lock it in.'

The location of the anomaly was recorded into the device's memory. Harper spoke out of the corner of his mouth, not wanting to turn his eyes away from the screen for a second.

'At least now we know we can find our way home. Drop a marker, just in case we need to find a way back in a hurry. Then take it back around and prepare to move forward.'

The floating electronic eye whined softly as its turned in the air.

'Give me maximum illumination'. Circling the camera lens, an extra ring of lights shone deeper into the tunnel.

'Jesus . . .'

Something the size of a large, pale, greasy-looking dog scuttled away into the darkness.

Takada grabbed Harper's arm. 'Did you see it?'

'Hmm?' Harper stared straight ahead. 'Yes, I see it. Look.' He tapped the bottom of the screen with his pencil.

For a moment, everyone was silent.

'The ground.' He continued to point.

At last, Takada murmured, 'I see it.'

There were footprints leading down the centre of the tunnel. Harper nodded. 'Size ten sneaker, wouldn't you say? Follow them, ASAP.'

Chapter 26

Find Me This Traitor

Grimvaldr paced in the castle courtyard while several Wolfen followed him with their eyes.

'Sire,' Andrejk said at last. 'We still need five days to bring in the entire outer ranks of Wolfen.'

Grimvaldr walked slowly towards his general. 'I fear that events are not going to be ours to dictate anymore. We now know that the Panterran are aware we are calling for reinforcements – if they are going to make war, they will either head off our far Wolfen before they arrive, or they will seek to attack us long before we are ready.'

Grimvaldr turned to another of his generals. 'Magnus, what say the scouts – where are the enemy encampments now?'

Magnus, a tall battle-scarred Wolfen, rested his hands on the hilt of his broadsword. 'They are two to three days out . . . but many of our scouts failed to return – captured, most likely, and therefore we have to assume we have blind spots. The Panterran and Lygon could be even closer.'

Grimvaldr grunted. 'They will attack us in two days. What will we have available?' He turned to Karnak, his most experienced soldier. The Wolfen warrior was of the same age as Grimvaldr, and like him had seen war many times before. He smiled grimly as he stepped forward.

'Ten thousand Wolfen elite, two hundred bowmen, five hundred fast riders . . . more than enough to roll over a million Slinkers, and just as many of their giants, sire. The Lygon caught our warriors by surprise in the fields. But it will never happen again. We'll equip the front lines with lances – the great blunderers' own body weight will carry them onto our pikes.'

Grimvaldr placed his hand on Karnak's shoulder. 'If only everything went to plan – we could win all our battles at the table.'

'Yes, sire. The mists of war sometimes blur all.'

Grimvaldr turned to the other Wolfen and spoke in a loud and strong voice. 'Valkeryn will not fall this season. Though I believe we have enough force to stop the enemy in their tracks, it is imperative that we hold them back for two, perhaps even three days, until our reinforcements begin to arrive. Then we will close around them like a fist.'

He turned back to Magnus. 'The far troops need to be fully equipped and briefed – we can't have thousands of Wolfen streaming into Valkeryn, unprepared. Ready some Wolfen to meet and organise them, so they are armed and ready for battle. Every Wolfen . . . and every second, will count. Go.'

The generals filed out, leaving only one remaining.

Grimvaldr sat heavily on a bench and rested an elbow on his thigh and his chin on his fist. He sighed long and wearily. 'Do you think we can hold them? Could they possibly overwhelm us?'

Vulpernix sat down beside the king. 'The Panterran have brought together every warrior in the land. All have been attracted by the thought of conquering Valkeryn.' He looked off into the distance, as if gathering his thoughts. 'The Lygon will come in their first attack – though Karnak may think we can spear the giants on our pikes, I fear that they will be ready with heavy armour. Their enormous strength will allow them to carry steel thicker than our weapons could ever hope to penetrate.'

He turned to Grimvaldr. 'The pikes will break . . . but still, I believe we can repel them. All will depend on the reinforcements getting here in time. If not . . .'

The king nodded slowly. 'If not, they will not be needed.' He inhaled deeply and let the breath leak from his long snout. 'I need to ask a favour of you, old friend.' Grimvaldr gripped the forearm of the ancient counsellor and looked deeply into his eyes. 'We cannot win this war, while our plans are being shared with the Panterran. Find me the traitor – find him quickly, before these devils are at our gate . . . and our throats.'

Vulpernix placed his hand over the king's. 'Trust me, sire.'

*****

148

Eilif bounced around her large room, pulling open drawers and opening boxes. The armour she chose wasn't her standard heavy battledress of polished steel with the crest of the raised wolf's head. Instead, she chose fire-blackened leather, toughened and hard enough to deflect arrows. Tight chain mail covered her arms and long legs – it too had been stained to blend into the shadows.

She belted a medium-length sword to her waist, paused, and then added several more blades. She then strung one of her shorter bows, looping it over one shoulder with a quiver of arrows over the other. She was about to bound from the room, when she stopped and went back to the shelf. She reached in among the bottles of potions and powders, and her hand closed on a small leather box. She rattled it and a hissing came from within. Nodding, she stuck the small box in a pouch that she had tied over the small of her back.

There was a knock on her door and she froze. She thought quickly and looked around her room at the disarray she had caused. If it was the queen, she could never explain her attire.

The knock came again.

Eilif went to the window and pushed it open. Without a second thought, she leapt out.

*****

The two brothers, Strom and Sorenson, moved quickly and quietly through the dark forest, making note of large trees and landmarks as they went. No moon meant tracking and travelling fast had to be accomplished with sharp night vision, smell, hearing – and caution. They needed to track their quarry, but not stumble into them. They also needed to find their way back, as they expected to be moving fast.

Both Wolfen knew that the Panterran's night vision was twice as good as their own, and if they were detected, their mission would be a failure. It would also mean capture and a very unpleasant death.

After a while, Sorenson stopped and motioned for them to still. He moved his head slowly in an arc, listening. 'Something,' he whispered to his older brother.

Strom's ears flicked forward and then back, and in another moment he whispered in response, 'I don't sense Slinker. We must keep moving.'

Sorenson nodded, but he turned back again briefly, his brow furrowed with concern.

The two Wolfen crept forward, staying low and moving as fast as their senses would allow.

*****

Eilif had been tracking the Panterran for hours, and in the last few moments she had picked up the almost imperceptible sounds of another party – smaller, but moving stealthily beside the main trail.

She took to the trees, moving along the thick branches that were less crowded than the forest floor. If there had been strong moonlight, she would have been more exposed, but as the night was dark and the path was heavily overgrown, it suited her to be able to move at greater speed, unencumbered by bracken and fallen trees.

Eilif increased her speed, sensing she was closing on the small party. She knew they weren't Panterran – she could not smell the acrid tang that the foul creatures left behind. If one of the creatures stopped to urinate . . . Even if covered, the smell was appalling. She shuddered as she remembered the disgusting creatures touching her face and body.

In another hour, Eilif knew she had managed to get ahead of the small party. She hesitated; she could outpace them and reach her quarry first, or she could wait to see who had been tracking them. She remembered an olden saying from Balthazar – something like, *my enemy's enemy is my friend.* She hoped that the party turned out to be her friends and not those of the Slinkers.

Eilif pressed herself into the limb of a tree just over the path, her night armour blending perfectly into the background. She sensed them now – there would be two of them. She waited, unmoving, and unafraid.

A large figure appeared . . . but strangely, only one.

*****

Strom stopped in the centre of the path, his hand on the hilt of his sword. He waited, his senses focused. He knew there was another being close by. His instincts were as sharp as any in the kingdom, but his large frame meant that, as silently as he could move through a forest, it was not easy for him to vanish like some of the other warriors.

That was where his younger brother was second to none – he could become like a forest wraith.

*****

Eilif knelt in the crook of a large branch. The massive figure was frozen like a statue. She sniffed the slightly acrid tang of the Panterran, perhaps because they had recently passed through, but she also caught the scent of her own kind. She continued to stare at the being; it stood there, unmoving, but not concealing itself. She had the feeling that it sensed her, that it knew it was being watched. That it had come out into the open area of the path, *wanting* to be seen . . . And if it wanted to be seen, then it wanted to draw her attention away from . . .

The small blade came down along the side of her throat.

'And what would the king say, young princess?'

She pushed the blade away from her face. 'He'd say that he's happy to give friends of Valkeryn to the hated Slinkers.'

Eilif dropped to the ground, with Sorenson landing lightly beside her. Strom had already sheathed his sword and joined them. He bowed slightly. 'Not a good night for hunting, my lady; there is no moon.'

'Depends what one is hunting. And what *are* you hunting, the two of you?'

Strom and Sorenson exchanged a glance. Nodding, Sorenson turned back to the princess. 'You need to go back to the castle. There is important business afoot.'

Eilif placed her fists on her hips. 'If that business of yours is rescuing the Man-kind, then I'm going with you. And if it isn't, then I'm going by myself . . . and you'd better stay out of my way.' She had raised her voice only slightly above a whisper, but still it seemed loud in the hush of the forest.

Sorenson reached forward and grabbed her snout and held it. 'Silence, or the only thing we'll find tonight is our way to the afterlife at the hand of the Slinkers.'

She pulled her nose free, and snapped at his fingers. 'My father would have you whipped for that. Though I struggle to think of him

151

as my father at all, after he has handed our good friend to those vile creatures.' She walked a few paces further along the trail. 'Well? With or without you?'

She heard Strom groan softly.

Sorenson turned to his brother and shrugged. 'At least she knows how to track and hunt.'

Eilif started foward. 'We need to hurry, or they'll be lost once they get to into the tangle brush – without a trail, we'll never find them.'

Strom motioned for the three of them to crouch, and he linked his large fingers across his knees. 'We don't have the time to explain what has and is occurring in the kingdom. But it is enough to tell you that the king risks everything by sending us out to rescue the princeling . . . and your friend.'

'Grimson? They've got Grimson?' Eilif tried to stand, but Sorenson grabbed her and pulled her back down.

'Captured by the Slinkers several days ago,' he said. 'Spirited away. Arnoddr-Sigarr offered to be part of an exchange – the Man-kind for the prince. We hope that they are taking the Man-kind to where they have Grimson. We have little more than a day.'

But why just the two of you? Why not the entire Wolfen army? Grimvaldr would normally not rest until he had rescued my brother – I don't understand what is happening.'

'No princess, you don't. There is war coming, and if he sent out his legions now, there is a chance they could be ambushed and pinned down, days from the castle . . . at a time when all of Valkeryn will need them. But Strom and I might be able to find the camp and infiltrate it.'

'I smell Slinker.' She flashed the brothers a questioning glance.

Sorenson held up a leather bag tied at his waist. 'The hide of a dead Slinker – it will at least cover *some* of our scent. Hopefully long enough for us to get close.' He dropped the bag and reached inside his vest, pulling forth a small cage. He gave it a little shake, and it started to glow. He held it up, facing back the way they'd come, and the beetle glowed dully. But when he held it in the direction they were heading, the glow intensified.

'A female fleet beetle.' Eilif snorted, nodding as understanding dawned on her. 'And Arn has its mate on him.'

'Hmm, not really *on* him, but he certainly has it *with* him. But we only have limited time – just over another day and night until we lose the beetle's guidance.'

Strom got to his feet. 'If you follow our instructions, then you may accompany us. Agreed?' In answer, Eilif started to move off down the path, and Strom grabbed her shoulder. 'Wait. You won't need all of these. We need to travel light.' He pulled a few of the daggers from her belt and cast them aside.

'I'd much prefer to see those buried in a Panterran, than in the dirt of the forest floor.' Muttering, Eilif headed off into the dark.

Strom shook his head, and Sorenson just chuckled softly.

Chapter 27

You Are The Monster Here

Arn's knees were bruised, and his neck chafed even though the rope had been looped around the outside of the bag over his head. The air inside was stiflingly hot.

From time to time, he felt something sharp prodding his rear, and he hoped the Wolfen brothers weren't too far away. Arn also knew what would happen if one of their sorcerers took the opportunity to probe his mind again – whether he wanted to or not, he might alert them to the fleet beetle, and betray his would-be rescuers.

He had no idea how long he had been forced to march, but as it was early evening when he was taken from the castle, and there was faint warmth touching his skin now and then, he thought that the sun must have been coming up. He felt fatigued, but he did not yet crave sleep – adrenaline must have been coursing through his system.

They marched on and on, and the rubbing of his boots became a damp, stinging throb – *burst blisters*, he bet. The hours passed, and finally there came a push in his back, and he was pulled roughly to his knees, the sack dragged from his head. Even though it was only mid morning, the weak sunlight blinded him and made him screw his eyes shut in pain.

Arn blinked several times, and his vision swam for a few seconds until at last his eyes adjusted enough for him to make out his surroundings. They were in a clearing with a large domed tent set up at one edge, and smaller tents scattered throughout. There were also cooking fires dotted in just about every vacant space. Black banners flew from the top of the tents depicting the head of a cat with yellow eyes and the familiar, merciless gaze of the Panterran.

Panterran and Lygon moved about the clearing. Arn watched as Orcalion swaggered over to the largest tent. Outside, a ring of guards in loose black robes watched as he approached. Two heavily armed Panterran at the entrance stepped forward to meet him. He spoke briefly to the pair, motioned to Arn and then to himself, before nodding and returning to their group.

Arn was still on his knees, and Orcalion reached for the tether around his neck and yanked it roughly. With his arms bound, Arn fell forward into the dirt.

'Mogahr sleeps. But do not worry, ugly one, I'm sure she will wish to see you when she wakes.'

Arn spat dirt from his mouth and struggled back up to his knees, 'Can I have some water?'

The corners of Orcalion's lips twisted in a cruel, disbelieving sneer. 'Water?' He grabbed the tether again, and yanked hard.

Arn pulled back on leather, defiance in his eyes. 'I won't be a pet for some monster. You'll be sorry for this one day.'

Ocralion used all his strength to pull Arn down over, and this time swiped him across the face, raking the skin with his needle-like claws. 'Monster? You are the monster here. You are the disgusting freak.' He kicked Arn, hard. 'A pet? She already has the princeling as a pet.' There was the hissing laugh, and he stepped in close and crouched to look into Arn's face. 'You won't need water, Man-kind. You won't need anything soon.'

Orcalion motioned to one of the Panterran that had accompanied them from the Wolfen castle. 'Stake him here, and make sure you guard him well.' He narrowed his eyes at the guard. 'Your life depends on it.'

The guard nodded jerkily, and bowed while Orcalion glided away. Then he hissed something inaudible, and probably treasonous, at the departing sorcerer's back, and spoke quickly to two of the other Paneterran, who scurried off and then returned with a wooden spike and mallet. They hammered the spike into the ground, and tied one end of the tether to it. The two Panterran retreated to the shade of some trees, and turned their backs on him to laze in the dappled light.

Arn sat cross-legged in the dirt. He had no shade, and already thirst was beginning to weigh heavily on him. He was hot, but had stopped sweating. *Not a good sign*, he thought. He bowed his head and felt the fatigue of the march catching up with him. His long hair fell forward over his face, and he felt himself about to doze. His eyelids drooped, and he swallowed painfully, forcing the dry lump of his fear down his throat, where it settled in his belly . . . and fluttered.

Oh, God no, he thought. *Not now, you stupid beetle.*

The feeling settled, and as Arn's eyes began to close, he caught sight of a single Panterran standing silently watching him, its golden eyes shining from under its cowl. Arn's head lolled forward, and he was asleep.

*****

Sorenson pushed the female beetle back within the folds of his vest. Even in the morning light, the glow from the bulbous insect was becoming blinding.

They crept forward, towards the sounds of the large encampment. Sorenson led, followed by Eilif and then Strom. All kept low to the ground, and moved stealthily through the heavy foliage.

Sorenson raised his hand, and his two companions froze. He pointed up at the tree line, and then held up two fingers – there, in the branches, were a pair of Panterran guards. Luckily, they were focused on something in the opposite direction, and the three were able to crawl past them.

In the heavy brush at the edge of the clearing, they stared into the busy camp. Eilif let out a small gasp at seeing Arn staked out in the sun. He was covered in dust, and there was blood on his face and along his throat from the rubbing of the tether. She snarled at the sight of it, but Strom placed his hand on her shoulder to keep her quiet and calm.

'The queen's forward encampment – heavily guarded.' Sorenson turned to Strom, who grunted but kept his eyes on the Panterran soldiers milling about.

Eilif curled her hands into fists. 'We have the element of surprise. I say we rush them now – they are less active during the day.' She looked from Strom to Sorenson. Neither acknowledged her.

Strom spoke in a low growl, 'I would like nothing more than to enter that camp, with sword in hand . . . But first we must locate the prince. Besides, a frontal assault would either result in three dead Wolfen, or if we somehow managed to free the Arnoddr, and dragged him beyond the perimeter of the camp, what then? Being chased by several hundred fully armed, fleet-footed Panterran are odds that not even I like.'

A deep snuffling grunt took their eyes beyond Arn, to the far edge of the clearing.

Sorenson cursed. 'Gravilents – heavily armoured. At speed, almost impossible to stop. They will decimate our front lines.'

A mountain of scale-covered flesh pulled on a chain holding it in place. The enormous creature stood two and a half times their height, on four column-like legs. Broad and flat, the creature had a hide of shingle-like scales so tightly fitted together that they formed an interlocking set of natural armour. The Panterran had further added spikes and blades to its body to make the beast more formidable and ill tempered, as the base of the weaponry looked to be embedded deep into the thing's flesh.

'And there are Lygon,' Strom spat. 'A war party, numbering in the hundreds –probably one of many spread across the outer rim of the kingdom. They'll converge on us from many different angles, all at once. We need to tell the king and the generals.'

There was a yelp from within the large tent.

Eilif's mouth dropped open. 'That was Grimson.' Her face was a mix of panic and anger.

Strom turned to the black dome and narrowed his eyes. 'Good. That's means he's alive.'

'We can tell my father of the war party, but first . . .' Eilif looked as if she was about to get to her feet, when Strom grabbed her again.

He pointed at the tent. 'Queen Mogahr – Orcalion said it was she who wanted Arn. That vile night-creature will sleep for many hours yet, and when she finally wakes, she won't leave her tent. Instead, they will take the Man-kind inside.'

'So?'

'There are hundreds of Panterran outside the tent, but I expect there will be only a few *inside* the tent. Much better odds, don't you think? We just need to wait until they have him in the tent, and then we attack.'

Eilif frowned impatiently, but eventually nodded.

Strom smiled grimly. 'So . . . we dig.'

*****

Eilif listened as Strom explained the plan to her, and what he expected her to do. She didn't like it, but she saw no sensible alternative – after all, her suggestions started and ended with her running across the open ground, sword raised, screaming a war cry . . .

The tunnel would need to be at least twenty longs, and deep enough so that it wouldn't collapse if walked upon, but shallow enough so that they could break through the surface, up into the tent. When she had asked how they might know they were directly beneath the tent, Sorenson had pulled free the glowing fleet beetle, and grinned. She had smiled back grimly. The fleet beetle was magnificent when it came to general directions, but it was hardly a precisely calibrated compass.

For her part, the task was quite simple. When the brothers burst out of the ground, there would be pandemonium in the tent, and they would have to rely on the element of surprise to overwhelm the guards. From her position at the edge of the clearing, she was to ensure that no one else entered – her arrows were to stop anyone or anything from joining the battle.

And then? From there, it didn't sound so very different to her plan – they'd need to flee through the forest while being followed by hundreds of angry Panterran . . . and probably a few Lygon for good measure. *Simple.*

Chapter 28

Grape, His Favourite

Arn was sitting on the bus, wearing a new shirt. The collar was too tight, and it chafed uncomfortably. He hated it when new shirts did that.

He saw Becky get up from her seat. She turned briefly to wink at him, and then began walking down the crowded aisle between the other students and towards the doors. He tried to get up from his seat to follow her.

It hurt. Every time he tried to stand, he was dragged back down, and his collar chafed even more. Steve Barkin was pinning his hands behind his back. It occurred to him that he should tell someone, but Edward sat beside him, absorbed in his comic book. Typical – when he was engrossed in his fantasy world, nothing else mattered to him.

Edward stopped reading to sip from a can of soda – it was grape, his favourite.

Arn had never felt so thirsty in his life. 'Can I have a sip?'

Edward ignored him.

'Can I have a sip there, buddy?'

Nothing. Nothing but the chafing of his neck, Steve Barkin pinning his arms, and that relentless, diabolical thirst.

Chapter 29

Life, But Not As We Know It, Jim

'Enlarge.'

Albert Harper sipped his twentieth cup of coffee for the day, and stared hard at the large screen. They had been following the boy's footprints through the desolate wasteland for what seemed like hours, and they had seen nothing to give him hope that Arn could have survived for any period of time.

The observation area was crowded with scientists, technicians, and military specialists. Several additional screens had been set up, and for the last four hours nobody had moved.

The sun had risen a while back, and, at any moment, Harper expected to come across his body – dehydration, sunstroke or a dozen other elemental or bacterial afflictions could have brought him down. But as their hope had begun to wither, the flat, unbroken line of the horizon rose up into a series of jagged peaks. There was something out there after all.

'It's a forest.' Harper punched the air in triumph. 'Give me full scope.'

The lens rotated, and a panorama was revealed that looked a combination of the Amazon jungle and a redwood forest. There were grass-covered hills, trees climbing hundreds of feet into the sky, and, beyond that, mountain peaks.

Takada, smiling, handed Harper another cup of coffee. 'Toto, I don't think we're in Kansas anymore.'

Harper grinned. 'Life, but not as we know it, Jim. Increase speed,' he said to the technician, then turned back to Takada. 'If the kid made it this far, he'd have made it to the forest. We're not that far behind him.'

After another twenty minutes, Harper called for the probe to slow as they came to the colossal tree line. The camera switched from its illuminated strobe to red-light vision as it swivelled under the dark and dense forest canopy, continually adjusting its focus to capture the detail.

Something burst from between the boughs and flew past the screen, startling everyone in the room.

'What the . . .? Did you see that?'

Takada spoke evenly to the technicians. 'Stay focused. Anything else on the motion sensors?'

'Are you kidding? There's *too much* on the sensors. This place is crawling with life.'

Harper clicked his tongue in frustration. 'Okay, push it forward, but be careful now; we can't afford to get the probe snagged on anything – can't exactly send in a maintenance team.'

It was mid morning on *SingerWorld*, as some were now calling it in deference to the missing young man. Shadows darted past them – creatures, some revoltingly weird, only partly recognisable, which crept, scuttled or flew in the semi darkness. None were particularly large, but already they had come across the torn carcass of an animal the size of a goat on the forest floor. Something even bigger must have taken it down, judging by the bite marks.

The hovering camera floated about five feet from the ground. Its single lens glowed a deep red, indicating that it was only monitoring the environment in infrared for the time being. Harper had refused all requests to go back to strobe in the event it startled the wildlife.

Harper held up his hand. 'Stop. Pan ninety degrees.'

The camera slowly swivelled.

'Angle down right here . . . Let me see the forest floor.' He squinted as the camera tightened its focus.

There, on the ground, lay something half buried in the leaves.

'Is that a silver dagger?'

Chapter 30

Soon It Would Be The Panterran's Time

The Wolfen dug fast. They encountered no roots or heavy stones, and after a few hours, by Eilif's judging, were shy of the tent by only two lengths. At the rate they were digging, they'd be underneath Mogahr's tent in only a few more minutes.

The plan was to complete the tunnel and wait until Arn was taken inside. Then everything was to happen quickly – they'd break through, praying they didn't do so right at the feet of an alert guard, or under a brazier of glowing coals – a lot could go wrong. Strom was to subdue any resistance, then release Arn, while Sorenson would see to Grimson. They would then drop back into the hole and escape.

If everything went as they hoped, the brothers, Arn and Grimson would return to where Eilif was waiting for them at the other end of the tunnel, and then together they would make their way back to the castle. Stealth would be irrelevant, and there would be no time to stop for sleep or food. Their lives would depend on their speed – and a lot of luck.

Eilif lifted her head slightly and peered through the branches of the thick brush. The Panterran guards were still in the trees, but like most of the Slinkers during the day, they were sluggish, inclined to doze rather than keep a keen eye on their surroundings.

Eilif reached for her quiver of arrows, and laid it on the ground beside her. Then she dragged the leather pack from her back, and reached inside to pull free the small box she had brought with her. Instead of rattling it, this time she was careful removing the lid. She peered inside at the occupant – a small multi-armed creature that could have been an octopus, except its body was dry and spikily armoured. Its head pulsated, and many black eyes turned to look at her. It coiled itself as though about to spring, and she picked up one of the arrows and dipped its tip into the box. There was a hiss, and she pulled her head back slightly, only peering in after a second or two. The arrow's tip came away covered in a greenish yellow liquid. She smiled; the vipod's venom was one of the most deadly substances known to the Wolfen, and would stop a Panterran's heart before he even knew he'd been struck – and certainly before he had time to raise an alarm.

Eilif repeated the process with six of her arrows, laying them side by side on the soil. She drew in a deep breath and closed her eyes, mouthing a silent plea to Odin, for good fortune.

She opened her eyes and looked up at the sky – the day was rapidly drawing to a close. Soon it would be the Panterran's time, and things would shift in their favour.

*****

Deep in the tunnel, Strom slowed his digging, and then stopped. He placed his ear to the soil above his head. Sorenson had just returned from dumping the last load of dirt, and Strom reached out to take his arm.

'We're here, brother. Less than a length straight up.' He tightened his grip; by the light of just the fleet beetle, he stared hard into his younger brother's face. 'Odin, give us strength this day.'

Sorenson placed his free hand over Strom's. 'And every day yet to come.'

Strom nodded. 'Now we wait.' He pulled some dried meat from his tunic and offered some to Sorenson. Both Wolfen leaned back in the dark tunnel and chewed, imagining their first actions when they emerged into the heavily guarded tent.

Sorenson held up the fleet beetle, its glow now making him squint. 'And thank you, my lady. Your job is done.' He opened the cage, and placed it in a little alcove he had dug in the tunnel wall.

*****

Steve Barkin tightened his relentless and painful grip. If Arn could only get one arm free, he'd be all right. But Barkin was too strong.

Didn't someone see? Didn't anyone care? He'd had enough. He craned his head around to look over his shoulder, just as Barkin leaned forward.

His teeth were like needles, his eyes yellow slits. Arn screamed.

He opened his eyes. Hours had passed, and his wrists, tied together behind his back, felt like they were on fire. Blood from the wound on his face had dripped onto the soil in front of him, and he noticed that a few of the carnivorous butterflies had arrived, to pick at it like a scab.

He lifted his head, and blinked to try and clear his blurred vision. Standing in exactly the same spot was the solitary Panterran figure. Its unblinking, golden eyes still fixed on him. From within the cowl Arn had an impression of its head turning slightly towards his guards. The figure then glided forward and knelt down in front of him.

Arn chuckled mirthlessly. 'Nice place you got here.'

The Panterran reached into its robe and pulled free a small wooden bottle that it uncapped and lifted to Arn's lips.

'Drink this.'

At this point, Arn didn't care if it was poison, or some revolting Panterran concoction, as he knew his body would soon shut down without moisture. He immediately drained the mouthful of liquid and then surprisingly, the creature reached forward with one clawed hand to wipe his forehead. Arn could smell the vinegary smell of the Panterran as it leaned in close to him, its golden eyes looking deep into his own.

'Do not hate all of us, as all of us do not hate you.'

'Who . . . are you?' Arn tried to make out the thing's face, but it pulled back, and then stood.

'The ones who watch.' The figure turned and glided away.

'Thank you.' Arn licked his still dry lips and watched as the figure disappeared among the trees. *The ones who watch? The ones who untie would be better.* He sat back to straighten his spine. It was cooler now, and the shadows were lengthening. Further down the camp, more Panterran were milling about, having appeared from wherever they had been resting, preparing for the coming evening. Many shot him hostile glances, their faces pulled into ugly masks of disgust, but only one took the trouble to spit at him.

A strange sound that started as a deep rumbling, and finished in an elephantine squeal, made him turn to look towards the far end of the camp. Arn thought he had seen enough weird wonders in this world, but this made his mouth fall open. A monstrous beast swung its head towards Arn, and emitted another squealing roar. Had Arn's hands been free, he would have covered his ears. The almost bovine eyes peered out from under a hood of scales, and a metal ring was buried deep into the flesh of its temples. Arn couldn't work out whether the thing had evolved from some sort of giant armadillo, elephant, or perhaps even a weird blend of both.

Its size and appearance was terrifying, but the thing that worried him most was that on its back there were fixed structures – simple T-shaped posts about three feet in height. He knew what they were; he had seen similar things in pictures, fixed to the decks of ancient wooden ships about to enter a war – they were there simply to give an archer or cavalry man something to hold onto as the pitching ship – or in this case, lumbering beast – advanced into battle.

A Panterran threw a thick rope over the beast's head, and ducked underneath to pull it through the metal loops on each side of its face. Then he leapt up onto its neck, yanking at these reins as he rode it further down into the camp.

The armoured tank of the future, Arn thought. He could picture this lumbering mountain tearing through the Wolfen lines. He lowered his head again, feeling a sense of doom wash over him.

Arn was losing track of time – was it minutes or hours later that Orcalion reappeared? Beside him scurried a portly Panterran carrying an ornate wooden stool. He placed it down next to Arn, and Orcalion sat on it and faced him.

'Are you well rested, hairless bag of meat?' His mouth twisted in a malevolent, needle-toothed grin.

Arn ignored him and concentrated instead on trying to blank out the pain in his shoulders and wrists, and also the odd fluttering he felt deep down in his belly – *very deep down* in his belly.

He wondered where Strom and Sorenson were, and hoped that if they did manage to stage a rescue attempt, he would be able to move quickly, or at all, after being hobbled and tied to a stake in the ground for so many hours.

Arn's lips were split from dehydration, but he knew that a request for more water would just give the wizened little Panterran more enjoyment, and another opportunity to goad or beat him. He lifted himself slightly, determined to try to stretch the muscles in his legs, and get some blood back into them.

Perhaps thinking Arn was trying to get to his feet, Orcalion grabbed at the tether hanging from his neck, just as the flap of the tent was thrown back and a tall figure appeared. The warrior, dressed in highly decorated black robes, fixed his yellow eyes on Arn, then Orcalion. He nodded.

Orcalion laughed. 'Time to perform, son of Man.' He dismissed the two Panterran who had been guarding Arn, and unwound the tether from the stake, dragging him to his feet and leading him like a broken horse.

Arn stumbled and fell twice, before his cramping legs supported his weight. He tried to blink away the dizziness as he was led toward the dark mouth of the black tent. Nightmarish images of what was to come danced in his feverish mind.

The fetid air at the tent's entrance was like a shot of smelling salts. The acrid ammonium smell made his eyes burn and his head snap back. Inside, there were braziers burning dimly, but still it was hard to make out anything more than shapes.

As his eyes slowly adjusted, he looked around. There were perhaps twenty Panterran standing guard – taller than any he had seen in the camp, and all with long curving swords hanging from their waists. Some held long-handled brushes, like brooms, which they constantly swept up and down the length of the most grotesque animal Arn had ever seen.

The tether around his neck was fixed to a metal ring at one end of a low bench in a corner of the tent. Orcalion sunk to his knees in front of the lumpy, sagging body of the queen. The horrific creature turned its luminous golden eyes on Arn, and yawned widely. A few blackened teeth showed in its cavernous mouth, but Arn winced and had to turn his head as the fug of its disgusting breath hit his face and made him want to retch violently.

'Arnoddr – I knew you'd come to save me!'

Arn recognised the small voice immediately. He searched the other corners of the tent; tucked away to one side, in a cage no bigger than a small packing crate, sat a cross-legged Grimson. His face broke into a wide smile as he reached through the bars to wave. Arn could see blood on his fur, and anger boiled within him.

'*Arnoddrrrrr-Sigarrrr.*' The words wheezed towards him in a long slow hiss.

Arn looked back at Mogahr, but had trouble maintaining eye contact. He felt as if even the sight of her might infect him with her corruption.

Orcalion, seizing him, forced him to his knees. 'Bow in the presence of Queen Mogahr the Magnificent, you disgusting hairless creature.'

Mogahr waved her hand at Orcalion. '*Leeavve usss.*'

Orcalion started to protest, but a glare from the queen sent him bowing, back-pedalling from the tent.

The queen sniffed. '*Youu ssstink of Woolfen, asss muuch asss the youung priiinceliiing.*' She turned briefly to Grimson. '*Youung tenderrr priinceliiing.*' She smacked her lips together over her blackened teeth, making Arn shudder.

Her golden eyes slid back to him. '*Wheere are the waar machinesss of Mann-kind? Wheere are the treesss of fire that reacched the sssky, and burnnned the land from mountain to sssea? If you teach usss your secretsss, we can be . . . friendsss.*' She paused, her head weaving back and forth like a cobra, as though trying to see him from many different angles at once. Her look became furtive. '*Whaat havve you taught the Woolfen? Did you also bring them . . . gifts?*'

Her hand went to her robe and pulled it open revealing a pair of sagging, leathery breasts and the magnificent diamond, now chained and clasped in silver. The blood red stone swung forward and she stroked it lovingly.

Mogahr's eyes seemed to stare right through to the marrow of his bones. Arn gulped and shook his head. A sound like a wet cough was hacked at him, and given the curve of her lips, Arn guessed she had just laughed.

'*Wordsss doo not need to comme from the tongue, ssstupid ape. You wiiill tell usss . . . or your waarm innardsss wiiill.*' She motioned with an arm, and two of the guards moved quickly to take hold of him.

'*I liiike yourrr eyesss – daaark liiike the niiight. I thiiink I wiiill keeeep them.*'

Arn's guts were churning. Suddenly, he doubled over, dragging the guards with him and almost throwing them to the floor. Embarrassed, one of them wrenched him upright by his hair, and the other buried his fist hard into Arn's stomach—

With a breaking of wind, a tearing of fabric, the beetle burst from Arn's pants and flew around the inside of the tent.

'*Fleeet beeetle – he'sss beeeing trackeddd.*'

One of the guards ran to the entrance of the tent, and pushed up the flap, opening his mouth to yell an alarm. But no sound came. Instead, he fell backwards like a plank of wood, an arrow protruding from his neck.

At the rear of the tent, a volcano of earth, teeth and fur erupted.

*****

Strom landed lightly on his feet, and shook the soil from his head. He raised his sword. In no more than a single breath, Sorenson sprang up out of the hole beside him.

The Panterran guards were frozen. The Wolfen brothers charged forward, slashing and hacking anything that moved. The queen hissed a single command that had half of the guards crawling on top of her to create a living shield of flesh, their swords pointed outwards, so that they resembled some sort of spiked sea creature. It suited the Wolfen, as this took them out of the fight.

Sorenson caught sight of Arn, hands bound behind his back, leashed by his throat to a bench in a corner of the tent. He fought his way towards him, slicing through the thick tether easily. Strom was now in the centre of a Panterran storm of swords and claws, and his own blade rose and fell, filling the tent with blood and shrieks of hatred from the furious Panterran.

Arn called for a blade, but instead Sorenson dragged him to where Grimson crouched, rattling the door of his cage impatiently. In another moment, Sorenson had freed the young Wolfen as well, and was herding both of his charges towards the yawning hole in the ground. Just before he was pushed into the pit, Arn shouldered over one of the fire-filled braziers; its coals landed in the folds of the tent, which exploded into flames.

The Panterran shrieked and fled the tent, dragging their grub-like queen with them.

'The one thing Panterran dread more than drowning,' Sorenson shouted over his shoulder as they hurried along the tunnel, 'is a good fire!'

As Arn dragged Grimson along with him, he looked down to see the female fleet beetle scurrying past them. Clinging to her back was the male.

So far so good, he thought.

*****

Eilif held up her bow with the last arrow nocked, but immediately lowered it. The tent was a magnificent inferno, and the entire camp were running about like ants. The queen was dragged from the tent, and if not for the crowd of supplicants surrounding her, the temptation to shoot an arrow into her ugly bloated hide would have been irresistible.

She could hear the others coming along the tunnel, and prayed that they were all unharmed. She took one last look back into the camp. The light was beginning to fade to a deep purple, and she saw that a group of the giant Lygon had thundered into the clearing, and began to push, shove and fight with each other, their roars outstripping the sounds of the panicked Panterran.

Eilif pulled her bowstring back as far as it would go, aimed high into the sky and fired her arrow. The silent and poisonous projectile was too dangerous to take with her now that it had the vipod venom coating it . . . She hoped that it would land among the Lygon, seeming to have dropped from the sky itself.

'A gift from Odin,' she whispered, laughing softly as waited, crouched beside the tunnel exit.

Chapter 31

A Life Saved Is A Life Owned

They ran through the forest in single file – Sorenson, Grimson, then Eilif, Arn, and finally Strom. They kept close together, with no more than an arm's length between them.

Strom had told them he estimated they had about thirty minutes before the fire in the tent died, and it was cool enough for the Panterran to enter . . . to find that there were no charred Wolfen bodies. The tunnel would also be found, and followed, and then all hell would be on their trail.

It was dark now, and thankfully the moon had risen enough for Arn to see clearly. As before, the rising moon filled him with energy, which he needed after the ordeal of the previous night and day.

Eilif had given him some water and dried beef. But there could be no stopping to enjoy his meal; they all knew that the night belonged to the Panterran, and until they were safe within the castle walls, they would run until they dropped.

In front of him, Eilif glanced over her shoulder, checking for signs of pursuit. Arn caught her eye; she smiled, slowing her pace a fraction so that they were running side by side. She nudged him with her elbow.

'Someone must be looking out for you, Arnoddr. Rarely does one escape from the Slinkers. But you have managed it twice.'

Arn laughed. 'You came to rescue me this time. That makes *you* my guardian angel.'

'Really, that makes us even,' she said softly. 'But a life saved is a life owned. Now I have a claim on yours as well.' She looked away quickly, and Arn bet that if there was a little more light, he'd see that the inside of her ears had turned pink.

*****

Sorenson raced through the darkness, trying his best to retrace their path back to the castle. He knew that soon he'd have to carry Grimson, whose panting was growing ever louder. Sorenson knew why – the young Wolfen had to run twice as hard as his long-legged companions.

Just a few moments earlier, Strom had passed word up to him that he could now hear the sounds of pursuit – the Panterran travelled fast in the dark, and their eyes were better suited to night hunting.

Sorenson counted trees and familiar landmarks, trying to ignore the creeping fatigue in his limbs, and was comforted at least to know that they were following the right path. If they could just make it back into the open fields of Valkeryn, they would be safe.

He slowed slightly, and stared into the darkness. There was a strange whirring sound up ahead – not something he had ever heard before, or could identify as a natural noise of the forest. As he rounded a tree into a small moonlit clearing, a horrifying beast reared up in front of him.

Like a giant cobra, with a flattened body and a single, burning red eye, the thing gave off an insect-like hum as it hovered in the centre of their path.

As Sorenson ground to a halt, a blinding light like a thousand candles flared from the beast's eye. Grimson screamed, and Strom shouldered Arn and Eilif aside as he rushed forward to drag the young Wolfen out of harm's way. The thing whined again, and rose up as though to strike. Strom snarled and raised his broadsword.

There was another bright flash.

*****

Sorenson stared down at the broken beast. In one mighty swing, Strom had buried his blade deep into its head, the light of life fading from its eye as it fell heavily to the ground.

Strom stood, rooted to the spot, hands still gripping his sword. The huge Wolfen shuddered and shook, his teeth chattering. The smell of burning fur and flesh filled the night air.

Some type of venom, Sorenson thought, and dived at his elder brother, pushing him away from the beast. Pulled free at the same time, the sword

171

slipped from Strom's hands and clattered to the ground, and the beast bobbed up and floated away, leaving them once again in the silence and darkness.

*****

'What was that?!' Arn crawled from the bushes where he had been thrown, and looked around warily. Strom lay on the ground, with the other Wolfen kneeling beside him. 'Was it a jormungandr?'

Sorenson shook his head. 'They don't come this far out of the caves. I've never seen, or have ever been told of any beast like that one.' He put his hand on his brother's shoulder. 'It attacked Strom, and has poisoned him.'

Arn looked at the giant Wolfen's burned hands, and sniffed. *Weird,* he thought. It reminded him of when old Mrs. Heming's Siamese cat chewed through the television cables.

Sorenson cradled his brother in his arms, and poured some water across his lips. Strom spluttered.

'Is it dead?' He spoke weakly, without opening his eyes.

Sorenson nodded. 'Or soon will be. You split its skull.'

Strom sat up with his brother's help. Arn could tell he was in a lot of pain. The giant Wolfen looked at his blistered hands, and shook his head. 'In a few hours, they'll be swollen, raw and useless.' His ears twitched and he sniffed the air. 'They're coming. Get me to my feet.'

Sorenson and Arn helped him to stand, while Eilif pulled a small leather pouch from her belt. Inside was a paste, which she rubbed on his cracked and blistered hands. *Feninlang,* Arn hoped.

Strom flexed the fingers, and nodded his thanks. He then dipped a finger in the paste and rubbed it onto his teeth, closing his mouth to work it around with his tongue. He shut his eyes for a few moments and breathed, seeming to swell with energy.

At last, he disengaged himself from Arn and Sorenson, and then stood swaying slightly in the dark. 'They're coming . . . and you must go now. The feninlang will give me energy for another hour; after that . . .'

Sorenson grabbed his brother's arm. 'Run for that hour, then the Mankind and I will carry you.'

Strom slowly shook his head. 'And Grimson? My brother, you must get back and tell them of the Panterran camp, of their war beasts, and of

Mogahr being so close to our kingdom. Get your charges to safety. I will only slow you down, and then we will all die.' He looked across Eilif, Grimson and Arn, and then back into Sorenson's eyes. 'And some more quickly than others.' His meaning was clear – death was not the worst thing that could befall you at the hands of the Panterran.

They all knew the giant warrior was right. Sorenson cursed and banged his fist against Strom's chest, then buried his face there for a few seconds, until Strom pushed him gently backwards.

'Go, brother.'

Sorenson gazed sadly up into the large face, and placed his hand on the crest of the wolf on Strom's chest. 'My strength to you, my brother.'

Strom nodded. 'And my speed to you, beloved brother.'

Sorenson turned away, and called to the others to follow him. Eilif looked up at Strom and placed her hand against the mark of the red-eyed silver wolf on her chest – the royal house crest.

'You were our finest champion, Strom.'

Sorenson called to her again, and she turned on her heels and followed, leaving the giant figure alone in the dark.

Chapter 32

Please Tell Me You Got That?

'Something coming at us fast – biological – go to strobe, sir?'

The room fell silent as the technicians pressed buttons and shifted joysticks to keep the camera hovering in the darkness.

Harper folded his arms and tried to remain calm, but his heart was racing. 'Not yet; we might frighten it off, and never actually see what it is.'

'Could it be Singer?'

Harper ignored the question, but kept his eyes on the screen. 'Recorders running. Prepare for evasive.' He turned briefly to another screen showing pulses of radar waves, bending around the approaching object. It was nearly on top of them. 'Hold at six feet vertical.'

'It's too dark; at the speed it's moving, it'll run right by us and we won't see it. We've got to light it up.'

'Negative. Hold . . .' Harper got to his feet, his wide eyes flicking from screen to screen. 'Hold . . .'

Shapes appeared as the radar blip converged with their position. In night-vision mode, everything was a ghostly green. But the apparition that emerged from the darkness was unmistakable: 'It's a freakin' giant wolf!'

For a moment, a second, human face was exposed by the greenish light, and then there was a ferocious snarl as a giant wolf creature, even more terrifying than the first, loomed up in front of them.

'Go to strobe!' The forest lit up – but for less than a few seconds, as something came down hard on top of the camera. The screen immediately melted into snow.

The entire room was on its feet. No one could speak, and the only sound was the static from the destroyed camera.

Harper turned to the recording engineer. 'Please tell me you got that.'
The engineer nodded. 'Yep, all of it.'

The loop was replayed for the first of many times, the technicians staring in wonder at the beasts' faces. And Arnold Singer was clearly there too; he looked frightened and thin, but otherwise seemed healthy.

Harper leaned back and smiled. 'Welcome back, son.' He spun in his seat and eyed the army personnel hovering over him. 'And now . . . we go and get him.'

Chapter 33

Know Who You Face This Day

Strom stood in the centre of the path, between two large boulders. This made it hard for his adversaries to creep up on his flanks, but still didn't mean he couldn't be overwhelmed by a frontal attack. He doubted the Panterran had the stomach for it.

He had torn his tunic free, and used the leather to wrap his hands; the blistering was painless due to the feninlang root balm, but was starting to weep. He would need a firm grip on his sword.

He stood staring into the dark, legs spread, holding his blade ready as the approaching horde bore down on him.

The first Panterran runners that broke through the forest onto the path were quickly cut down, and their squeals of surprise alerted the rest to be cautious. In a few more seconds, more of the small warriors had appeared, but stayed back, just out of reach of the large Wolfen's sword.

Strom held his position – he didn't really care if they fought him; he just needed to slow them down.

The snarls and hisses of the tangle of Panterran built quickly. Strom bared his teeth.

'Craven worms of the night, your cowardice is why you will never truly defeat the sáál of the Wolfen.'

The snarling fury of the Panterran quietened, and the boiling mass of flat-faced creatures parted to allow Orcalion to glide through.

'*Ah*, of course . . . mighty Strom. We thank you.'

Strom frowned in confusion, and Orcalion nodded and continued.

'You broke the agreement, champion of the Wolfen – made in the presence of your king: the Man-kind for the princeling – that was our deal. Now who is the most deceptive?'

Strom kept both hands on his sword, and snorted in contempt as more and more Panterran crowded in around him. 'You would never have released our prince.'

Orcalion grinned. 'Now we shall never know. But history will record that the Wolfen provoked this war . . . and for that, we thank you.'

'Wolfen don't fear war, or death, you vile little creature. We will never fall to your steel and claw, or to your deceptions.'

'You think not, berserker? You will fall, and fall this night, to us . . .' He leaked a hissing chuckle. '. . . Or to our large and hungry brothers.'

So saying, he stepped to one side to allow three enormous Lygon to thunder onto the path. They held huge stone mallets in their taloned hands, and dagger-like fangs curved back from faces as ugly and fearsome as monsters from Hellheim itself.

Strom, snarling, backed up a step. Up close, the Lygon were more terrible than the clay model Balthazar had made at the castle. Their orange and black-striped fur rippled over massive columns of muscle. Like giant striped ogres, they roared and raised their weapons, bringing them down onto the ground with so much force, Strom could feel the impact through the soles of his feet.

Strom sucked in a huge breath, then let loose a roar that made the Panterran shrink back behind the Lygon. He pointed his sword at the brutes before him.

'Know who you face this day. I am Strom, son of Stromgarde, descendant of the very first guardians! If I die this day, so will many of you.'

'Kill him!' Orcalion screeched at the three giant creatures, then slunk quickly out of sight behind them.

The Lygon each were twice Strom's weight, but they hesitated in the face of his ferocity. They were used to warriors fleeing from them in fear, and never had they faced a being who would stand up to three of them.

In the end, it was Strom who charged.

When they came together, there was an explosion of muscle and steel that shook the trees around them. A severed Lygon head flew through the air as the Wolfen's broadsword flashed in an arc. The Panterran shrunk back further into the brush as blood sprayed in all directions.

As Strom had expected, they were enormously strong, but slow.

Another of the Lygon suffered a deep gash to its arm, causing it to roar its pain to the sky, and pull back temporarily from the fight. Orcalion screamed until his eyes bulged and spittle flew from his black lips. The Panterran pulled his own curved sword, and prodded the giant beast in the back.

The huge Lygon wouldn't budge. The remaining beast swung its stone mallet, striking the earth thunderously, splintering trees – but never once touching the Wolfen. For the first time, fear gripped the spine of the Panterran.

Orcalion dropped his sword, and snatched a bow from one of his cowering warriors. He nocked an arrow and fired it into the Wolfen's leg. Strom grunted and sunk to one knee.

With the feninlang stimulant wearing off from his already battered body, Strom knew his fight was done. He lowered his sword and raised his face to the sky, smiling, knowing he had given his brother time to get his charges well away.

He opened his arms wide, and yelled with all the strength he could muster, 'For Valkeryn!'

Emboldened at the sight of their stricken enemy, the two Lygon came at him with their weapons raised. With his last vestige of strength, Strom lifted his blade and plunged it deep into the gut of one of the charging giants, its own weight ensuring that it impaled itself to the hilt.

The dead creature fell on top of Strom, pinning him flat, while the other put one large foot on his free arm. Orcalion crept closer and stood cautiously over his prone body.

'I'm glad you will be dead soon,' he hissed. 'You have slain many of my people, champion puppet of an old king. And one cannot be champion forever . . .'

Strom regarded Orcalion with glazed, staring eyes. 'Another champion already rises, vile creature from the mire. And thousands more like me wait for you on the plains of Valkeryn.'

Orcalion laughed. 'Valkeryn? *You* won't see it again . . . but *it* might see you.'

He turned to the Panterran who had finally gathered enough courage to creep forward.

'Take his head.'

Chapter 34

I Fear It Has Only Just Begun

They crashed through the last line of brush at the edge of the fields leading to the castle, its spires just visible over the rolling hillsides.

After running through the night and most of the day, they stumbled and shuffled forward. Fatigue weighed heavily on their bones. Sorenson put Grimson down onto the ground, and the young Wolfen woke as his feet touched the grass. 'Are we home?'

'Soon. Look.' Sorenson pointed. 'Riders already approach.'

Arn was half carrying Eilif, who was breathing raggedly.

'Thank Odin, it's over,' she murmured, as the banner of the king's riders appeared over the hill.

Arn looked at Sorenson, whose face looked grim. 'It's not, is it?'

Sorenson shook his head. 'I fear it has only just begun. They had gravilents in their forward camp. They are hard to control, but very effective in breaking through an army's front line. They wouldn't have them so close to the kingdom, if they didn't intend to use them . . . soon.'

Arn and Sorenson stood in silence. The Wolfen warrior's eyes were glassy – and Arn wondered whether it was fatigue, or regret for leaving his brother behind.

Arn reached out to grasp his shoulder. 'I'm sorry about Strom.'

Sorenson just grunted.

'Do you think that he could still be . . .?'

'No . . . they wouldn't take him alive. Strom wouldn't let them.' He gripped Arn's forearm. 'You are a brave creature, Man-kind, and you have a good and strong heart. Worry not about Strom. He is crossing the rainbow bridge to sit with Odin and the other champions of Asgaard. When the time is right, his sáál will return to us again.'

Arn turned and tilted his head. 'You believe in an afterlife then, and *ahh*, reincarnation?'

Sorenson spoke without turning. 'I don't understand that word, but all Wolfen believe that a good spirit will be granted a place in Valhalla, and when Odin calls upon that sáál again, he may be granted another life. Perhaps again as a Wolfen.'

He looked at Arn. 'Perhaps you were once a Wolfen in a previous life . . . or maybe will be one in a life yet to come.'

Arn smiled, but could see no humour in Sorenson's features – the Wolfen believed what he said.

The Wolfen riders were upon them then, and the first few leapt from their horses to run the last steps to embrace Sorenson. Arn saw that one young Wolfen, the dark-furred one he remembered from the king's banquet, also dismounted and raced up to Eilif.

Arn was left by himself. He watched as Grimson was lifted onto one horse, and the tall dark Wolfen led Eilif to another. A horse was then brought for him, and Arn climbed up into the saddle, at first with difficulty, but finally he managed to sit upright.

Instead of simply lifting Eilif into the saddle, the dark Wolfen leapt up first and reached out his hand to her. Arn didn't know why, but he suddenly felt awkward and intrusive for watching this moment of intimacy. It felt weird; he didn't like it, and . . . what? He didn't quite know what he was feeling. He turned away, but couldn't help looking back.

Eilif eyed the offered hand, and then shook her head and waved it away. The dark Wolfen looked taken aback – humiliated, even.

Eilif glanced about, and then spotted Arn staring at her. She marched purposefully towards his horse. In a moment, she was beside him.

'Scoot forward.' Arn did as he was told, and she leapt nimbly up into the saddle behind him. She wrapped her arms around his waist.

He cast a furtive look at the dark Wolfen. The expression, *if looks could kill,* came to his mind as the spurned warrior's eyes burned into him like twin flamethrowers. At that moment, Arn knew that not all in Valkeryn were happy to have him as part of their inner circle.

Arn tore his eyes away and spoke over his shoulder. 'Who's the dark rider? Is he a special friend?'

'No one but an ambitious warrior.' Eilif snorted dismissively and kicked her heels into the horse's flanks. 'Let's go – I need a bath.' She pretended to sniff Arn's neck. '. . . And so do you, *phew*.' She laughed and hugged him tighter.

Arn smiled. He couldn't help it – he liked her.

Chapter 35

What Happened To My People?

After returning to the castle, Arn was led to his room, and found it filled with food. He suddenly remembered he hadn't eaten in days, and gorged himself until his stomach felt like it was going to split. Then he undid his belt and lay on the bed.

He breathed deeply. *Safe . . . again*, he thought. Then his thoughts turned to home, and he wondered about his parents, Edward and, of course, Becky. He imagined her long hair, and as she turned and smiled at him, he saw her eyes were silver blue, and her face was covered in fur . . .

Arn shook the image from his head and rubbed his face, feeling the dirt and grease on his skin. His clothes itched, and looking across to a low bench near the window, he saw that there was a cloth and a large bowl of water.

I should at least wash my face, and under my arms, he thought. He closed his eyes for a second. *Maybe, I'll just wash my face . . .*

He slept for nearly a day.

*****

He awoke to find Morag removing the remains of his meal, and wishing him a good day. The sun was already high in the sky and Arn reckoned it must have been close to noon. He sat up and eyed the cold leftovers as they were taken away, feeling hungry once again.

Morag returned with a pile of towels. 'And now, sir . . . Bath.' She dropped a sack onto the ground. 'And please put all your clothes into this bag.'

Arn laughed. 'Do I smell that bad? Are you going to burn them?'

Morag laughed in return. 'Yes, and yes.'

He stopped laughing, suddenly feeling a little awkward. He had no idea how he really smelled to the Wolfen. They had an undoubtedly excellent sense of smell, so for all he knew, his odour was totally repulsive. He started peeling off layers and dropping them into the open sack.

Morag watched him carefully, seeming to sense his embarrassment. 'It's the Slinker smell. We can't stand it.'

Of course, he thought. *Just as the Slink . . . Panterran couldn't stand the smell of the Wolfen.*

'Can I ask you something? Have the Wolfen and the Slinkers ever been friends? Have you ever tried to make peace with them?' Arn wrapped a small towel around his waist.

Morag's face grew dark and she stared for a moment as if thinking carefully. She nodded slowly.

'Yes, we have tried. We have tried treaties, sent emissaries, entire peace delegations; for many centuries we have tried, but nothing has worked. Nothing ever works with them.'

'What happened?'

'Wolfen die. Always the Wolfen die.' She hefted the bag and straightened. 'Their hatred runs deep. They do not want peace; they want only one thing – a world without us.'

'I'm not so sure. I think there may be some . . .' Arn closed his mouth. He saw the sadness in her eyes, and wondered whether she had lost someone in their eternal war. *And we thought we had differences*, Arn thought.

Morag pushed open the door and held it for him, waiting to lead him to the bath chamber.

Arn raised his hand. 'I know the way. Thank you.'

She smiled, then headed in the opposite direction down the stone corridor. Arn passed a few other Canite females in the corridor, who stopped to stare, or held hands up over their faces to titter at his hairless body.

The bath chamber was once again filled with steam, and a large tub filled with soapy water. New clothes were laid out once again – he noticed this time there was a dagger already hanging in the scabbard.

Someone cleared their throat from within the cloud of mist, and Arn's eyes were drawn to the other side of the chamber. Balthazar emerged from the steam like an apparition made solid. He bowed to Arn, then smiled and stepped to one side, gesturing to another figure standing mute behind him.

Arn gasped – it was *him* – moulded from clay. Just like the mould of the Lygon, Balthazar had crafted a likeness of him in fantastic detail. Arn winced.

The likeness was naked.

'What do you think, Man-kind? Is it not like an image in a looking glass?'

Arn bobbed his head from side to side. 'It's really good – the best I've ever seen. But where are my clothes?'

Balthazar looked confused for a second, then pointed to the pile laid out for Arn nearby.

'No, I mean on the likeness?'

The court counsellor shrugged. 'It is as you are, and as I observed you. Is it not correct in its anatomical detail?'

Arn pointed to the model's middle. 'Yeah sure, but I don't really like that everything about me is on display. Can you . . . Uh, can you put some clothes on it?'

'I suppose so. But the King and his family approve of it. They want it in their private gallery.'

'The king?'

Balthazar nodded. 'And the Queen.'

Arn screwed up his face as if in pain, and spoke the next words slowly. 'And . . . Eilif?'

Balthazar nodded again, this time more vigorously. 'Of course – she liked it the most. She said it was . . .' He searched his memory for her exact words. '. . . Exciting.'

Arn groaned. 'Just put some clothes on it . . . please. We Man-kind have a thing called modesty, and don't like to walk around naked.'

Balthazar shrugged again, and gave a small surprised laugh. 'And I thought that was just to stay warm without fur. Well, as you wish, young sir.' He threw a sheet up over the statue, and sat down. 'But until you arrived, we only had legends, and some old artefacts from the caves in the dark zones.'

Arn climbed into the bath, keeping his towel wrapped around his waist until the last moment. He wasn't keen to give the counsellor any further glimpses of his anatomy, which might make for future art or science exhibitions.

He relaxed into the hot water, closing his eyes and sighing as his knotted muscles unwound. His eyes flicked open.

'Caves, artefacts?' He turned to look at Balthazar. 'You mentioned those before, and . . . Vidarr, the archivist. I need to speak to him – find out what really happened.'

Balthazar had the sheet off the model again, and was making some adjustments to Arn's . . . *bits*. He spoke over his shoulder while he sculpted.

'I can take you to him – or at least I can take you to where he *should be*. Actually finding him is another matter.' Balthazar laughed and stood up. 'Bathe, rest, and then eat. After that, if you still wish it, we shall try our luck.' He nodded a farewell, and then left.

Arn sank lower in the water, and looked again at the clay model. 'And you put some pants on as well.' He closed his eyes.

*****

Arn pushed his long hair back off his face and took a deep breath. Washed, clothed and fed, he felt human again. *Human – I'm probably the only one in the world who feels that way now*, he thought.

As he strode down the stone corridor looking for Balthazar, Eilif silently fell in beside him.

'You smell nice again.'

'Not a Slinker stinker anymore?' He raised his eyebrows.

She laughed lightly at his words. 'No, just the Arnoddr-Sigarr smell – nice.'

Arn looked her up and down. She wasn't wearing any of the clothing she normally wore around the castle – no heavy velvets, satins or embroidered silks. Instead, she had on a similar outfit to that which she had worn when she had rescued him from the Slinkers – pants, leather vest, and a fine chain mail – light but formidable. Her outfit was finished off with a sword strapped to her belt.

'You going out again?' He reached out and pinched the material of her vest.

Eilif looked from his hand to his face. 'Valkeryn is on a war footing now. All must be ready to fight at short notice.'

'You're seriously going to go into battle?'

'Of course.' She frowned, not understanding his question.

'But you're a princess.'

She knocked his hand away. 'And just a female – is that it? I don't know what females were like in—'

'No, I mean that you're royal. It is important for you to be safe, for the good of the Canite population's morale. Will the king go into battle as well?'

'Yes. The king is a great warrior. It would be a waste of his skill for him not to fight . . . and *bad* for the population's morale.'

'But what if he falls?'

She shook her head slowly. 'The king may fall – but Valkeryn will not, must not. All know what to do. All must fight.'

Her eyes bore into his like chips of silver blue ice. He could see that she didn't just believe she *had* to fight; she *wanted* to fight. After another few seconds, he nodded. She folded her arms and looked him up and down.

'And where do you go in such a hurry, son of Man?'

Arn motioned down the corridor with his head. 'Looking for Balthazar. He's going to take me to the archives, where we hope to find Vidarr.'

'Why?'

'Looking for clues.'

She stepped closer to him. 'What sort of clues?'

'I'm looking for something—'

'Like treasure, weapons or food?' Her eyes lit up with excitement.

'Something far more valuable than that, at least to me. I'm on the trail of what happened to my people.' He started walking again.

She skipped a few steps to catch up with him. 'I'm going to help. I think I'll like looking for clues, and finding out what happened to your pack.'

*****

Bergborr stepped back into the shadows.

Neither Arn nor Eilif paid any attention to the dark corridor as they passed it – both were too engrossed in each other's company.

He stepped out again, knowing they wouldn't see him. *Why would they?* he thought. *She doesn't even know I exist anymore – I might as well be vapour rising from a dying fire.* His bitterness boiled inside him.

He peered around the corner. His mouth turned down in distaste, and his hand rested on the hilt of his sword.

The Slinkers should have finished him. The Man-kind needed to disappear, one way or another. Until then, Bergborr knew that *he* would be no more than an annoyance to the princess.

He shook his head. When the Man-kind first arrived, he had taken Eilif's infatuation with the hairless creature as being one of simple curiosity. He shuddered. It was turning out to be much more. Moving back into the shadows, he leaned his head against the cold stone wall.

One way or another, he thought.

*****

Arn and Eilif met Balthazar in the courtyard and he walked them to the castle keep – the most ancient structure within Valkeryn's walls.

Arn was taken aback by the age-old building. While the walls, towers and castle of Valkeryn were old, it was still formidable and obviously well maintained. But this smaller structure reminded him of the old castles or temples that sit abandoned in unexplored jungles or on miserable hilltops in Scotland. The hard granite was weathered to a melted smoothness, and where once there were probably sharp spires and ornate carving it was now crumbled and degraded.

Arn imagined it had been a grand hall and set of rooms for the king and his family and perhaps that was about all. Maybe long ago there had been other buildings surrounding it for guards or servants, but now they were either long disintegrated or their bones had been incorporated into the massive edifice that Valkeryn had become.

Balthazaar turned to Arn.

'In the first days of our empire, this was all that Valkeryn was. The main halls were built over a natural maze of tunnels and caverns that were further excavated down many levels. The lower we descend, the older the artefacts we find.' He smiled. 'The problem is, the tunnels are near endless, and the only lighting is what we carry. Without the archivist's knowledge, a Wolfen could search for a lifetime . . . as Vidarr already has.'

Arn turned to Eilif. 'Have you met this Vidarr?'

Eilif shrugged. 'Maybe when I was younger, but I can't recall him.'

Balthazar chuckled. 'Not many have. He was old, even when I was a youth. And that was many, many years ago. Some say he is as old as Valkeryn itself, but that can't be true, can it?' He turned and winked at Arn.

Balthazar stopped at a huge wooden door, with a ring for a handle and heavy brass rivets, giving it a solid, armoured appearance. He raised his fist and knocked. A deep echo could be heard from within. The echo died away, and they waited. Nothing.

Balthazar looked at Arn, shrugged and then banged his fist once more. He leaned forward until his ear was against the wood. As before, there was no response, other than the lonely echo bouncing around the cavernous interior.

Balthazar took hold of the ring, first with one hand, then with both. The ancient metal mechanism grated and squealed, but eventually turned. He put his shoulder to the door. 'Give me some assistance; this weighs more than a veldoxer.'

Arn had no idea what a veldoxer was, but guessed it was something heavy. He nodded to Eilif, and the three of them pushed on the door. There was a popping sound as the time-welded seals gave up their hold on the wood, and then the massive door swung slowly inwards, releasing a wave of odours – mouldy paper and mushrooms, or something else long dead.

'*Phew.*' Arn had his hand up over his nose. 'When was the last time anyone saw Vidarr alive?'

Balthazar looked around slowly. 'Ten years, maybe more – he never leaves. But wait, he's here. Look.'

He pointed to a torch that was burning at the far end of the entrance hallway, its flame looking tiny in the enormous chamber.

Everywhere Arn looked, there were stacks of papers, books and scrolls, and bottles of things dried or floating in fluids. It resembled a cross between a magician's workshop and a very disorganised library. He felt a cold draught; the chamber had arched doorways leading away in all directions.

'Vidarr.' Balthazar looked around, smiling, but tapped his foot impatiently. He raised his voice. 'Vidarr, it's Balthazar; I've brought someone interesting for you to meet.'

The three of them stood in silence, listening as the echo of Balthazar's voice died away.

Eilif edged closer to Arn in the gloom. He felt her elbow touch his.

Balthazar was about to call again, when a shuffling sound swept through the silence. They turned, trying to find its source, but it seemed to be coming from all around them. Then it stopped.

'Is it the young Man-kind?'

Balthazar laughed softly. 'Perhaps. But you will have to come and see.' He whispered to Arn, 'Even though he spends his life within these dark and dismal walls, he misses little. Answer him truthfully, young Man-kind, and he may just help you.'

A small cough emanated from one of the arched doorways, and then the most ancient creature Arn had ever seen shuffled into the dim light. He barely came up to Arn's shoulder, and he wore a robe that swept the floor behind him.

Arn felt Eilif take a small backwards step, and then she spoke softly into his ear. 'Loki's beard, he must be a hundred.'

Immediately the ancient creature responded, 'I was over a hundred when Balthazar was but knee high.' The words drew out into a wheezing sound that could have been a laugh. Balthazar bowed deeply.

'Vidarr, I am honoured that you would join us.' He straightened and motioned to Arn. 'May I present a youthful representative of the Old Ones, the human race, the last of the Man-kind . . . Arnoddr-Sigarr.'

Balthazar stood aside, and Arn felt awkward and exposed. He bowed, not knowing what else to do.

'Arnoddr-Sigarr? Do you know what that name means in our land?' Vidarr shuffled forward.

Arn nodded. 'I do now.'

'And you came to us after falling through a magical doorway?'

Arn remembered what he told Balthazar when they first met. He nodded, and Vidarr grunted softly but didn't look convinced. He kept his eyes on Arn as he shuffled lightly forward.

'This door – is it still open now?'

'I don't know. I honestly don't know. It might be; I mean, I certainly hope it is. And if that's the case, then I expect my people are looking for me.'

Vidarr nodded. 'Good. A race that cares when a single one of its kind is missing is a good race.' He pinched Arn's cheek, then his arm, then poked his chest – performing a quick examination. 'And this magic door . . . How was it opened?'

189

Arn shrugged, but stayed still as the little Canite prodded and poked. Truthfully, he didn't really understand all the science behind the technology at Fermilab, and had no idea how he could describe it to a medieval society of creatures. His explanation might end up sounding like sorcery – something attributed more to the Panterran.

'*Ah*, it was an accident.' He looked down at the ground, avoiding Vidarr's gaze.

Vidarr gripped Arn's forearm, and turned him sideways. 'An atomic accident?'

Arn felt his breath lock in his chest, and he stared squarely into the eyes of the ancient creature. 'How . . . How do you know about atomic energy?'

Vidarr chuckled softly in his wheezing manner and shuffled away towards the rear of the chamber. 'Lots to discuss.'

He paused, and looked back at Arn silently for a few moments, then said, 'Man-kind were a mighty race, or so legend has it.' He paused again, closing his eyes and intoning softly, as if reciting scripture, 'Not only will atomic power be released, but some day harness the rise and fall of the tides, and imprison the rays of the sun.' He opened his eyes and smiled. 'Do you recognise that, young Man-kind? You may have, because it was a human who said it . . . so long ago, that even his memory is now dust. Well, except to old things like me who keep all good memories alive.'

When Arn didn't respond, he seemed to be a little deflated. 'A Humankind called Thomas Edison said it – have you heard of that one?'

Arn nodded vigorously. 'Yes, of course. He was a great scientist and inventor. The father of the light bulb.'

Vidarr clapped his hands together, seemingly satisfied at last. 'A great scientist from any species, I think. And did you?' He raised his eyebrows. 'Imprison the sun? Harness the tides?'

Arn pictured the enormous power of the machines he had seen at Fermilab. He thought of the energy of nuclear reactors, and laser power. He saw in his mind mighty dams built to hold back a trillion gallons of water, or steep-stepped canals allowing ships to sail across continents. He then remembered Hiroshima, Nagasaki, and Chernobyl. He nodded slowly. 'Yes, yes I guess we did. But sometimes things didn't always go to plan.'

Vidarr smiled. 'Do they ever?'

*****

Vidarr led them all to a large round table overflowing with ancient texts. He lit several candles, and shuffled off, returning almost immediately with a jug of liquid and several wooden mugs.

He poured a mug for Eilif first. 'I was at your birth,' he said to her. 'You've grown into a strong and beautiful princess. You remind me a little of Queen Freya, and a *lot* of King Grimvaldr.'

He patted her shoulder. Next he served Balthazar.

'And the Lygon, young Balt – is it true the Panterran have drawn those stumbling brutes from the dark lands?'

Vidarr was probably the only Canite in all of Valkeryn who was old enough to refer to Balthazar as 'young'. The counsellor nodded gravely.

'We fear they are literally at our door. Once again, war bares its teeth at us, old friend.'

Vidarr nodded. 'Then some things need to be discussed, and some things need to be preserved in the event we are overrun.'

Finally, he came to Arn, who could smell the liquid's underlying metallic odour, mixed with something sweet, something ripe. *Honey, cloves and yeast, maybe*, he pondered.

'And you, Man-kind – you have come with questions, questions about yourself.'

Arn wondered at the perceptiveness of this little old creature that made him feel like an open book. The questions were on his lips, but Balthazar lifted his mug.

'To Valkeryn, and the king.'

Arn raised his mug and sipped the heady brew – warm, gritty, yeasty-sweet. *Not bad . . . but not good either*. There was some underlying flavour he couldn't quite pick out.

'It's called *yogunburr*,' Vidarr offered – seemingly reading his thoughts again. 'I brew it on the rooftops, so the sun can warm the vat. It's also close to the pidhen roosts; their bodies help in the fermenting process.'

'Magnificent,' said Balthazar, smacking his lips. Even Eilif raised her mug in a salute. Vidarr went to pour them a little more.

Arn groaned inwardly; that was the extra ingredient he had detected – decay. He grunted and nodded . . . and put down his mug.

191

'I do have questions,' he said. 'I believe my time was long ago, and the accident somehow threw me forward . . . to your time, *this* time. But there are no traces of humans having been here at all.' Arn looked across the table to his friends. 'Balthazar has told me of the legends, about man somehow rising up to the sky, in body or spirit. But I'd like to know if there is anything more substantial? Some kind of records?'

Vidarr sat down, leaned back and laced his fingers across his stomach. '*Hmm*, and there are other stories that tell of Man being *released* by a great fire. Perhaps the Great Fire that delivered the very first Wolfen.' He closed his eyes. 'I do not know. There are several ancient Man-kind texts and artefacts here, but nothing that provided an insight into the final days of your species.'

Arn sat thinking through Vidarr's words. 'Balthazar also mentioned that there are other libraries, other caves.'

The archivist nodded. 'They are located in a remote and inhospitable region, well beyond the Valkeryn kingdom. Some are still sealed, and strange symbols mark the barriers that cannot be dented by the strongest Wolfen steel. Many generations have tried to enter, but none have succeeded. They must contain great secrets.'

Vidarr rose and leaned across the table, pulling a pile of papers and a stick of charcoal towards himself. He spent several moments scratching, rubbing and shading something on one of the yellowing pages, before holding it up and examining it carefully. Satisfied, he slid it across the table to Arn.

Arn felt a small thrill as he looked at the charcoal image. It was rough, but clear enough – a gauntleted fist holding a thunderbolt.

Could it be? he wondered excitedly. Could it be the military base at what was once North Aurora, where these very symbols were marked on the outside of the blast doors? If anything was going to be preserved, it'd be in underground bunkers like those.

Arn calculated his distances: Fermilab in Batavia was more than an hour's bus ride from North Aurora. Mr. Jefferson usually pushed the bus at about forty to fifty miles per hour, so . . . It would be a long and difficult trek through the wild forest, but he had already made it out of the wasteland. He could find it.

He stared into the ancient Wolfen's eyes, and held up the picture.

'I know it.'

Chapter 36

The Shape Of Things To Come

Each frame of the image feed had been cleaned up and enhanced – every pixel had been illuminated, magnified and scrubbed so that a detailed analysis could begin.

Harper and Takada had been ordered to attend a meeting at an unmarked base just outside of Chicago. When the black helicopter that had been sent to collect them touched down at Fermilab, Harper had a sinking feeling that his project was suddenly not so much *his* anymore.

A briefing room had been set up, and a dozen stony-faced men and women sat at a long table and watched as selected images were projected onto a large screen. It seemed that the images from the probe had already preceded them. Now it was expected that Harper and Takada would explain them.

Takada stood nervously beside the images. When he spoke, his voice sounded tight in this throat. 'The being is approximately six and a half feet tall. And . . . we firmly believe that it is not wearing a mask.' The physicist paused and let the small audience take this in.

There were murmurs among the group, and one sat forward clearing her throat. Her green jacket had numerous stars pinned to the collar and her face was hard as the table in front of her. 'How can you be so sure?'

Colonel Marion Briggs looked around at the others. 'Does anyone else here remember that young Chinese guy who wore the old man mask onto the plane? It looked so real, he managed to get right through customs and immigration. Even fooled the person sitting next to him for several hours.' She jabbed a finger at the screen. 'So, how can we just rule that out?'

Takada cleared his throat, already wilting. He turned to Harper, who nodded and got to his feet. Harper signalled to a technician at the back of the room, and immediately the screen showed five pictures lined up next to each other, creating a time-sequence panorama. They were all of the face of the lunging beast, the images only milliseconds apart, and only changing fractionally in angle from first to last. Following enhancement, they were brutally clear, right down to every single hair follicle and fold of flesh.

Harper look at Briggs, then the others. 'Look at the eyes – notice anything?'

There were a few shrugs.

'We went from night vision to white light – only for a second, but we lit the forest up like a stage. Note the contraction of the pupils; if the subject was wearing contact lenses, there wouldn't be any. Those eyes are real, ladies and gentlemen. Now, in humans, light can be reflected back from the eye as a red glow – the bane of wedding snaps the world over.' No one laughed. 'In any case, that's due to the light reflecting back off a blood vessel layer behind the retina. But in wolves, the retina has a reflective layer behind it called the *tapetum lucidum*. This layer acts like a mirror, reflecting light at the back of their eyes. It's what helps them in the dark. It's also what gives their eyes that silver shine.'

Warming to his lecture, Harper paced around the table. 'We've analysed every life form image we were able to isolate, and not a single one matches any of the known genera, family, species or order we know or understand. Sure, there are things that look like birds, like squirrels, but they're not. We might be looking at a new dimension, a new planet or time – pick any, or all of them, and you could be right. But if someone were to ask me . . .'

He signalled to the technician again. The screen changed to a background shot of Arnold Singer – he looked haggard and frightened, and there were bruises over his face and deep marks around his neck.

'Mister Singer here is either in these creatures' care, or being held as their captive. But the thing is, he's alive. Does anyone know the odds of finding another habitable planet in our universe? I'll tell you: it's about 0.01% over 4,000,000,000 years. And the young man just happens to fall onto one? I think not.'

He turned back to the screen. 'I think Arnold Singer is right here, in this country . . . In this state. The big question is: *when?*'

Colonel Briggs stood up and placed her cap under her arm. 'Good enough for me. The doorway's still open, we can survive there without suits, the indigenous defence technology is primitive . . . and of course, Mister Singer is still alive and needs to be rescued . . . if we can find him. I'll recommend to the general that we mount a mission.'

Harper raised his hand. 'Wait. We need to find him, *and* the diamond. Without it, we may not be able to shut down the anomaly. There's also the scientific imperative to do more research. This is a pristine environment; we can't barge into it with modern technology.'

Briggs clicked her tongue. 'Who said we want to shut it down? Besides, you said yourself, Harper – it's already our world. And how can our technology be modern when they're the ones from the future?' She smiled without humour. 'More importantly, if we don't claim it, someone else will.'

She strode towards the door, and then paused. 'We'll be needing some technical advice, so you, or one of your science team, will be coming with us.' She glanced at Takada, who visibly paled. 'The team will be operational and prepared to go in twenty-four hours. Be ready.'

The door slammed behind her.

*****

Harper slumped down into his chair, his mind spinning. The lights had come up and the rest of the room had filed out, not giving the two scientists a second glance.

He thought about what the colonel had said, and despite himself felt a thrill of exhilaration coursing through his veins. Though he didn't like the idea of culturally polluting a pristine species and environment, the thought of an expedition made him shake with excitement.

He was mentally ticking off what he'd need to take with him, when reality sank in. He wasn't a linguist or cultural specialist; not having either specialisation wasn't a deal breaker, but the real kicker was that, if anything went wrong there, he was really the only one who could diagnose and rectify the problem – and for that he needed to be behind a console.

He sighed. How many scientists get to go and meet a whole new race? Or maybe meet a whole new species? He turned to Takada.

'I envy you.'

*****

In the long black car that silently sped along the freeway, Colonel Briggs kicked off her shoes and spoke slowly into the phone.

'Yes sir, a Type A environment – indigenous personnel warlike, aggressive, but in my judgment, limited in offensive and defensive armaments.'

She paused, a smile spreading across her face. 'Yes sir, I agree. Just a look-see for now. Maybe bring back a few . . . specimens. One team of Green Berets should do just fine, sir.'

She ended the call and tapped her driver on the shoulder. 'You know how many colonels will be bringing the President a whole new conquered world this year?'

The driver knew better than to answer. She laughed and leaned back in her seat.

'Just one, I think.'

Chapter 37

Legends Upon Myths Upon Tales

Arn shivered in the cold darkness. Vidarr had led the three of them deep below the castle through a number of tunnels that were fast turning from excavated passageways into natural caves. Glistening limestone columns of lilac and mineral green danced and shivered as the tongues of flame from their burning torches flickered in the dark.

From time to time, plate-sized fungi growing from moist grottos intruded across their path, and Vidarr stopped to tear loose a chunk from one of the largest stalks. He took a bite.

'Like meat,' he said, holding it out. Arn shook his head, understanding now where the pervasive mushroom smell came from.

The next tunnel opened out into a cavern, and in every nook and cranny there was an overflowing chest or table piled high with debris that was rotting down to sparkling orange dust – small mountains of wood, metal, stone and waxed paper.

Vidarr stopped and shifted uneasily in the darkness. 'It has been many, many years since I have had reason to venture this far down.'

Arn laughed softly. 'So much stuff . . . It's endless.'

Vidarr hummed his agreement, and held up his torch. 'Items accumulated since the dawn of Valkeryn. From time to time a traveller will have something strange to trade – and if it is of interest, then it usually finds its way to me.'

Arn noticed that the old archivist kept looking over his shoulder to some of the darker areas of the caves. Arn held out his own flame and squinted, taking a dozen or so steps away from the group. He noticed that this passage ended not with a rock face, but instead with heavy bars set from floor to ceiling.

Vidarr answered his unspoken question. 'The deeper caves are home to all manner of things.'

'I've met them.' Arn grunted. 'The jormungandr.'

'Yes. And . . . others.'

Arn recalled his arrival deep below ground, and the glistening thing in the dark that had looked like a giant hairless rat – and most disturbingly, had giggled.

Vidarr shuffled off, and Eilif came over to take Arn by the hand, pulling him along. He looked back once more to the bars sealing off the deeper caves, and thought he heard sniggering away in the darkness.

They followed Vidarr, ducking through various passages, around pillars, and soon entered a cathedral-sized opening that swallowed their torchlight. Even though the ceiling was hidden in the blackness, there was a sense of openness, of hugeness, which staggered Arn. *They could hide an army down here*, he thought.

Vidarr lit the torches that were protruding from rings embedded in the rock, before finally placing his own into an empty holder. He turned and opened his arms wide, and walked out towards the centre of the cavern.

'And now . . .' He turned to them, his breath steaming in the chill air. He motioned to the mountains of artefacts piled, stacked and bundled everywhere. '. . . Now it would help if you knew what it was you sought, young Man-kind – a thing, a word, or even just a thought – down here, I can help.'

'We're looking for clues.' Eilif nudged Arn, and winked at him as if sharing a secret. He realised she was still holding his hand, and he gently extricated his fingers from her warm grip. Once free, she immediately began pulling things from among the piles of artefacts. She stopped, frowned and held something up to sniff.

'What's this?' She held up something that might once have been metal. Now it was an L-shaped lump of rust and verdigris that weighed heavily in her hand.

Arn took it from her, and rubbed away some of the corroded crust. He snorted softly. 'It is . . . It *was* a gun. A small weapon of sorts.'

Vidarr took the gun and held it out, sighting along the barrel. 'Ah yes – the pistol. I believe it expels a metallic pellet faster than the eye can see, which could penetrate any armour known to Wolfen-kind. A small weapon, but one with formidable power.' He registered Arn's surprise.

'As I said, Arnoddr-Sigarr, I have studied these objects and scraps of history my entire life. I know what they are, and where they are, but unfortunately how they could ever work is still a mystery to me.' He held the gun out to Arn. 'Perhaps that is where we can help each other?'

Eilif snatched the pistol and brandished it like a club. 'Imagine if we had some of these – the Lygon would be sent straight to Hellheim in a blink!'

'Does it help you?' Vidarr folded his bony arms into his robe.

Arn looked around. 'Sort of. It tells me that my people were here, but at a different time. And now they're gone – at least, from this part of the world, as far as we know . . .'

Vidarr nodded slowly. 'It's true that the dark lands hold their own secrets, and adventurers who have entered those realms tell of all manner of strange beasts living there, but . . .'

Arn stepped closer. 'But?'

'But nothing. Legends upon myths upon tales. You must realise that you are the last of your kind, Arnoddr-Sigarr.'

Arn turned away, feeling deflated. Balthazar placed a hand on his shoulder. 'I'm sorry, Arn, but *we're* glad you're here. Tell us what we're looking for.'

Arn realised that he didn't really know. He'd probably recognise it if he saw it, but he needed their help as well if he was going to make any headway.

'Something with writing on it, I guess. If it looks interesting, set it aside in a pile, and I can look it over.' He picked up what appeared to be the handle of a cutlass, its blade long since disintegrated. 'Are the artefacts organised in any way?' It didn't look to Arn as though they were.

'Yes. This room contains all the most modern pieces. Everything you see here comes from the periods you call the twentieth and twenty-first centuries. After that, there is nothing. But for before that . . .' He pointed down a dark tunnel. '. . . We will need to go to another chamber to look at the eighteenth and nineteenth century items. And then—'

'Wait.' Arn stared in alarm at the old archivist. 'The twenty-first century is the last era of my kind that you've come across? But that's my era! Is that when we were wiped out?'

Balthazar shrugged. 'Or departed. Remember the legends, Arnoddr.'

Arn frowned. A memory was surfacing – Edward, or was it Beescomb or Dr. Harper, talking about the possible dangers of using the accelerator

... A disquieting thought bubbled up in his brain, but he tried to push it down, squeezing his eyes shut. Once again, he heard the mocking whisper that had tormented him on his trek through the wastelands. *Was it you? Was it your fault? Did you kill them all when you fell through the wormhole?*

'Here.' Balthazar pulled back some dusty oilskins to reveal several wooden chests that were as large as bathtubs. He grabbed the metal lock of one of them, but it fell to red dust in his hands. Wiping the residue from his fingers, he grabbed the lid and swung it back – instead of opening smoothly, the lid crashed to the floor as its hinges broke apart. 'Oops.'

'Don't know your own strength, counsellor,' Eilif laughed, kneeling beside the chest.

Inside were individually wrapped packages, all of varying shapes and sizes. Balthazar picked one up and unwrapped it, revealing a book with a cover made of simple boards. Arn leaned over him holding the torch.

Balthazar's hands shook slightly as he opened the book, which immediately began to disintegrate. He cursed under his breath.

Vidarr grabbed his wrist. 'Take care; the air in the archives preserves most things for many millennium. But as soon as light, heat or shaking hands touch them, they immediately show their age.' He pulled a blade from its sheath on his belt and used it to lift several of the pages at once.

Arn and Eilif crowded in to look over his shoulder. Arn lifted his torch a little higher. 'Looks like a diary.'

Tight cursive writing filled the page. Arn read what he could make out.

'Something, something ... Okay, here we go. *The town has been sealed off. No one knows anything, not even Daddy. The government has stopped anyone saying anything on the news, and I can see soldiers on every corner.*' Arn skipped a few faded lines. '*The sky is all wrong. I'm scared.*'

'I'm scared,' Eilif repeated. 'Scared of what – the sky?'

Arn looked at the numbers in the upper right-hand corner of the page. It was dated just a few months after he had left. If the book was found close by, then something happened right in his old neighborhood – maybe even started there. He thought of Fermilab again and the accident. Once more the voice tried to whisper its mocking torments into his mind. He shut it out.

He tried to read further, but even as he watched he saw the words disappear. The light, heat, or perhaps the steam of their breath was lifting the ancient ink right off the pages.

'Turn it over, quick.'

Vidarr used his blade to lift and turn another of the pages. The next was only half full and, as before, the words started to fade. Arn read quickly.

'The soldiers have told us we all need to go to the shelters now, but I don't know how we can, because the car won't work, and neither will anything else. Daddy says it's because there's a magnetic disturbance close by. The sky is getting worse – it's dark purple and full of lightning, and it looks like a giant tornado is growing over the science base. It's sucking the clouds into its centre, and they're going down into the base somewhere. I have to hurry, but I don't know what to take. It's so windy outside that I think we'll all get blown over anyway. I don't want to go out there – I just saw a tree get pulled down, and it's sliding down the street towards the tornado thing at the base.'

The words faded away, and Arn urged Vidarr to quickly flip to the next page. There was one final entry.

'Daddy says I can't take my diary, but I can wrap it carefully and place it in the cellar. I can get it when we return. And hey, if you're reading this, don't steal it, or even read it!!!'

Like magic, the words faded, faded, and then the entire book melted into a pile of powder. It was as if the small diary had waited countless millennia to give up its message, and now its soul had been released.

Eilif stuck her finger in the dust and lifted her hand to stare at the powder as if looking for the lost words. She rubbed her finger and thumb together. 'They never came back . . .'

Arn kept looking at the pile of dust, imagining the weird tornado sucking everything into the base, which he assumed had to be Fermilab. He backed up a step, feeling a little nauseous.

'Let's see what else we can find.'

*****

The hours passed rapidly. They searched most of the cavern, finding little more of interest to Arn, but in the process managed to turn a lot of the items to dust. Eilif and Balthazar kept up a continual volley of questions about everything they pulled free – in-line skate boots without wheels, broken beer bottles, a dented aluminum baseball bat that Eilif scoffed at because she thought it was a weapon, a set of false teeth. Balthazar held up the teeth and grimaced.

Arn sat down wearily and folded his arms. Again, there was something nagging at him, and when Vidarr pulled the remains of a doll from another pile of debris, it hit him: *Bones. Where are the remains of the billions of people?*

Arn got to his feet and walked over to where Vidarr was holding up to the light a sealed bottle, shaking it to see what effect it had on the contents.

'Have you ever found any skeletons?'

Vidarr nodded. 'Sometimes, but they are in the older caves. We come across the stones that you used to place on top of your dead – things like crosses, and Man-kind with wings. Cemeteries, I think you called them.'

Arn shook his head. 'No, not the already dead and buried bodies. I mean the ones who disappeared – who flew away. I mean, it's not as if that tornado over Fermilab could have whisked away seven billion people . . .' He sunk down onto the ground, exhausted.

Eilif sat next to him, patting his knee. 'I don't know if I'd want to see the remains of all my people as nothing more than piles of bones.' She reached over and grabbed his hand and squeezed it, looking into his face. 'What is a Fermilab?'

'It's where I came from,' Arn said wearily. 'And it's somewhere I need to try and get back to.' He thought for a moment, trying to decide whether that was actually true. Finally, he made up his mind. 'Vidarr, do you have any maps? Can you show me where the gauntlet and lightning bolts were seen? I have no idea where I am now, but I should be able to plot my path back to the lab from there.'

The ancient archivist nodded. 'Yes, I think I can show you exactly where the iron doors were seen. I also . . .' He stopped and stared up into the ceiling. In another moment, they all heard it – a voice calling them.

Vidarr made a small sound of delight in his throat. 'Two visits in twenty years – this is strange. Well, we have been down here now most of the day, and I need my dinner. Let's see who else has paid us a visit. Come.'

*****

A tall, thin Wolfen bowed as they approached – Arn came last, lost in dark thoughts, and he only heard the Wolfen's voice when the latter addressed him directly.

'The king requests your presence, Arnoddr-Sigarr.'

Arn frowned and nodded. 'Okay, we'll just have some . . .'

'It is a matter of urgency.'

Eilif took Arn by the elbow. 'I'll come too.'

'Forgive me, princess.' The messenger bowed again. 'King Grimvaldr requires an audience with the Man-kind . . . alone. He asks that you grant them some privacy.' The Wolfen kept his head bowed, and Arn wondered what would happen if Eilif decided to disobey.

She eyed the tall warrior for a few moments, before putting her nose in the air. 'I *will* come – but I'll wait outside for the king to finish. It can't be anything more than another boring talk about the Slinker encampments.'

'Thank you, princess.' The messenger sounded relieved. 'I'll be outside; please hurry, sir.' He pushed his way out through the heavy doors.

Arn turned to Eilif. 'Maybe if I'm lucky, I'll get to swallow more fleet beetles.' He chuckled and nudged her.

She turned, her silver blue eyes flashing. 'There will be no more secret missions for you, Arnoddr. Not without telling me. Promise.'

Arn was taken aback by her anger. 'Huh? Of course . . .'

'It is said that the Panterran have more than one life. But I can tell you, Wolfen do not. I'm not sure about Man-kind, but you have escaped death twice now.' She stared hard into his eyes. 'I will not lose you.'

'Okay, okay – calm down. I'll tell you if it's anything important.'

Vidarr cleared his throat. Under the small archivist's arm was a sheet of rolled parchment.

'Before you leave.' He cleared a space on the table and unfurled the sheet. 'See here – this mark is the centre of our kingdom, where we stand now.' He pointed with his stick of charcoal at a small area marked with a wolf's head crest. Then he pointed to the far side of the map, where the detail and place names were sparser. 'The beginning of the dark lands, the area you seek.'

Arn could see that the area Vidarr indicated was past a mountain range, and across an enormous lake. In the other direction was an expanse of featureless yellow and brown – the *wastelands* he had trekked across.

Vidarr looked up at Arn. 'A long and dangerous trip, young Man-kind.'

Arn nodded with some resignation. He traced the edges of the lake with his finger. 'Are there many Wolfen towns by the lake? Maybe we can borrow a boat.'

'There are some outposts, but none by the lake. It would be wise to give the waters a wide berth.'

'*Huh* – why?'

'Because of what lives in the lake.'

Arn rolled his eyes. 'Oh, great. Does every lake, forest and desert have things that eat people . . . and Wolfen?' He sighed and was about to turn away, but Vidarr snagged his arm.

'You have a good spirit, Man-kind. And I am glad that in my long life, I have had a chance to meet one of you before I pass on to Valhalla. But there is much you don't know about this world. It is true that the surface holds many dangers, but below the surface, below the dark waters, and deep in the dank caverns, there are things that shun the light. Things that Wolfen and even Panterran never mention.' He released Arn's arm. 'What is found, cannot be unfound.' Vidarr stared up into Arn's face. 'Promise that you will never travel into the earth below fifty longs.'

Arn did a quick calculation – a *long* was the basic Canite unit of measure, and roughly equated to about a foot and a half. So fifty longs was about seventy five feet. But the military base would surely stretch deeper than that . . .

Vidarr must have seen the indecision on his face. 'At least stay in light the entire time. Deep in the dark earth, there are things that have crawled up from Hellheim itself. Maybe they were surface dwellers once . . . but no more.'

'Sir.' The Wolfen messenger poked his head in through the heavy doors. Vidarr rolled the map, and pressed it into Arn's hand.

'May Odin protect you, *Master Arnold Singer.*' Vidarr stepped back and ambled slowly to the rear of the large room. Arn thought he glimpsed the ghost of a smile on the old archivist's lips as he melted into the gloom.

Chapter 38

The Forges Of The Enemy

It was dark outside when the Wolfen messenger led them through the narrow laneways, up onto a small stone bridge over a river that ran through the castle grounds. The river flowed deep and swift, and provided much of the drinking water for the castle inhabitants.

The small party had to stand aside as dozens of Wolfen warriors ran past carrying shovels and picks. 'Preparations,' Balthazar explained grimly.

The warriors rushed towards the main gate, and then out onto the plains in front of the castle. In the distance, Arn could make out a glow on the horizon. He frowned and turned to Balthazar. 'Wrong place for the sun to set . . . Looks more like a forest fire.'

Balthazar's face grew dark. 'Hundreds, thousands of fires, I'm afraid. It is the Panterran. Listen.'

Arn concentrated, and could hear a faint, rhythmic *clunk-clang* of something heavy and metallic being smashed together.

'What is it?' He looked to Balthazar, but it was the tall, thin messenger who answered.

'The forges of the enemy. They are making weapons in readiness for their attack.'

The Wolfen, too, were preparing themselves. Some of the castle's smaller gates had already been closed, and masons worked to brick them up. The main gates were reinforced with crisscrossed wooden beams, locked together with massive iron studs. When it came time to close them, a metal bolt as thick as Arn's leg would be threaded through several large iron rings.

'Could they lay siege to the castle and starve us out?'

Balthazar chimed in. 'Doubtful. We have plenty of supplies, and we also have the river. Though we can't stand the flesh of fish, we can survive on it. Also, as the far Wolfen join us, we will grow stronger while, hopefully, the enemy weakens.'

Arn looked down into the water. The river was deep and flashes of silver glinted in its depths. It rushed beneath them, and disappeared through an arched tunnel into the ground.

Anticipating Arn's next question, Balthazar pointed to where the water flowed into the tunnel. 'The river travels underground, and we have placed a gate across the tunnel. Have no fear: no Panterran will be sneaking up on us. Besides, they can't stand water.'

Arn nodded, watching the river as it swirled away into the darkness.

*****

Once again Arn found himself seated before the sealed doors of the king's main hall. He and Eilif sat together on a polished wooden bench, and Arn rested his elbows on his knees and his chin on his hands. He looked across at Eilif's face – she seemed calm, but her breathing was rapid.

'Are you afraid?'

The silver blue eyes turned to him. 'Afraid?' She seemed to think for a moment. 'Of dying? No. Of living, yes, if it meant a lifetime of Panterran oppression.'

Arn starred at her for a few seconds, wondering at the depths of her people's desire for freedom. He knew there were always things worth fighting for . . . and dying for – his own heritage had taught him that. He rubbed his face and then ran his fingers up through his long hair.

She put her hand on his shoulder, and shrugged. 'Perhaps the Panterran were created to provide some sort of balance in the world – light against dark, good to bad, peace and war. She sighed and sat back. 'Perhaps we are not supposed to know peace. Perhaps, from time to time, we Wolfen need war to remind us of where it was we came from – born of pain and fire. I think that ruling a land is not a right, and it must be fought for every single day. My father taught me that.' She turned to him. 'Did your people know peace, Arn?'

Arn thought for a moment before answering. 'Mostly, but there was always conflict. We had world wars, and small wars, but we always wanted peace. We all lived in the hope that one day war would be a thing of the past.'

'You had no Panterran, or Lygon, or even Boarex. Who did you fight?'

Arn snorted. 'Other humans. Different countries – sometimes even within our own country.'

She frowned in confusion. 'You fought other Man-kind – why? You would have been the same. Did you want to eat each other, or make slaves from your brothers? Did you not have shared dreams and goals and a common lore?'

'No and no, we were a fractured race. I guess you could say, we were still evolving.'

'Ha, it sounds like you were more warlike than the Wolfen or Panterran. You must have been fearsome warriors.'

Arn sighed and nodded. 'Yes, but the problem was, we humans became very good at war – too good.'

Eilif screwed up her brow in confusion, and was about to say something else when the huge double doors pulled inwards. Vulpernix appeared, and with his single eye, looked from Arn to Eilif and then back again, before bowing slightly and motioning with his hand for Arn to enter.

Eilif got to her feet, but Vulpernix stopped her. Instead she mouthed something he couldn't make out, which Arn assumed was a wish for good luck. Vulpernix watched Arn enter, but didn't follow, and pulled the heavy door shut, leaving him alone in the large hall.

*****

The heavy doors closed shut behind him.

Arn stood alone in the large hall. He walked forward cautiously, his footsteps sounding heavy on the stones and echoing in the high-ceilinged room. The last time he had been here by himself . . . He just hoped that if the king was going to ask anything else of him, it didn't involve eating insects.

It didn't bode well that the hall was as dark as it had been the last time. Arn was beginning to wonder whether he really was alone in the room, when a slight scrape of a heel on the stones drew his eyes to one of the windows. He could make out a large figure leaning against the sill, and looking out into the dark night – a dark night with a rim of red on the horizon.

The figure spoke without turning. 'Not long now. I would wish for more time, but there will be none given.' He raised one large fist and pounded it onto the sill. 'We need hold them for only a few days! Just until the Wolfen arrive from the far outposts. Only then, may I dare to believe that we can defeat them.'

Arn stepped a little closer. 'But why don't you just shelter behind the walls? Surely you have a better chance of staying safe and holding them off then.'

Grimvaldr shook his head, but kept his eyes on the red horizon. 'We are Wolfen. The strength of the kingdom is not in her stone, but in her blood and flesh. We will face them in battle, eye to eye – our courage, our skill, and Odin's will, will define our victory, not our ability to cower behind brick and mortar. The walls will be our last refuge, not the first.'

'And . . . if you can't hold them?'

Grimvaldr turned and looked at him with weary eyes. 'A king may fall, but a kingdom may not. While a single Wolfen lives, then so too will Valkeryn.' He smiled. 'We *will* hold them.' He turned and stared once more at the glowing horizon. 'I must call on you again, young friend. All Wolfen must fight when the kingdom is threatened – not just because it is our duty, but because it is in our blood.'

'All?'

The king nodded. 'Male, female, old, young. All who are strong enough to wield a sword, axe or pike will heed the call. The very young, the sick and very old have already been spirited away to somewhere safe, but there is one who must also be kept safe – one who is the soul and future of this mighty kingdom.'

'You mean Grimson.'

The king nodded solemnly. 'In the short time you have been here, you have proved your courage, honour and skill – all things that are valued and needed now. Grimson must be taken from the castle and hidden. No one must know where he is . . . not even me.' He glanced at Arn again. 'The Panterran have methods of interrogation that go beyond physical torture. But they found it difficult to drag secrets from *your* mind, a *human* mind. It is enough for me.'

Arn remembered the claws digging into his mind, and how the old sorcerer had been unable to clearly read his thoughts. But this thing the king asked, the responsibility of it, made him feel overwhelmed.

'What about Sorenson? He is better able to find his way through the forests. And besides, I want to fight as well.'

'Yes, I hear that your skills grow rapidly, and I would have valued your sword. But after Strom fell to the Panterran, it would take a brave Wolfen indeed to tell Sorenson that he is not to fight them, and gain an opportunity to avenge his brother.'

'And Eilif?'

'Will fight at my side.'

'But . . . I was planning to take her with me to—'

'To the dark lands. Arnoddr, you could not stop her from entering the battle even if you wanted to. But you must take Grimson there; it might be the one place the Panterran will not follow. But I do not want to know any more, in case . . .'

Grimvaldr tugged a ring from his finger and held it out to Arn – a large silver wolf's head, its ruby red eyes glowing. 'There is not a Wolfen on this world who will not recognise this ring. Please . . . take it, and you will have passage anywhere. And when the time is right, give it to Grimson.'

Arn looked at the ring, then reached into his pocket and pulled forth the ring that Eilif had given him when they first met. 'There is no need, sire. I have one.'

Grimvaldr's stared down at the small piece of jewelled silver. 'I should have known. What did the princess tell you when she gave you this?'

'That it would keep me safe – as you have told me.'

'And that is all?' The king stared at him, hard.

Arn just nodded, feeling a little confused.

Grimvaldr turned away. 'It is of no consequence. There are other more pressing matters. Tell Grimson . . .' He searched out the words. 'Tell him . . . any Wolfen, servant or king, would be proud to call him his son. Tell him . . . I will always be looking over him.'

Arn nodded even though the king couldn't see him. 'I'll keep him safe.' He turned to leave, then stopped, silently regarding the large figure, silhouetted against the glowing red horizon.

'My strength to you, great king Grimvaldr.'

*****

Eilif sprang to her feet as Arn slipped quietly back out into the corridor. No sooner had he closed the doors, when an eerie howl echoed behind them. Concerned, she tried to push past him, but he grabbed and held her fast.

'He is sad about the coming battle. He just needs . . . some time alone.'

He felt her muscles relax, but couldn't bear to look her in the eye. Keeping his eyes fixed on the ground, he spoke softly as he led her away from the door. 'You're going to fight, then?'

She squeezed his hand tightly. 'Oh yes! I can't wait for the battle to begin. Will you fight by my side, Arnoddr?'

Arn frowned. 'What if you're killed?'

'I will acquit myself honourably – if I die, many Panterran will die first. Besides, all Wolfen have no greater wish than to die in love, or in battle.' Her voice softened. 'I can do both.'

Arn was horrified, but she went on. 'After all, we all die, and is it better to die old and sick, or to cross the rainbow bridge to Valhalla as a young warrior?' She was almost skipping like a child.

'But we could . . .' He stopped, remembering the wishes of the king.

'Together we will make the Panterran quake in fear. They will sing about us for a hundred generations – the great Arnoddr and Princess Eilif.' She kissed his cheek. 'I need to prepare my battledress and weapons. The war should be upon us by morning – I shan't be able to sleep tonight.'

Arn watched her skip down the stone corridor.

And neither will I, he thought dismally.

Chapter 39

Reconnaissance Mission-1

Colonel Marion Briggs had taken over the command centre, and now walked up the line of five rod-straight men and one woman. All wore green fatigues and cradled M16s. The six elite Green Berets stood like statues as she gave them their final briefing.

'This is a reconnaissance mission: take a look around, get me some intelligence on the terrain. If you see the kid, grab him. But I also want . . . samples.' She paused. 'The indigenous inhabitants are approximately human-sized, and have little more than knives and swords. But I don't need to tell you not to underestimate them – if you're threatened, shoot to kill.'

Briggs stopped and stared at Albert Harper, her expression hard enough to break stone, her voice lethally soft.

'Once we confirm that my team has survived the jump, your man will be going through.' Her eyes challenged him to object. When he didn't, she turned to look at the bank of screens beside him; each of the six small displays showed an image of her – taken from the corresponding cameras mounted on the helmets of each of the soldiers.

The vision was clear – her team was ready. Satisfied, she shouted, 'Good to go, ladies and gentlemen. Let's do this.'

*****

The Panterran camps were advancing on the castle. Trees had been felled for their fires and war machines, and huge swathes of forest had been flattened as the main army moved forward like a living mass of fangs and steel. Behind them was a wasteland, crushed and burned to ashes.

Advance parties of Panterran and Lygon scouted ahead. Goranx led his party of ten Lygon up a hill, atop which stood a single tree. At close to nine feet in height and weighing more than a thousand pounds in his battle armour, he was a fearsome sight, even to his own kind.

He held up one large, clawed hand, signalling for the patrol to halt. He could sense something – a vibration deep in his gut. In the dark, his eyesight was exceptional, but he could find no cause for this strange feeling anywhere on the barren hilltop.

But there was something coming. His giant warriors, sensing it too, began to breathe heavily. Six-inch claws extended from the ends of their thick fingers, tightly gripping axes and clubs that were nearly as long as most creatures they battled.

Then, from out of the dark, six strangely dressed bipeds crested the hill, pointing small metal sticks, the other ends of which they cradled against their shoulders. One of the Lygon shifted, his huge belt clanking at his waist. The creatures froze in surprise.

'Man-kind,' Goranx muttered.

One of the creatures fled back down the other side of the hill. Goranx roared at the sudden movement, drawing back an arm thicker than a tree, and flung his club at them.

The humans screamed in a tongue he couldn't understand, and then a noise like thunder roared from the ends of the small sticks they carried.

Goranx responded with his own roaring scream as he felt the small projectiles bounce off the plates of his armour, or embed themselves in his thick hide. The Lygon reacted in kind: they charged.

*****

Captain Chris Masters was first through the *rift*, as they were now calling it. The sensation was unpleasant and disorientating, but not debilitating. Jumping from a bright white laboratory room, to the darkness of the dank tunnel . . . It was a surreal experience, to say the least.

The team moved quickly to the hole in the ceiling, and Masters pushed his M16 up over his shoulder. He pulled a long-barrelled hand gun from his belt and aimed it up the shaft, firing a tungsten-tipped bolt straight up, which embedded itself in the rock wall, a rope trailing behind the spike. He tugged it once to see if it held, and then turned.

'Fuentes, you're up first with Doctor Takada. Jenson, you're last. Let's move, people.'

In a few minutes they had pulled themselves up out of the deep shaft. Masters checked his compass, and was relieved to see it still worked.

Fuentes offered Takada some water, which he refused. 'Take it, Doctor,' she said. 'This party has only just started.'

Masters motioned towards the sterile landscape and led them out in a jog. It would be many hours until they saw the lines of trees signalling the start of the forest.

Time passed, along with the miles of sand beneath their boots. Night had already begun to fall when the horizon rose up into an enormous green, buzzing, slithering presence around them. The forest dwarfed anything Masters was used to back home, and though this was a recon mission, personally he would be happy with just locating Singer and evac'ing immediately. He'd leave the sightseeing for the next guys.

He heard a soft wheezing behind him, and turned to see Takada bent over with his hands on his knees – the man had done well, but desperately needed to catch his breath. 'Let's get to the top of this hill for a look-see, and then we can take five. Okay there, Doc?'

Takada nodded.

'Good man.'

They moved to the top of the small hill with a large tree at its apex. Masters raised his hand and they slowed.

Fuentes sniffed. '*Phew*, what the hell is that smell?'

Takada straightened and frowned. 'Like ammonia – cauxin, I believe – it's in cat urine.'

Masters still had his hand up, and now made a fist – the team stopped. Watery clouds passed across the moon and then cleared, bathing the hillside in a silvery glow.

Fuentes looked up. 'That is one big mother of a moon.'

The trees shifted slightly. Masters sucked in a breath. There was a metallic *clank*. They froze.

'Holy Christ – tighten up, people. We got company.'

The giant creatures were armed with clubs and axes, and armoured with what looked like thick metal sheeting – way too heavy for even a large man to carry.

Masters cursed – he and his team had packed standard rounds – not tipped for armour piercing.

So much for human-sized inhabitants, he thought. *Typical crap military intel.*

No one moved, or even breathed. The large, luminous green eyes locked onto them, and some of the ogreish creatures growled.

Chris Masters, captain in the Green Berets, had thought he was afraid of nothing.

'Oh God, oh God, oh God.' It was Jenson, behind him. 'We need to evac, now.'

'Hold your ground!' Masters hissed. 'Don't move a muscle . . .'

Jenson ignored the order and sprinted back down the hill.

The sudden movement caught them all off guard, and the lead creature opened its mouth wide enough to fit Masters' entire head inside. Teeth like a bear trap flashed in the moonlight as the thing roared. The noise was so loud, it chilled Masters and his team down to their very marrow.

Something struck Fuentes, who was standing beside him, and she jerked backwards with a grunt and a sound of crunching bone. Fear shot up Masters' spine, but his training took over.

'Engage! Engage!' The four remaining M16s sprayed streams of lead.

*****

Colonel Briggs watched with cool detachment. One by one, the cameras were destroyed by things that could have torn themselves from the pages of a horror story. In the darkness, their features were unclear, but what *was* clear was how little effect the M16s had on these massive, fur-covered creatures.

She couldn't tell what happened to the scientist, as he hadn't been wearing a helmet-cam. But when Fuentes was taken out, he had been standing there with his hands to his head, and his face ripped with shock. She doubted there'd be any need for a rescue mission.

She looked across at Jenson who had come back through the rift, and her mouth curled slightly in distaste. He was still shivering uncontrollably. *Some Green Beret*, she thought.

She turned to her military aide. 'Three things: one, get an armed guard on that rift – heavy-calibre weapons – I don't want anything paying us a visit unannounced.' The aide nodded. Briggs jerked her thumb over her shoulder. 'Two, get that pathetic, gutless worm out of my sight . . . and out of my army.'

Jenson looked up for a second, then buried his head in his hands and sobbed.

'And three, I want two squads of Delta Force, and some bigger ordinance. And make sure you get Samson on the team.' She half saluted, dismissing the aide. Her lip curled slightly as she rewound the image loop. 'We'll shown 'em we've got our own monsters.'

Briggs gritted her teeth and spoke at the screen. 'Military Rule-1 – when pushed, push back harder. *Brigg's Rule-1* – if you want something done right, do it yourself. This time I'm going too.' She looked across to where Harper knelt beside the shivering soldier. 'I mean, *we're* going too.'

She smiled at the chaos and destruction on the screen. 'Thank you. Now I have no reason to play fair with you at all. I'm coming, and I *do not* come in peace.'

Chapter 40

At This Most Dire Time

Bergborr entered the gatekeeper's armoury, and called loudly to the key master. A short, brutish-looking Wolfen ambled out, covered in soot and wearing a leather apron. His hands were scarred from working with fire, hammer and steel his entire life.

'Drengi.' Bergborr bowed slightly. 'I've come to conduct an audit of the castle keys. All must be double checked and secured.'

The ironmonger stared hard at Bergborr. 'Where is the order? I have already secured all vital keys in the heavy vault.'

Bergborr raised his voice slightly. 'I am charged by Grimvaldr himself.'

Drengi lifted a rag and wiped his hands. 'I will need to see—'

Bergborr exploded in rage and roared into the squat Wolfen's face, 'By Odin's wrath, we are at the moment of war, and you want a bureaucrat's signature? Retrieve the keys for audit *immediately*. Or at this most dire time, do you want Grimvaldr himself to come and beg you personally?'

The squat key master grunted, nodded, and disappeared for several moments, returning with several wooden boxes. He opened one lid after the other, displaying large ancient keys, almost identical except for engraved Wolfen words on their shafts, which identified what they opened and where.

Bergborr ran his gaze over them, and then pointed to the boxes. 'Count them off.'

Drengi nodded again, and performed a quick audit, knowing each key by heart, having kept them in order and in good care. He went from one box to the next, and as he moved down the line, Bergborr placed his hand in the boxes, lifting out one key after the other and turning it over in his hand. He stopped and held one up to the light, noting its deeply etched lettering.

'Please sir, keep them in good order, in the event we need to reach for one, or all, in haste.'

Bergborr placed his hand back in the box. 'Of course. Carry on; I have other tasks to complete before this day is ended.'

Drengi continued his count.

Bergborr had replaced *a* key in the box, but he had used his other hand, and this key had no lettering on it.

*****

Arn stuffed clothing into a leather bag, leaving room for some food. Eilif had baked him a loaf of bread, and he took a small bite. It was dry and tough, but he savoured the yeasty flavour and smiled at her effort. He next packed spare boots and a flask of water.

He had dressed in a leather jerkin and pants, boots and a vest. He looped a belt around his waist, from which he hung his dagger and several pouches. Lastly, he tucked his pocketknife inside one of the pouches.

He lifted the sword he had been given by Sorenson and half pulled it from its scabbard, admiring the gleam and sharpness of the blade. He laid it on the bed. Next, he picked up a heavy cloak, trying to decide whether he would take it – they'd need to travel light and fast. Once outside the castle walls, the son of Grimvaldr would be fleeing for his life. Still, the targets on their backs would hardly keep them warm . . .

He held onto the cloak as he walked to the window, and looked out. Within the walls of the castle, thousands of Wolfen were forming up into ranks. They were orderly and without panic. They made him feel both sad and proud.

But from his vantage point, he could see beyond the walls, where smoke was curling high into the air over the ruined earth. The smudges of light he had seen on the horizon, from the distant forges of countless Panterran, had now become thousands upon thousands of surging bodies.

In among these, he could make out larger animals – the gravilents, he presumed. The whole scene reminded him of the carcass of a dead animal being consumed by maggots and carrion beetles.

Arn breathed slowly, closing his eyes and trying to blank it all out. But the whining and hissing of the approaching army of merciless creatures made his blood run cold.

Then another sound, behind him, made him jump.

Eilif stood in the doorway, regarding him curiously. She stepped inside and closed the door behind her. The sheen of her polished metal armour was startling in the candlelight. The raised crest of the red-eyed wolf adorned her breastplate, and her silver war helmet was pushed back, its wolf-faced visor snarling at the ceiling. He remembered something similar when he had first seen Grimvaldr on the hill. It seemed so long ago.

She walked forward slowly with her hand on the hilt of the sword. The armour moved perfectly with her, the chain mail fitting snugly to her body. She looked athletic, and fearsome, and . . . beautiful.

Eilif looked him up and down. 'Why aren't you ready?'

Arn threw the cloak over his bag, and sat down on the bed.

Eilif frowned and moved a few paces closer. 'Do . . . Do you need help getting into your armour? I can do that for you.'

Arn shook his head. 'I'm okay. I can do it. Just had a few things to prepare, and I guess I got distracted. Still a lot on my mind right now.'

'Is it the homesickness spell that ails you again?'

He smiled at her. 'Sure, a bit.'

'Father said you cannot fight by his side, as he needs his generals close. I'm sorry.' She looked away for a moment, then turned back quickly. 'But when the battle starts, I'll look for you. I want you by *my* side. Fighting together, it will be glorious – no one shall best us.'

He took her hand. 'It doesn't matter.'

'But I want to look out for you.'

Arn was filled with such a sadness then, it threatened to well up inside him and pour forth in a wave of tears and confession. This amazing creature – this amazing race of beings – all could be gone in another day.

An old quote from his literature class floated into his mind, and before he knew what he was doing he spoke it aloud:

'Every *parting* is a form of death . . .' He paused as his voice threatened to crack. She seemed spellbound by the words, and he managed to finish. '. . . As every *reunion* is a type of heaven.'

She placed her hand over his. 'That's beautiful. What is a heaven?'

He smiled again, and swallowed the lump in his throat. 'It's our Valhalla. A place of peace where all good spirits go.'

She nodded. 'I would go to heaven, because I am a good warrior. So will you.' She drew her sword and raised it.

'Death to the Panterran! Death to the Lygon! And long live Grimvaldr and all the mighty Wolfen!' Her eyes glowed with excitement. Then she sheathed the sword and headed for the door.

'I'll find you on the field.' She paused as if waiting for something, and Arn rose from the bed, meaning to shake her hand, or hug her, or something.

As he drew close, he saw her lips just curve into a shy smile, and the inside of her ears darken to a shade of pink. She grabbed hold of him, and pulled him to her. He felt her face against his cheek as she hugged him hard. She pulled back, and made a fist over her chest as though grabbing something.

'My heart . . .' She moved her closed fist from her chest to his, and opened the fingers. '. . . Is now your heart.'

She quickly pressed her lips to his for a second, and then spun away without another word.

Arn watched her go.

Chapter 41

Not All Can Be Honourable

The figure moved silently along the cobbled street. It wore no armour or clothing of any type, and if it had stepped out of the shadows, the moonlight would have shone on a coat of dark fur.

As it made its way to the edge of the stone channel that carried the stream through the castle, another, older figure emerged from the gloom.

'A Wolfen without clothes – either you go to meet your love, or you do not wish to have your family crest seen by others. Which is it, young Wolfen?' The older figure stepped closer. 'Ah, Bergborr of the house of Bergrinne.'

Bergborr straightened, but kept one hand behind his back. 'Vulpernix.' He bowed. 'Lurking in the shadows could get one into trouble.'

'Only with those who look for trouble. You haven't answered my question.'

Bergborr nodded. 'I go to meet Eilif.'

Vulpernix laughed softly. 'She would rather marry a Lygon than be in your embrace.' The old Wolfen lowered one of his hands to the hilt of his sword. 'If I was a traitor, I might be tempted to give an enemy a way into the castle. Perhaps . . . by unlocking the river gates?'

Bergborr bared his teeth and growled. 'You dare accuse me? It is your own plan of which you speak. Besides, Panterran will never go near water.'

Vulpernix nodded. 'That is very true. But unfortunately for the kingdom, we are not just at war with the Panterran. Everyone knows the Lygon have no such fear of water. You are cunning, Bergborr – but do not take me for a fool.'

Vulpernix drew his sword, pointing at the chest of the younger Wolfen. 'I have been watching you for days. You slip out to meet with the Panterran. I know the secret meeting places, for I have used them too. I know those creatures better than you, young fool. I feed them useless information, and watch for it to be used to the detriment of their accursed Panterran queen. You also deliver them Wolfen knowledge, but it is solely for your own betterment, and to the detriment of our great race.'

Bergborr lifted his chin. 'Not all Panterran are as you believe, there are . . .'

Vulpernix suddenly leaned forward. 'Fool! What is it you think you will accomplish? They don't make deals with Wolfen – they use them, and then crush them, as they surely will do to you . . . and the Princess Eilif.'

Bergborr fell to his knees and reached out his hand, beseeching the older Wolfen noble, 'You are right, and I am a fool, and perhaps made more so by love. Do you know what it is like to love another, who barely knows you exist? What it is like to be the perfect suitor, but then be scrubbed from your love's consciousness by a creature that shouldn't even exist? If I am a fool for love, then I am one rendered deaf, dumb and blind to everything and anything but that love.' He shook his head. 'Perhaps it is a sickness.'

Bergborr beat his chest with one hand, punishing himself, over and over, his face a mask of humiliation and sorrow. Vulpernix kept his sword up, the point only a few hand spans from the young Wolfen's torso.

'Love makes fools of some, and heroes of others. Get up.' Vulpernix watched as the young Wolfen's hand beat his chest again harder, and he made a sound of disgust deep in his throat, at the dark Wolfen's lack of dignity. He was about to order Bergborr to his feet again when on the next motion, instead of the hand striking his body, it shot out and grabbed the tip of the sword. The razor sharp edge would have bitten deeply, but the weapon was locked, only momentarily, in a steel grip.

It was enough.

Bergborr gritted his teeth from the pain, and stared into the old Woflen's eyes as he spoke. 'But if there is a chance for that love, then would I not be a greater fool not risking all for it?' He lunged forward, swinging his other arm up from behind his back, the full length of the metal key protruding between his knuckles. The blow struck Vulpernix in the neck, piercing deeply, and crushing his windpipe so that no sound other than a strangled hiss fell from his gaping mouth.

Bergborr whispered into Vulpernix's ear, 'What do I hope to accomplish, old fool? I do not just hope; I *will* accomplish Grimvaldr's downfall, and in his place will rise King Bergborr, with Queen Eilif at my side. The king believes the Panterran can never be made into our allies – but he's wrong. I've already done it.'

Vulpernix looked up to the sky, to the tiny pinpoints of light, which he knew to be the candlelight from Valhalla's golden hallways. He'd be there soon.

A final thought drifted across his mind as his single clear eye began to cloud over. *Sorry, my king. I have failed you. May Odin give you luck and strength on the morrow.*

Vulpernix sped to Valhalla.

*****

Bergborr slipped over the side of the bank, dragging the old Wolfen's body with him. He paddled silently to where the river flowed into the arched, gated tunnel. Sucking in a few deep breaths, he ducked below the surface, dragging the body with him.

The slight murmur of the river masked the sound of heavy, ancient iron gates being unlocked and forced open.

Later, Bergborr would tie a length of dark cloth to a flagpole on the highest turret of the castle – that would be *the signal*. His job would then be done.

Chapter 42

One World, One Race To Rule

Orcalion bowed deeply and crawled forward on his knees. He knew that the queen was still furious for his role in allowing the Man-kind to escape.

He looked up into the golden, slitted eyes. 'We are ready, almighty Mogahr.'

The eyes didn't blink. *'And whaat offf the Wolfen traaaitor? Did heee open the hiddeen gate into the cassstle?'*

'The sign is there. The colours of Grimvaldr have also been taken, as well the Wolfen scouts we captured. They will be put to good use.'

'And the Lygonsss – can we trussst thossse ssstuumbling bruutesss tooo hold tooogether long enough for the attackkk?'

'The Lygon want flesh – but as long as we do not bring them up too soon, we may be able to hold them until the charge is sounded. Once they charge, anything in front of them will be destroyed.'

'And wheeen theeere is no mooore Wolfen flesssh to consssume? Yesss, theen weee will deal with them alssso. One world – one race to rule it, Orcalion.'

Orcalion nodded. 'As you wish, my queen.' He tilted his head. 'I wonder: how exactly does our pet Wolfen imagine he will live to claim his prize?'

Mogahr's mouth opened, revealing the decayed remnants of her long fangs. *'We promisssed him that he and the princesss would not be killed. We promisssed him that heee would rule over the remaining Wolfen. The Lygonss will need rationss for the long marccch back to their homeland. Perhapsss our traitor can be king of the prisonersss taken for fooood.'*

Orcalion hissed out a laugh and bowed deeply. 'But they shan't meet their deaths at our hands. We Panterran *always* keep our word.' He laughed again.

Mogahr raised her head and sniffed the air. *'It will sssoon be the darkessst hour of the night – we attack then.'* Her eyes narrowed and she leaned forward. *'If you fail me, Orcalion, at thisss, the most important hour for all Panterran kind, then the Lygonss will have more than Wolfen-kind for their fooood.'*

Orcalion, cringing, got to his feet, but remained bent over. 'King Grim-valdr will fall, and Empress Mogahr will rise and reign supreme over all of this unworthy world.' He continued bowing as he hurried from the tent.

Once outside, he glided away, pausing only to cast a glare back over his shoulder. 'You will not be queen forever, old witch.' He continued mut-tering to himself as a giant figure emerged from the darkness in front of him.

The Lygon general towered nearly a head above his own kind, and dwarfed the smaller Panterran. With his battle-scarred face and ogreish physique, Goranx was a monstrous devil, to be sure. Orcalion was re-lieved that the beast fought on their side.

He looked at the newly taken heads hanging from the Lygon's belt and frowned. 'Man-kind? There are more?'

Goranx shrugged. 'Perhaps. They were good . . . Soft and sweet.'

Orcalion's eyes narrowed slyly. 'There is another in the Wolfen castle. The queen wants this one alive, but in battle things become confused . . . and lost.'

Goranx stared for a moment, as if trying to pull the hidden meaning from the small Panterran's words. His broad mouth twisted into a cruel smile.

Orcalion knew that the queen would not get everything she wanted this day.

Chapter 43

Come The Far Wolfen

Onwards they ran – females, males, young and old – all those strong enough to wield a weapon. Foam flecked at the corners of their mouths, and tongues hung from fatigue.

Some ran in full armour, some in a leather battledress that was little more than a vest and a belt with a scabbard. Small bands in their dozens joined up with others, to form groups in their hundreds. The hundreds then joined together, until a bristling, jostling horde poured down from the hills, down into the outskirts of Valkeryn.

A howl echoed through the night air – then another, and another. From one side of the hills to the other, thousands were answering the call.

Some miles ahead of them, past the forests at the very foot of the hills, the fields crawled with the slow surge of bodies pushing through the long grass. Thousands of almost silent creatures snaked their way forward, and at a designated point they fanned out.

Prisoners were brought forward; their mouths tied shut and hands bound behind their backs. Grimvaldr's colours were raised, and stakes were quickly hammered into the ground.

The prisoners were readied and then the horde sank down and waited for the coming tide of warm Wolfen bodies.

Chapter 44

The Long Night Of War

Grimvaldr watched the approaching line of fire as it devoured the far hills beyond Valkeryn. The air rang with the sound of large drums beating out their advance, and from the stamping of thousands upon thousands of feet upon the hard-packed earth.

The king now wore his full armour, and the silver shone in the moonlight. He turned to his assembled generals.

'The halls of Valhalla will be full tonight, and blessed are those who are first to make their way to sit before Odin.'

As one, the generals strucks their fists against their armour-plated chests.

'Our enemy is not like us. Where we show mercy, they are cruel. Where we hold out our hand, they clutch the assassin's blade. They have no sáál, and Hellheim waits for their twisted minds and bodies.'

In response, the generals beat their chests again.

'If a Wolfen king falls, the pack will fight on. If he falls, Valkeryn lives on. For inside every Wolfen, the spirit of Fenrir burns like the Great Fire at the beginning of all things.'

The fists were now beating continuously.

'But the Panterran – if their Queen falls, they will be like a serpent with no head. Our goal is to capture Mogahr, or take her head. Even if we fail in this, the Panterran will fall back to defend her – and give our far Wolfen warriors time to swell our ranks. The dark is their friend, so they will attack when the moon sets and before the sun rises. If they like the dark, then we will be the light.' He smiled grimly and looked slowly around the room. 'We will be Fenrir's fire with all its blessed light and heat, and we will give them war.' His voice rose, and he crushed his hand into a fist before them. 'We will give them a war to end all wars!'

Grimvaldr bared his long teeth and roared, and the Wolfen responded in kind, their roars a deafening cacophony in the large throne room.

The king held up his fist. 'Generals of the Wolfen pack, assemble your warriors. The hour is here.'

Swords were drawn and shouts for Valkeryn, Grimvaldr, and death to Mogahr echoed around the room as the Wolfen departed to prepare their troops. Grimvaldr watched them go, and waited for the heavy doors to be closed. Then he turned to the remaining figure, standing silently in the room.

Queen Freya, dressed in her own battle armour, smiled at her husband. He walked towards her and removed one of his heavy gauntlets, so he could reach out to stroke her cheek where it showed beneath her helmet.

'Freya, beautiful Queen Freya. I remember when I chased you through the castle grounds when we were both little more than younglings. You have been my blood and sáál, my fire for an eternity.'

She reached up to take his hand, and hold it against her chest. 'If this day we are to travel to Valhalla, then I have no regrets. Mighty king, you have given me everything I could have ever wished for.'

Grimvaldr reached inside a pouch at his side and drew forth a small box, which he opened to reveal a tiny painted likeness of himself, and one of Freya, Eilif and Grimson. 'Give this to our son. Send him away with the Man-kind now, before he is trapped here by the horde. I fear if these walls fall, then none will survive.'

Freya took the small pictures, looked at them for a moment, her lips turning up in a small smile. She pressed the box to her lips, as a single tear rolled down the fur on her face. 'I pray, one day he returns to take Mogahr's head . . . To take all their heads.'

Freya grabbed Grimvaldr and clung to him, rubbing her cheek against his. He held her close for a moment, before pushing her gently away.

She nodded. 'I'll see you on the field, my lord. The enemy will pay a heavy price this day.'

*****

Bergborr was the last of the Wolfen to leave the throne room. The dark warrior felt nauseous. Fear, perhaps . . . or was it guilt? He couldn't tell anymore, as things were so jumbled in his head.

He wanted to fight, and fight for Valkeryn – home to his ancestors for countless generations. But as he walked down the corridor, looking at the pictures of the kings past, he knew that his likeness would never grace the walls while Grimvaldr lived. Or for that matter, while Eilif thought she had a choice of suitor.

He grimaced at the thought of the attention she had been giving to the Man-kind. His hairlessness and short face were repulsive. It was unnatural and it was sick.

He was walking heavily down the corridor, cursing beneath his breath, when Eilif suddenly appeared in his path, making him start. She threw back her head and laughed at him, and the sound made his heart melt within his armoured chest. He had loved her since he had first seen her in the king's court, and now that she was at the cusp of being an adult female Wolfen, he wanted her even more as his life mate.

He devoured her with his eyes – her tall form, strong and lithe in her battle armour. Her eyes, that were large and shining pools of both flashing silver ice, reflected his own image back at him.

She raised her chin. 'You look like you have seen a wraith, brave Bergborr. One so large should not be so afeared, especially on the eve of a great battle.' She folded her arms and raised an eyebrow.

He laughed in return and took her hand. 'I would fear a single harsh word from you, over a thousand Lygon death warriors, my beautiful Eilif.'

Her smile evaporated, and she pulled her hand away. 'I'm no Wolfen's Eilif.'

'Of course, I just meant—'

'I'm to see the king now.' She nodded. 'Until the battle, then.'

He stepped towards her. 'Are you . . . Are you fighting close to the king? I shall look for you.'

She turned away. 'No need; I already have someone to fight by my side this day. Look to your own Wolfen brothers, Bergborr. And may Odin protect you.'

'May Odin protect us all,' he replied automatically. He bowed as she danced lightly away down the corridor.

Already have someone to fight by my side. The words burned him deeply. Any stirring of guilt he had felt earlier was swept away with the loathing he felt for the Arnodrr-Sigarr – from the moment he arrived, everything changed. And in turn, Bergborr had been forced to change his plans to suit the circumstances.

The queen of the Panterran had ordered that none were to harm the Man-kind. She now wanted him even more than she wanted Grimvaldr to fall. Bergborr shivered in anticipation. He couldn't imagine what the vile queen would do to the Arnoddr when she finally had him in her taloned grip, but it soothed his bitter heart to know it would undoubtedly be bloody.

*****

Eilif entered the throne room and was surprised to find her mother there. She walked quickly to the queen, took her hand, bowed, and then turned to her father.

'You called for me?' She looked up into his face, noting that the strong features looked slightly drawn, as though a great pain was burning inside his breast.

'Yes, Eilif. This one last time I call.' He took her hand and led her to a large throne-like chair, sitting her down and staring at her, as though collecting his thoughts. Freya came to stand beside him, and placed one hand on his shoulder.

Eilif looked up into his eyes; his solemnity was making her nervous.

At last, the king drew in a deep breath and spoke.

'Grimson will be safe.'

Eilif nodded and waited. She already assumed that Grim would be kept away from the battle. But this couldn't be why they had called her on the eve of war.

'He'll be taken to the far lands, then?' she asked.

The king smiled sadly. 'You are very perceptive. Yes, he will go to the far lands . . . and well beyond them. In fact, he is leaving now. I apologise for not allowing you your farewells. But time is not something we have to spend freely. In fact, time is something that is controlled more by our approaching enemies.'

She nodded and smiled at the queen. Freya smiled sadly in return.

What of it, Eilif wondered? The battle would be decided quickly, and when the mighty Wolfen were victorious, Grimson would be sent for, and then he and his escort . . .

The thought ended abruptly, as if it had fallen off a steep dark precipice in her mind. She turned to the king.

'Who accompanies our prince on his journey?'

Grimvaldr didn't respond.

Eilif rose slowly from the chair. Her knees shook, but she stared unwaveringly into the king's eyes.

Grimvaldr reached out for her as he murmured, 'The Arnoddr-Sigarr.'

Her breath momentarily locked in her chest, and then exploded in a howl that pierced the long throne room. She batted his hand away. 'No! He was to fight by my side. He is . . .' She balled her fists. 'There were a hundred others you could have chosen – why him?'

'There were others, but Grimson trusts him – and I trust him. He has already proven his willingness to risk all for us. Who better to protect our future, than one brave sáál from the past?'

Eilif howled again and fell to her knees. She let her head fall and closed her eyes. 'Was there no one else to go with him?'

Grimvaldr knelt down next to her. 'As you said, Eilif, I could have sent hundreds, thousands. But I believe that stealth will succeed, where force would not.' He paused, and then lifted her chin. 'You know, there is a strength in that one, the likes of which we have not seen for an eternity. He is the right choice.'

Eilif got slowly to her feet. He was right. Grimvaldr was always right.

The king tried to embrace her, but she pulled away and ran towards the doors.

'He's already gone, Eilif. He will return when the time is right, and the land is safe once again.'

'And who will keep *him* safe?' Eilif cried, pushing through the doors, leaving the king and queen standing in silence.

Perhaps he had left something for her, something telling her where they had gone? She tore through the stone corridors, her armour clanging like cymbals as she barged through doorways, bounced off walls, not slowing until she came to his room, and shouldered open the door.

'Arn, my Arn!'

The room was empty. She rushed about, searching, rifling through drawers – there was nothing. She balled her fists and squeezed her eyes shut, refusing to give her suffering a voice.

Every parting is a form of death, he had said. Now the words made sense – *that* was his message to her. Eilif sank down onto the bed, burying her face in the sheets and drawing in his scent. Through the window, the moonlight washed over her.

She lifted her head and screamed her agony.

Chapter 45

There Will Be No Saviours

The first wave of the far Wolfen burst through the trees into a large clearing. They skidded to a halt, their eyes wideneing first in disbelief, and then in triumph.

Several Wolfen elite stood waiting for them, their hands tight on their sword hilts, with bodies nobly erect, and their demeanour calm. The banners of Grimvaldr fluttered in a breeze beside them.

A roar went up from the travelling warriors, who were now piling up in the expansive clearing, dozens deep, each craning over the other, to see the armoured warriors they would soon be joining.

'Grimvaldr comes to meet us. Long live the king!' A roar went up and they rushed forward. It was only when they were within a dozen paces of the motionless warriors did they see them for what they were – caricatures of living beings. Their mouths were sewn shut, and blood leaked from under armour where they had been pierced a hundred times. In addition, the elite warriors had been lashed upright, with even their necks bound to hidden stakes, giving them a proud posture.

The far Wolfen, confused, slowed, but only for a second as a screech tore through the air, followed by the hiss of hundreds upon hundreds of arrows in flight.

By the time a warning was roared, hundreds of bodies lay twitching on the grass. The same scene was repeated along a dozen slopes.

There would be no far Wolfen joining the battle this day.

Chapter 46

To The Dark Lands

'I could have fought. I'm big enough.' Grimson trailed behind Arn as they threaded their way along the winding path. He pulled his sword free and slashed at a hanging vine.

Arn spoke over his shoulder. 'Stay quiet. There are Panterran about. And I know – I've seen you practise – you're very good. But I am on a quest, and I needed the help of a stout heart. The king said you were the best man – *ahh*, Wolfen – for the job.'

'A quest? Yes, I'm the best one for that!' Grimson sheathed his sword and ran to catch up with Arn. 'What *is* the quest?'

'It'll be long and arduous . . . and very dangerous.' Arn looked down at Grimson. 'I guess you could say, we're looking for me.'

Grimson frowned in confusion.

Arn patted him on the shoulder. 'We're looking for traces of my people. I don't believe that they all flew away one day . . . or that our spirits did. Some would have stayed; some would have hidden from whatever happened. I need to know what that was. I just need to prove I didn't cause . . .' Arn swallowed hard, but that voice in his head wouldn't be silenced. *You just need to prove it wasn't you who caused the extinction of humanity, that's all . . .*

Grimson nodded. 'I wish Eilif could have come.'

The name felt like a dagger wound. 'Me too, Grim.'

'My name's Grimson. Only Eilif is allowed to call me Grim.' The young Wolfen thought about it for a moment, and then said, 'But you can call me Grim, too, I guess.' He nodded, satisfied with his decision.

Arn didn't hear him. He stared distractedly into the distance, where Eilif stood, sword raised, facing down a horde of Lygon that pounded across the ground towards her.

'Arnoddr, did you hear me?'

Arn shrugged, not wanting to talk anymore. He felt tired and depressed.

'This quest – where will it take us? Arnoddr, this quest – where will it take us?' This time, Grimson tugged at his arm.

Arn glanced down at him and blinked, seeming almost surprised to find that he wasn't alone. He reached instinctively for Vidarr's map, folded in a pocket sewn into his vest. 'The dark lands, and you will need to help. You will need to tell me if there is anything you recognise as being dangerous. I might not see it. This is your world now, Grim.'

The young Wolfen sighed, and then nodded. 'I can do that.' He thought some more. 'The dark lands – I wish we had more Wolfen with us. I wish we had Strom with us.'

*****

Strom's head bobbed above the slavering crowd, his staring eyes towards the distant castle. Goranx stood at the front of the horde and shook his grisly trophy. Both Panterran and Lygon cheered.

Mogahr raised an arm to silence them. She looked at the pike with the Wolfen champion's head impaled upon it, and her lips parted in a grotesque smile.

'*By the time of theee next sssun'ss risssing, I want a thousssand, thousssand more Wolfen headsss upon my ssspikesss.*' She held out her hand and a Panterran thrust something into it. This, she held up to the horde.

It was a long metal sword, with a jewel-encrusted pommel and leather-wrapped handle. '*Creeeated by the Panterran blacksssmiths, and harder than the ssstrongessst Wolfen sssteeel. Made from a block of the ancient's hardest iron*'

She turned the sword over and sliced the air with it. '*The weaponnn of a true championnn.*' She sat forward, her near hairless body cloaked by the darkest hour of the night.

'*The championnn who brings me Grimvaldr'sss head, will have thisss weapon as proof of hisss mighty deeeed.*'

The crowd roared, and the sound washed across the hilltop as news of the reward passed along the ranks.

Mogahr lowered the sword and looked to Orcalion.

'*Begin the attttack.*'

Chapter 47

They Do Not Know Who It Is They Fight

Grimvaldr stood in his stirrups and looked along the line of warriors. His elite were organised into two hundred phalanxes, five deep and ten long. Rows of archers stood in position behind them, and then two columns of another twenty thousand Wolfen.

The castle once had rolling green plain spread out before it, gentle hills rising into forest along its sides. Now, the plain was churned, the forest burning; the king surveyed the horizon, knowing that after several days of preparation, they were out of time. There would only be one chance.

Grimvaldr turned to two of his generals, Lon and Karnak. 'The east and west columns must not break. You must keep the Panterran attack funnelled down the centre of the plain. If too many of the gravilents get in among our troops, their armoured hide will take too long to penetrate, and we do not have the time or troops to spend on bringing them down.'

Karnak nodded. 'Mighty stones have been piled high, and on top of that will be Wolfen spears – they will not break on our eastern side, sire.' He looked at Lon. 'And if the general needs help, I'll make sure they don't break on his side as well.'

Lon laughed and struck Karnak's armour with his fist. 'You'll be singing in Valhalla long before they break my line, oldling.'

The generals both turned to Grimvaldr. 'Ready, sire. On your word.'

'Take your positions.'

Karnak and Lon turned to each other and gripped gauntleted hands at shoulder height as they stared into each other's face. Lon spoke quietly. 'May Odin allow us to spill rivers of Panterran blood before he calls us.'

Karnak grinned. 'Odin's strength, brother.'

Both pulled on their reins and wheeled their horses, racing them to either side of the plain.

Grimvaldr watched them go as Sorenson rode up beside him. 'The scouts report that no sign of the far Wolfen have been sighted.'

Grimvaldr looked to the sky. 'They will come . . . If they are able, they will come.'

The Panterran's drumming stopped, and horns blared eerily across the plain.

'They come.' Grimvaldr turned his horse back to the front of the ranks with Sorenson beside him. He rode along the lines of Wolfen, holding up his fist. In turn, the Wolfen thumped gauntleted fists against their chests as he passed.

'This day, we face a threat from vile creatures of the dark. They will give no quarter – neither must you. The Panterran would seek to bring this kingdom down, and crush the Wolfen into dust.' The king roared, 'But they do not know who it is they fight!'

A roar rose all along the ranks. The sound of fists being beaten against armour was deafening as Grimvaldr rode along the lines of his Wolfen.

'I will lead you into battle, and I will see victory, or I will see you in Valhalla. Odin be with the mighty Wolfen!'

Grimvaldr lowered his visor. The silver snarling wolf covered his own fearsome visage, making him seem like a shining automaton made for war.

Along the lines, one after another, steel visors clanked down into place. The Wolfen were ready.

*****

Mogahr was carried in a sedan chair to the highest point on the hill, so she could watch the chaos from on high. She smiled, counting the ranks of the Wolfen warriors, knowing she had them enormously outnumbered.

'*The foolisssh king waitsss in vain for hisss warriorsss from the far landsss. Perhapsss he will be joining them, before they will be joining him.*' Her hissing laugh carried in the air, but was drowned out by the sound of the massive gravilents, lumbering out onto the plain.

The giant creatures were fully armoured now, their heads were covered in iron helmets that had long sharp spikes welded into their flesh to the sides and front. In battle, they would swing their low skulls from side to side, decimating the tightly packed troops.

These living tanks swarmed with Panterran archers and Lygon warriors. The beasts' objectives were simple – break through the forward ranks of the Wolfen, so the Panterran could rain arrows down on their heads, and then allow the Lygon to drop down and bring hell in among their midst.

And this would only be the first wave of the Panterran attack.

Mogahr hissed, *'Take me a little clossser, I wisssh to sssmell the blood as it flowsss.'*

*****

Sorenson watched as the colossal beasts started to pick up speed. Still in almost total darkness, the moving mountains were unmistakable. To the east and west, Lon and Karnak's columns had done their job. By piling boulders high, they created an uneven battleground that did not suit the low, heavy war-beasts. For now, their riders would choose a path that allowed them to pick up speed – right down the Wolfen elite's throats, and right where Grimvaldr wanted them.

Sorenson looked to the king next to him; like the rest of the front-line Wolfen, their expressions were unreadable behind their helmets, but all waited on Grimvaldr's word. Beside the king sat Freya, her hand already on the hilt of her sword, and next to her was the smaller figure of Eilif, her head bowed.

Sorenson moved up beside the princess, and could hear the small whisper of a voice drifting out from behind her visor – perhaps a prayer. He reached out to touch her shoulder. At first, she jumped at the contact, but then settled back in her saddle. He leaned across to her.

'There was an old philosopher who once said, "Use an enemy's strength against it, and make that strength its weakness."' He lifted his visor and smiled at her. 'Fear not, princess. We have a few tricks to play yet.'

Eilif nodded jerkily and she drew in a shuddering breath.

The Wolfen on horseback pulled at their reins as the horses started to become agitated. By now, they could not have failed to catch the scent of the strange beasts approaching them. Every Wolfen could feel the thunderous impact of the gravilents' feet as they struck the ground, each now reaching speeds akin to a horse's gallop. Unchecked, they would easily crash through the Wolfen lines.

Grimvaldr raised a fist. 'Hold.' His voice was strong and steady.

Sorenson lowered his visor.

*****

Eilif felt smothered beneath the steel of her helmet. She looked left and right along the line of riders; all faced the coming attack bar one – a dozen warriors down the line, one looked back towards her. It was Bergborr; she could tell by the dark crest and black horse tail streaming from the rear of his helmet. He raised a fist to his chest and opened his hand towards her.

My heart for you, the gesture meant. She was supposed to catch it and press it to her chest. Instead, she looked away.

She felt a deep sense of dread in the pit of her stomach, and closed her eyes – wishing that when she opened them again, she would see Arn somewhere along the ranks, his long hair blowing back from his shoulders, his glowing bare skin and eyes alight with laughter. He would do something that would make her laugh, even now.

She opened her eyes, and the dread remained. She used all her strength to stop herself fleeing immediately to find him, to be with him – torn between her sense of duty and her desire to see him, just once more. She hoped that he and Grimson were safe.

Eilif reined in her horse as the tremors intensified. She had been trained since birth for battle, and practised most days in the art of the sword and bow, and even unarmed combat, but the approach of the massive creatures, bristling with spikes, and covered in Panterran and Lygon warriors, made her doubt her abilities and sapped her confidence.

She swallowed with difficulty and held her head high. *I am the daughter of the king, a Wolfen princess*, she thought. *I will not fail this day.*

The king roared once again, 'Hold!'

And then, 'Pull!'

*****

Thick, buried ropes, trailing out onto the plain, and hidden in the dark, were lifted and pulled by dozens of Wolfen warriors. Straining at first, and then picking up speed, as if whatever held them, was ripped away.

In the dim light Eilif watched in bewilderment, and then felt her heart soar – huge areas of the flattened and churned land in front of the castle were sliding away as logs bound together and covered in soil were dragged from the top of deep pits.

Of course – the Wolfen with shovels, she remembered.

To the sides, Karnak and Lon's warriors had done their jobs, and kept the mighty beasts funneled up the centre of the plain. The Panterran screamed warnings, but the speed and mass of the creatures was too much to allow them to slow or even turn, and their enormous bodies fell into the pits. Of the fifty monstrous beings bearing down on the Wolfen, more than forty tumbled into the voids.

Use an enemy's strength against it, and make that strength its weakness, Sorenson had said. She caught his eye, and he threw back his head and laughed.

'And now their weight will do the rest,' he roared.

The bottoms of the pits were filled with sharpened spikes and the weight of the gravilents forced them deeper into the impaling traps. Lygon and Panterran could be seen climbing out of the pits, and the king held up one arm, and then swung it down. 'Fire!'

The Wolfen archers fired a deadly volley of arrows onto the plain. Some Panterran tried to run back to their ranks, but the Lygon charged ahead. It didn't matter – the plain was too long, too open. As arrows rained down, it became their burial ground.

The archers fired their next volley at the remaining gravilents who were nearly upon them. Their target was not the charging giants, but their riders.

In took only seconds for the last few moving mountains to be at the Wolfen front lines. Once again, the king's arm came down, and ranks of Wolfen stepped to the sides, revealing the tips of sharpened tree trunks. Each of the shaped logs was forty feet long and mounted on a simple slide, with ropes tied off and straining at their base – in effect they were giant arrows.

Axe blades fell, and ropes were cut, flinging the thick trunks forward, like the mighty bolts of Odin himself.

240

Few of the giant spears found the soft flesh between their armour plates, and many were simply trampled to kindling beneath their tree-trunk legs.

The far killing was now at an end. This time, when the king's arm came down, it was to draw forth his sword.

The war was here.

*****

The gravilents were pulled by the chains linked to metal rings embedded in either side of their head, and though they roared in frustration, anger and pain, they were forced to follow their rider's commands. Their broad heads swung back and forth, the huge spikes and blades cutting a swathe through the warriors not fast enough to leap out of the way. Giant Lygon leapt from the backs of the creatures into the melee, and Panterran fired volley after volley of poison-tipped arrows into the seething mass of Wolfen.

Though the Lygon were enormously powerful, they were few in number and no match for the front ranks of the Wolfen elite. They were soon brought down, and the Panterran, after firing their arrows, slipped from the backs of the beasts and sprinted in retreat across the plain.

A cheer went up along the Wolfen ranks. Though dozens had been crushed and cut down by the blades and spikes of the gravilents, they had managed to withstand this first wave.

The Wolfen whoops of bravado fell silent, as the drumming of Panterran resumed, and with it the more sinister rhythm of giant axes and maces banging against armour. The signal for the next attack had been given; even in the darkness, the wave of bristling orange-and-black shapes could be seen flooding across the plain. This time it was the turn of the Lygon – and this time there would not be dozens, but hundreds upon hundreds . . . thirsting for Wolfen blood.

Eilif had seen the Lygon in the camp when they had freed Arn, but in their battle armour they seemed twice as large and frightening. She felt her heart beating like the wings of a small bird trying to escape her rib cage.

The challenging roars of her kin tore through the air, and Sorenson's voice rose above all others.

'For Valkeryn! For Grimvaldr!' He drew his sword. 'And for the mightiest Wolfen who ever lived – for Strom!' He charged, and was followed by the hundreds of Wolfen horsemen down onto the now bloody plain.

When the two sides came together, the sound rolled across the kingdom of Valkeryn like thunder in the midst of a great storm. The clang of steel and the roars and shouts of the Wolfen and Lygon, and the frightened screams of the horses, was shockingly loud.

Eilif spurred her horse forward, her fear beginning to dull and her training taking over. As she approached the battle, one of the charging Lygon swung a club as wide as she was, at her head. She dragged on her reins, swerving her horse as she lay back nearly flat in her saddle, the club passing harmlessly over her. Lightning quick, she was upright again, slicing her sword down the creature's back, opening a long, deep wound in the orange-and-black fur.

The infuriated beast screamed, and wheeled, but she was already moving on through the dense press of bodies and flashing steel. All around her, Wolfen and Lygon battled; bloody bits of both littered the ground, and the air was dank with the spray of blood.

She moved closer to Grimvaldr, who was still on horseback, and now ringed by a circle of his best warriors. Sorenson was among them, and she marvelled at his skill and strength, delivering mortal blows that severed snarling heads and removed limbs from brutish bodies.

She became aware of a whistling sound, and then what she thought was the fall of a heavy rain. But then it became clear: it was rain, but of a more deadly kind – Panterran arrows. Thousands were loosed, and of those, hundreds penetrated deep into the bodies of Lygon and Wolfen alike.

At shouts from the generals, the Wolfen dismounted. The horses galloped back to the rear Wolfen line, and each time the deathly whistle heralded the approach of the Panterran's arrows, the Wolfen raised their shields above their heads, forming a protective roof of steel.

More Wolfen now joined the fray, and the king and the generals quickly organised them into their fighting ranks. Solid walls of Wolfen, five deep, fought in waves.

The first line fought until fatigued, and then fell back behind the next line, and on it went. The generals yelled commands, the arrows continued to fall, and the Lygon kept coming. Then there was more drumming, and the arrow fall ceased. Immediately, in among the tree-trunk legs of the Lygon, the smaller bodies of the Panterran swordsmen whipped through like wisps of smoke, slicing at the Wolfen with their curved blades.

For every Lygon, or dozen Panterran, the Wolfen cut down, twice that many seemed to take their place.

The storm of battle raged for hours, and those Wolfen who paused to draw breath and look to the far hills of the Panterran camps, saw nothing to raise their spirits – the dark tide of bodies continued to pour down towards the Wolfen front lines.

Eilif's arm was a leaden weight, and as she drove her sword into the chest of one Panterran, another caught her in the back, its curved blade finding its way between the plates of her armour. As she whirled and cut her attacker down, she could feel the warm wetness of her blood soaking her fur.

She gritted her teeth. *It may be a while now before I see you, my Arnoddr.* Hoping that heaven and Valhalla were the same place, she fought on towards her father.

*****

The head of Strom hung in the darkness – like some horrifying totem – at the top of Goranx's pike. Holding it aloft with one hand, in his other the monstrous Lygon wielded a massive broadsword, which swept through Wolfen and Panterran alike as he cut a path towards the Wolfen king.

Grimvaldr had his back turned, but Sorenson saw the danger and pushed his way forward, roaring a challenge, his fury unleashed when he saw what the great beast carried.

Amidst the bloody carnage, the giant Lygon heard the challenge, and roared in return. He planted the pike in the earth, and charged.

Sorenson was a solid warrior, but considerably outweighed by his opponent. Now fighting at her father's back, Eilif feared for her warrior friend as she watched him engage the beast, diving and rolling under the first swing of its blade. In return, his own sword slashed through the air and cut deeply into the back of one of the giant's legs.

Again and again, the Lygon's massive blade swung at him, but each time Sorenson ducked and weaved, leaving deep cuts in the Lygon's hide. The orange-and-black fur was becoming matted with blood.

Sorenson circled the Lygon, his sword held firm and unwavering before him. He reached up, pulled off his helmet and threw it to the ground. He pointed to his brother's head, impaled on the pike.

'Your head will soon take its place, mindless brute from the dark lands.'

The Lygon smiled, delighted at seeing the face before him. He responded in a voice that was as deep as Hellheim.

'I know you, brother of Strom, son of Stromgarde. And now know me: I am Goranx, taker of heads, slayer of armies.' He swung his blade back and forth, the huge weapon making the air swirl around them, and forcing Sorenson to duck one way, then the other. 'Did you know your brother begged for my forgiveness?'

The effect of these words on Sorenson was only momentary, but it distracted him enough that he didn't notice the body of a fallen Wolfen behind him. The Lygon swung his sword, and as Sorenson stepped back, he stumbled.

Goranx took his chance: lunging forward, he brought his sword down again, and this time all Sorenson could do was raise his own sword above his head to try to block the blow. But it was as if a tree trunk had fallen on him – his blade shattered into pieces as the other blade smashed through it and embedded itself into his armour, and deep into the flesh beneath.

Goranx seized Sorenson by the throat and lifted him up, squeezing until the Wolfen's tongue began to protrude. He pulled him close, and hissed into his face, 'It was always going to end like this.' Tossing the fallen Wolfen back onto the ground, he placed one giant foot on Sorenson's chest, then threw back his head and roared.

In one swift move, he dragged his buried sword from the Wolfen's shoulder and raised the blade high into the air.

Eilif screamed Sorenson's name, and the sound of her own voice snapped her out of the paralyzing shock of watching the giant destroy her friend. The monstrous Lygon seemed to be savouring his moment of victory, and it gave her precious seconds to act. Sighting a fallen Panterran archer, she dived towards him, snatching the bow and arrow from his dead fingers.

In one smooth motion, she nocked an arrow and fired. Goranx screamed – in shock more than pain – and he tore out the shaft protruding from his side. He snapped the arrow like a twig between his fingers, and raised his sword to battle the circle of Wolfen elite that now closed in around him.

Eilif rose up to her feet, intending to join them – but staggered, dizzy, the leaden weight of fatigue dragging her back to the ground.

I'll just rest awhile, she thought, the bloody mud cool against her face.

Strong hands dragged her up to her feet. It was Bergborr.

'You must come with me immediately, princess.'

She shook her head. 'No, the king . . .'

'It is he who commands me. You are to be kept safe until the far Wolfen arrive. It is his order.' He swept a hand behind her legs and picked her up.

She was weak, confused. Her eyes had begun to play tricks, and it seemed to her that, as Bergborr carried her through the carnage, from time to time a Lygon would loom up in front of them, then, for no apparent reason, pull back and turn away.

She stared past his shoulder at the battlefield. The Wolfen lines were thinning, but were still holding for now.

Bergborr pulled her to him.

'We are to enter the forest, and use one of the secret trails to make our way to a hidden camp for the wounded. Soon the far Wolfen will come, and then we will see what the Panterran, and their Lygon mercenaries, are truly made of when our numbers match their own.'

She frowned for a moment, looking from Bergborr, to the forest, and then back to the battle. She could make out the figures of her father and mother, fighting side by side, the giant Lygon slashing and hacking his way towards them. She struggled against him, but Bergborr held her tight, and she had no more energy to fight.

'Don't worry,' he whispered. 'Those vermin will be no match for the Wolfen elite. But we must hurry.'

He carried her past the castle walls, and she heard a shout go up from inside. There was a roar and the sound of steel – swords being pulled from scabbards, and the pounding of thousands of feet.

As she slipped into unconsciousness, she heard the castle doors being thrown open, and a small smile touched her lips.

She whispered softly, 'Odin, bless the far Wolfen.'

Chapter 48

Valhalla, He Whispered

Grimvaldr swung his sword in an arc, bringing the sharpest blade in the kingdom down on the sword arm of a Lygon. Both the arm and sword fell to the ground. The king's silver armour was now dark, coated with congealing blood, and in one brief moment, he felt an oasis of calm settle in his chest.

He drew in a breath, and sighted first the line of Panterran flooding down towards them, then turned back towards the castle, where his Wolfen, though vastly depleted, still held their ranks.

Both Karnak and Lon's forces had now been committed, and were also being ground down. But still he felt strong and confident. There were no more Lygon entering the battle, and once these giant brutes were brought down, the Panterran, no matter their numbers, would have no more stomach for battle.

He saw Freya leap and weave, and smiled with pride – she was graceful and beautiful, even in battle. He loved her with a clarity that seared his heart, and he fought his way towards her. As if his movement had broken some sort of spell, the battle crushed in on him once more.

He dropped down, just before a blade as thick as he was passed a hair's breadth over his head. Grimvaldr stared up at the creature that towered over him.

As he expected, it was a giant Lygon, looming and snarling. Around its waist, it wore a thick leather belt, from which hung the heads of many creatures – including several Man-kind. He prayed to Fenrir that the Arnoddr-Sigarr was not among them.

Two of his elite leapt forward to grasp each of the giant's arms, and momentarily hauled him back. But the strength of this creature could not be denied, and the Lygon threw each to the ground, and turned to face them.

Grimvaldr regained his feet as a heavy gong resounded within the castle, and he paused to raise his head to listen.

The gates of the castle were thrown open, and time stood still as thousands of creatures collectively held their breath. The king raised his sword high, preparing to command the second charge, but instead his arm fell by his side.

A boiling multitude of bristling fur and curved fangs exploded through the gates. It was another Lygon army; somehow they had made their way into the castle grounds, and now had both the higher ground, and a position at the flank of the Wolfen.

The horde smashed into the rear Wolfen, and the Lygon front line pressed forward with renewed ferocity. Floating over the swarming mass of cursing, fighting and dying creatures, Grimvaldr thought he could hear the merciless cackle of the Panterran queen. Perhaps she had been brought forward so she could watch the final moments of the Wolfen as they were hacked and slashed and crushed from all sides.

In this darkest moment of distraction, the king sensed that menacing presence behind him once again. He tried to turn, but this time it as too late. The massive sword, thrust with the brute strength of the giant Lygon, pushed through the hardened Wolfen steel armour on his back, and burst from his chest. He felt his feet lifting off the ground as he was held aloft as a bloody, still-breathing trophy.

His own sword fell from his hand, and he reached to grasp the blade protruding from his chest. Grimvaldr wished he could speak, so he could yell one last order to his Wolfen.

Be brave – fight on! he would roar to them. Instead, as his vision began to cloud, he could only watch as Freya, his beautiful queen, screamed his name and rushed towards him, only to be cut down by a dozen Panterran.

Grimvaldr crushed his eyes shut. No more orders would come from him now, no saviours of the Wolfen race would come this day.

As he was lifted higher above the heads of the last few battling Wolfen, he saw the sun begin to rise at the far edge of the horizon – rising in the far lands, where he hoped his son was making his way now.

Grimvaldr felt the rays on his face, and in that fresh red warmth, he saw golden doors opening.

Valhalla, he whispered.

Chapter 49

The Fall Of The Wolfen

Arn paused and grabbed Grimson by the shoulder. The sun was coming up, and a slight breeze blew up from behind them, carrying with it a sound he could just make out. It was like a gong or bell being struck over and over.

Grimson lifted his head to sniff the air. 'My father – I can't . . . I can't *sense* him anymore.' He looked up at Arn. 'Can we go back, Arnoddr?'

Arn shook his head. 'Not this day.' He drew in a deep breath and closed his eyes. He hoped somehow that Eilif had survived, that the far Wolfen had arrived in time, and that Grimvaldr had triumphed. But even though the sounds of the gong probably signalled the end of the battle, deep down he knew the day did not belong to the Wolfen.

He watched the sun rise up over the horizon. He might have travelled a million years, and might have arrived just in time to witness the last night of the Wolfen. *It isn't fair*, he thought.

He patted Grimson on the shoulder and glanced at him, and for a moment the youngster looked like a normal boy. He blinked and the mirage dissolved. Grimson looked up and smiled, and Arn turned away. 'C'mon, we have a lot of ground to cover.'

The two small figures pushed their way through the brush. One was human, possibly the last of his kind. And for all Arn knew, the young Wolfen beside him was possibly the last of his kind, too.

CPSIA information can be obtained
at www.ICGtesting.com
Printed in the USA
BVHW072353070920
588213BV00001B/43